RATTLING THE BONES

Also by Ann Granger and available from Headline

Fran Varady crime novels

Asking For Trouble

Keeping Bad Company

Running Scared

Risking It All

Watching Out

Mixing With Murder

Mitchell and Markby crime novels

Say It With Poison

A Season For Murder

Cold In The Earth

Murder Among Us

Where Old Bones Lie

A Fine Place For Death

Flowers For His Funeral

Candle For A Corpse

A Touch Of Mortality

A Word After Dying

Call The Dead Again

Beneath These Stones

Shades Of Murder

A Restless Evil

That Way Murder Lies

A Rare Interest In Corpses

RATTLING THE BONES

Ann Granger

headline

First published in 2007
by HEADLINE PUBLISHING GROUP

1

Cataloguing in Publication Data is available from the British Library

978 0 7553 2045 5 (hardback)
978 0 7553 2046 2 (trade paperback)

Typeset in Plantin by Avon DataSet Ltd,
Bidford-on-Avon, Warwickshire

Printed and bound in Great Britain by
Mackays of Chatham plc, Chatham, Kent

Headline's policy is to use papers that are natural, renewable and
recyclable products and made from wood grown in sustainable forests.
The logging and manufacturing processes are expected to conform
to the environmental regulations of the country of origin.

HEADLINE PUBLISHING GROUP
A division of Hachette Livre UK Ltd
338 Euston Road
London NW1 3BH

www.headline.co.uk
www.hodderheadline.com

To my dear husband . . . forty years on!

Chapter One

My late grandmother, Erszebet Varady, more or less brought me up. My mother walked out one day when I was seven and didn't reappear for fourteen years. Grandma was what's called a formative influence. I learned to like good coffee and spicy goulash, never sit on the seat in a public loo and beware of anyone in a uniform. She knew how to read the omens like an ancient shaman. 'Sometimes when things get bad you just have to run,' she would say philosophically. It would have been a good thing if I'd inherited her instinct but bad situations have always held a fatal lure for me. The more sticky the circumstances, the more I want to pitch in there. There's no way it makes any sense. It's what dramatists call a fatal flaw.

Grandma had vivid personal experience of running away from a bad situation, having fled the aftermath of the 1956 Hungarian uprising with her baby (my dad) in her arms. She also had my grandfather with her but he was inconveniently recovering from a bad bout of influenza and not much help. He kept sagging at the knees at awkward moments. My grandma often expressed the opinion that no situation was ever so difficult but that any Varady male couldn't make it worse.

Despite the fact that my grandfather was himself a doctor, his health couldn't have been too good. He was dead by the time I was born. I have a photograph of him taken when he was about the age I am now, twenty-three. It's a professional portrait done in Budapest in a studio that had probably not changed its props since the days of Franz Josef. My grandfather is posed with one arm resting on a stump of Grecian pillar and the other propped dashingly on his hip. He is turned three-quarters on towards the camera and has a slight smirk on his face as if he couldn't decide whether to smile or not. Or it might just be he was pleased with his appearance. He is wearing a single-breasted suit jacket secured by one button mid-ribs. In the breast pocket there is an artistically folded handkerchief and in the opposite lapel a carnation. His shirt collar looks tight enough to choke him and he has a striped tie. He also has a neat little moustache and for some reason is wearing a hat.

This portrait held pride of place on our mantelshelf when I was a child. I decided early on that my father (who died about ten years ago) resembled him. Apart from the carnation and hat, that is. My father was also no great help in an emergency. After my mother's defection, he had remained physically present but mentally he had left with her. In between a string of jobs all begun with great expectations only to fold shortly afterwards in failure, he just hung round the place. He was a nice man, friendly and kind-hearted, but in truth no great help. It's always been down to the Varady women to take care of things and sort out problems. I sometimes wonder if it was the realisation that she would have to bear the entire burden of their marriage that resulted in my mother giving up the whole thing as a bad job, although I haven't the slightest idea why she went. On the few brief occasions we spoke later when she reappeared she didn't enlighten me and I didn't ask. She's dead too, now; so is Grandma. All those questions hover unanswered in the ether . . . taken to the grave as the Victorians liked to say. Some people try and discover old secrets. They rattle the bones and hope some inkling will fall out. I never have.

However, perhaps that's why, although my intention is and has always been to make a career in the performing arts, I have morphed into a part-time private detective. Possibly the above-mentioned high rate of mortality among my few relatives has something to do with it. After all, it left me alone in the world and homeless at sixteen. It abruptly called a halt to the drama course I was following. But I have another theory.

From childhood I have always had to try and work out for myself what's going on. In my family a child was to be loved, fed and taught good manners, but not included in important discussions. So they never explained where my mother had gone apart from some pathetic invention about 'a holiday' which wouldn't have fooled anyone, let alone a seven-year-old with a child's uncluttered logical mind. My father and grandmother, together with the motley collection of visitors who turned up at our door, communicated information of a sensitive nature by winks and nods and knowing looks. If it was necessary to speak they went into a huddle in the kitchen and got highly agitated in Hungarian which they had omitted to teach me. I used to think it just an oversight that they failed to instruct me in the language of my ancestors. Now I wonder if it wasn't just cunning.

The result of all this was that I learned early to look for clues. I sneaked around the place trying to find odd bits of paper and kept an ear tuned in for phone calls. I studied the expressions on the faces of both my father and Grandma when they thought I wasn't watching. I searched through drawers when I was alone at home. Once I found a cache of old photos. I went through them looking for one with my mother in it but she didn't appear in a single picture. Again, to this day, I don't know if that was chance or whether someone had culled the snapshots of her and committed them to the fire. No one ever told me and, of course, I didn't dare to ask. I'd have got the runaround instead of a straight answer, anyway.

Old photographs have continued to fascinate me. They open a tantalising window into the past. Those silhouette pictures, too, which people made before they had cameras. I've seen brilliant ones in antique shops. Even though the features are blanked out I'm sure the sitters were instantly recognisable to those who knew them. Faces aren't the only thing other people know us by. Body language is individual or a habit like twisting a lock of hair round a finger, even just a way of standing. Some people are identifiable the length of a street away and that's how I recognised Edna the bag lady.

Edna and I had once, in a manner of speaking, been neighbours. I had been living in a squat in Rotherhithe at the time, Edna in an abandoned churchyard nearby with a family of feral cats for company.

Events recounted above had led to my living in a squat and I supposed some other misfortune had consigned Edna to the world of the truly homeless. She was one of those who had fallen through the holes in the safety net of social services, either by choice or through oversight on the part of the authorities. One of the lost tribe who have floated away from the shores of sanity to sink or swim alone; if not condemned to care in the community, which in effect is often little better.

Not so long ago I took the first step out of the lost world and the Rotherhithe squat by a roll of Fate's dice. City planners in bright modern offices decreed that progress and redevelopment should move us all on, little caring where we went. The houses of Jubilee Street and surrounding roads and Edna's churchyard fell beneath the contractor's bulldozer and it had led to the parting of our ways. I was now living in comparative comfort, but until that morning I'd had no idea where Edna had gone or even if she was still 'with us', as my Grandma Varady used to say. People referred to death very delicately in our house, as if it was something that didn't happen in respectable families, another of those problems they had confronting reality.

Edna might have been 'with us', in the Rotherhithe days, but she'd never been 'with it'. Her mind had already moved on to inhabit a plane somewhere beyond anyone's reach or comprehension. Unkindly we called her 'mad Edna' which was not only insensitive but inaccurate. If Edna's mind did not work as others did, it was by choice. She wasn't ill; she had opted out. A small figure dodging from tombstone to tombstone like a crab among the rocks, she'd always appeared incredibly ancient, though it had been hard to tell given the layers of clothing she wore and her liking for woolly hats crammed over straggling uncombed grey locks.

I really had thought I'd never see her again, but there she was, not a shadow of a doubt, wobbling up Camden High Street towards the Tube station. Her gait had always been as distinctive as the rest of her. She moved both sideways and forwards at the same time. I wouldn't have called it a waddle because that suggests moving a considerable weight. Edna's bulk was due to her clothing and not obesity and she was light on her feet. She shifted her frame nimbly from one side to the other while pushing ahead of her the foot which had the weight taken off it, so that when she shifted the weight back again, she came down a few inches further than where she'd been to start with. It was a kind of hop, almost like a dance step. I once had a toy clown that whirred round the living room in the same way until someone trod on him.

I broke into a trot and caught up with her easily. 'Edna!' I called out. 'Wait! It's me, Fran!'

She kept her woolly-hatted head down and refused to look round or give any sign she had heard me. That was normal. Edna had never liked being hailed. She preferred to choose the moment of making contact and used, in the old days, to jump out disconcertingly from behind wonky gravestones giving people 'a very nasty turn', as they often complained afterwards. I returned the favour now, jumped in front of her and obliged her to stop. I'm not tall but she was shorter and the woolly hat only reached my chin.

'Come on, Edna,' I coaxed. 'You remember me.'

She wasn't trying to edge round me and I was sure she had heard me. But she still said nothing, only stood there sullenly with her chin tucked in.

'I'm Fran,' I repeated to the grimy bobble of wool under my nose. 'Fran Varady. I used to live in Rotherhithe, remember? In the squat in Jubilee Street where the girl was murdered.'

It was unfortunate that a couple of tourists were passing at the time I spoke and because Edna was always a trifle hard of hearing, or affected to be, I had uttered the words loudly.

The tourists looked at me aghast and hurried on.

I got a reaction from Edna at last. 'No,' she muttered.

'Yes, you do, Edna. Oh, come on, don't sulk, please!'

She changed her mind. She looked up at me, her sunken eyes gleaming with mischief. 'Yes, of course I remember you, my dear. How are you? What do you want?'

Her voice had always been extraordinary, totally at odds with her dishevelled appearance. It was quite deep and beautifully modulated, undeniably posh. Proper posh, I mean, not put on. I trained to be an actor and I know about voices. Once you heard Edna speak, she wasn't the same elderly down-at-heel bag lady. In the old Rotherhithe days I'd seen coppers, who had tried to move her on, change their attitude and tone immediately once they heard her.

I still am an actor, by the way. I might be 'resting' and I might fill in the time with odd jobs and a bit of detection, but I haven't given up my dream.

'I don't want anything,' I said, 'only to say hullo and glad to see you.' I noticed she had no bags with her. 'Where are you living?' I asked.

'In a hostel,' said Edna with disgust. 'They put me in a hostel. First of all they put me in a home with a lot of old people all sitting round a television. The wretched contraption kept on flickering in a way that hurt your eyes and blaring out its nonsense fit to deafen you. Mind you, some of the old folk were already deaf and the others were asleep all the time. I wasn't going to stay there, I told them that straight. So then they put me in the hostel. It's no better except that they don't make you watch that dratted box. But half the people there are bonkers and they don't allow any animals! I don't need *people*. I like *animals*.'

The last words were spoken fiercely.

'Sorry,' I said, 'I expect you miss the cats.'

'They took 'em away.' Edna was in full spate now, moved by remembered anger. She flapped her arms and shuffled her feet in frustration and looked as though she was making doomed attempts at lift-off, although more like some stranded and bedraggled bird oil-smeared on a beach than anything as sleek as a rocket.

'Something that called itself a cat charity took 'em, after chasing them all over the churchyard and trapping them in nasty little boxes. How could it be a charity? It took them from their home and from me. I looked after them.' She abandoned the attempt to levitate, sidled a little closer and her faded eyes glinted up at me conspiratorially. 'You know what they did with the cats? They did away with them, that's what. *Murdered 'em.*'

'Perhaps they rehoused them?' I suggested.

Edna showed that there was a difference between living in a parallel universe and not having your mind in working order. 'Rehoused the kittens, maybe,' she said sternly. 'The older cats, no. They weren't house-trained, they were used to roaming free and they were too old to change their ways.'

'Right,' I said.

I was glad she was as sharp as ever she had been beneath that skilful pretence of battiness. If she had still been living in the old people's home, sitting hour after hour before the television set, I doubted that her mind would still be in such good order. Hostel living might not suit her taste but in some ways it had benefited her. She was distinctly cleaner, skin washed and pink, clothes tattered but not whiffy, and she appeared generally better nourished.

She cheered up and uttered an unexpected cackle of laughter. 'They rehoused me, that's what they did, just like the kits. But I'm no kitten. I'm one of the old 'uns, too old to change my ways.'

She shook her head and looked baleful again. 'I don't hang around that hostel. It smells of baked beans. I spend my days walking round,' she concluded in a satisfied tone, 'like I always did.'

But obviously she had not always done. Once, decades ago, Edna had had a different life. I wondered how much of it she remembered and how much she had consciously suppressed. But she hadn't finished yet.

'They even took the old tom.' She returned to the topic of the cats. 'He led them a merry chase before they trapped him with a bit of meat. I hope he scratched them all. He had a grand set of claws and his teeth were good 'uns. He'd crunch up mice bones like they were made of jelly.' Her expression and tone became wistful, 'He went down fighting, that's what he did. They should have put me down with him.'

'I've got a flat, now,' I told her. I made myself sound as cheery as possible because she was grumpy and seemed still so upset about the cats. 'It's in a house that belongs to a charity that provides cheap housing for people like me. There are seven flats and a garden of a sort at the back. It's really nice. Come and visit me.'

'I might leave my card,' said Edna vaguely, drifting off to that other world, or appearing to do so. It was her way of refusing the invitation. She returned disconcertingly to the present. 'How is your young man?'

'You mean Ganesh,' I said. 'He's not my young man. He's a friend. He's very well. He works for his uncle now, a newsagent.'

Ganesh's parents had run a greengrocer's shop in Rotherhithe but they'd been disposed in the same way as the rest of us and had relocated to High Wycombe. Ganesh had been left behind and scooped up by another family member to be enrolled in another business. I know Ganesh objects to being passed round the family in this way but at the same time, he seems unable to break away from it. It comes under the heading of things that Ganesh Will Not Discuss.

'I was engaged to be married once,' said Edna in a conversational tone.

Used as I was to the 'hop, skip and a jump' way in which Edna thought, this was so unexpected I took a step back and wondered if I'd heard her correctly. Edna had never ever volunteered any personal information or even given a sign her previous life meant anything to her or that she even had any recollection of it.

I looked down at her, studying her more closely. It was impossible to tell how she had once looked. The general shape of her face was round but her chin was pointed. Heart-shaped, they call that. Only in Edna's case the whole thing had sagged. Her eyebrows had fallen out and were represented only by a sparse scattering of grey hairs. She'd compensated by growing a few hairs on her chin. Her eyes were deep-set and heavy-lidded and the eyelashes had gone the way of the eyebrows. Yet I noticed for the first time that her skin was very fine, like a piece of crumpled silk. Perhaps she had once been a very pretty youngster with a heart-shaped face, flawless skin and long eyelashes and someone had fallen in love with her.

Her brow wrinkled into a furrow. I thought at first she frowned because I was studying her so closely and so rudely. But it was because she was rummaging in her mind.

'I think I was,' she said, less certainly. 'I'm almost positive I was. Who could it have been, I wonder?'

Her gaze drifted past me and sharpened. Her whole expression and attitude changed. Panic crossed her features. Her eyes glittered with fear and their gaze darted about like a trapped animal's.

'I'm going!' she said.

She shuffled sideways and in a burst of unexpected speed outmanoeuvred me. I darted after her scurrying figure and caught her arm.

'Edna? What's wrong?'

'Can't stay!' she said irritably. 'Go away!'

Edna twitched her sleeve from my grip and made off, burrowing her way through the crowds like a demented mole. She rounded the corner where the Kentish Town Road meets Camden High Street and wobbled off along the Kentish Town Road until she was lost to sight among the pedestrians and traffic.

I let her go and turned back to the Camden High Street, looking round to see what on earth could have spooked her like that.

The usual hustle and bustle went on around me, images flickering and changing like a kaleidoscope pattern. But no, not every shape moved. One thing, or rather one person, was stationary.

He was standing diagonally across the road, on the far side of the traffic island, on the corner of Parkway in the shade thrown by the frontage of a bank. He was the kind of person you probably wouldn't notice in the ordinary way of things but once you had noticed him, his image imprinted itself on your brain like a snapshot.

I can see him now in my mind's eye, lurking in the shadows, pressed against the bank's respectable wall. It was as if he was anxious to remain unnoticed but, if noticed, hoped to gain some legitimacy from the business behind him. Everything about him was pale and so still that he looked just a little bit ghost-like. I could see he appeared young, fairly tall and spindly in build and I got the impression of a skin untouched by sunshine even though we'd had quite a lovely hot summer. His clothes were either white or very pale; at a distance I couldn't be sure which. He wore knee-length shorts with large square buttoned pockets on the sides of the legs. With them he wore a white T-shirt with the sleeves cut off and a white cap with a sharp peak, more like a tennis cap than a baseball cap. He was staring towards the Tube station entrance and me. As soon as he realised I had noticed him, he reacted as quickly as Edna had done, turning and disappearing round the corner, in his case into Parkway, taking him away from the area in the opposite direction to that taken by Edna.

He should have stayed where he was. I would probably just have dismissed him as one more oddity. Camden High Street is full of eccentric characters. Even if I'd thought he looked a bit suspicious I could have done nothing about it. If I'd marched over there before he slipped away and accused him of watching me and Edna, he could well have replied that I was off my trolley and he was waiting for a mate. Quite possibly he would have tried to sell me drugs. His whole body language spoke guilt but I decided quickly it couldn't be because he was a pusher and I doubted he was an undercover cop. Drugs Squad turns up in all shapes and disguise but they always look like cops. Partly it's their standard of physical fitness and very straight posture. They never look relaxed.

No one would ever mistake me for anyone official. I'm too short, relaxed to a fault, and anyone can see I'm the type usually at odds with authority. This is not by my choice, I might add. It's just the way things have worked out.

I act on instinct and it's not always wise, as my friend Ganesh is fond of pointing out. But I was never one for standing around watching life go by. I want to grab it by the throat. So I took advantage of a gap in the traffic and dashed across the road in pursuit of Ghostly Apparition. I wanted to ask him what his game was and I needed to see where he was going for my own satisfaction. Call it curiosity, call it meddling, call it what you like.

By the time I got into Parkway he was well ahead of me, walking quickly and purposefully with his arms swinging. In a way I was relieved to see him. At least he was real. I can move, too. I scooted along and came level with him, out of breath and probably red in the face. He knew I was there, knew I'd followed him, but he gave no sign of it other than lengthening his stride. His paleness was now even more apparent. I wondered if he'd been ill that his skin had that fish-belly translucence. His eyes were fixed in a rigid blank stare, apparently seeing nothing, making no contact with anything. I did wonder for a moment if he was schizophrenic and, if so, if he was taking his pills. That was a worry. The only thing I could be sure of was that, without breaking into a trot, he was definitely running away. I wondered if he was making for Regent's Park. There he could break openly into a jog and soon leave me behind.

Even this power-walking was doing me in. I struggled for the breath to hail him and managed to croak, 'Hey!' but too late.

Without warning, he wheeled right into Gloucester Avenue and almost immediately right again into Gloucester Crescent. His legs were long and his stride correspondingly so. My legs had to work double time to match his progress. I did my best, wondering, as my breathing became more laboured, how I got to be so out of condition. I pursued him past the curve of expensive homes in the Crescent. That's how it is in Camden: the wealthy and the homeless are jumbled up together in a unique ecosystem.

We proceeded at such speed that before I knew it, we were at the top of Inverness Street and he had turned into it. Here the fruit and veg market was busy. My quarry had lengthened his stride even more so that I dog-trotted along gasping in his wake like a fairy-tale character chasing someone wearing seven-league boots. I skidded on squashed fruit. I dodged shopping baskets trailed by doughty old dears heedless whose shins they cracked. Little kids, in and out of buggies, littered my way ahead.

The man in white had led me round in a circle and we

emerged, he still that tantalising distance ahead, into Camden High Street once more. Too late I saw his purpose. He ran across the road and disappeared into Camden Town Market. I realised he was clever and I'd been caught out.

In Camden Town Market space is at a premium and visibility down to only the immediate few feet ahead and the stalls to either side. They effectively cut out the light. It is a maze of shadowy narrow alleys between packed merchandise, browsers, tourists and genuine shoppers. He had already vanished among the crowded stalls. I plunged after him although a sinking feeling told me I was probably wasting my time.

Obstinately I pushed on, stallholders' cries ringing in my ears, people jostling me in their efforts to reach the goods. Loitering teenagers gathered before a jewellery stand blocked my way as they discussed the merits of strings of brightly coloured beads. Ahead of them I glimpsed a white baseball cap. There he was!

I thrust the teenagers aside ignoring the glare of the stallholder and the girls' indignant protests. Brightly-coloured clothing exotic with sequins and glitter dangled from racks and swayed into my face bringing with it the acrid and musty smell of the dyes. Between the racks, from time to time, I glimpsed my quarry or thought I did. A flash of white baseball cap, was that him? Or was it someone else? To anyone watching from above our chase might have appeared as one of those computer games where one character pursues another through a maze strewn with dead ends, obstacles and booby traps. Then he was gone.

I had been so long in pursuit, sticking to the trail despite all my quarry's tricks, that at first I would not believe I had really lost him. The realisation that he had shaken me off struck me like a painful blow. I scurried round a few corners, scanned the alleys in vain for a gangling white figure or a baseball cap. People pushed past me. Music rang tinnily in my ears and chatter in half a dozen languages. But I was alone.

I guessed what he might have done. Probably he had snatched off the tell-tale cap. He had ducked down and cut through the middle of one of the clothing stalls, squeezing between the tightly packed racks out into the parallel alley beyond. He was probably already back in the High Street.

I retraced my steps there although I knew it was useless. I looked up and down it in both directions but there was no telling which way he had gone. Perhaps even back to the Underground station and even now he stood on some platform way beneath my feet. He knew his terrain and had used it well to outwit me. But it is my terrain too, and I was furious with myself for allowing him to do it.

In a teeming metropolis you meet and part from people all the time. Lives touch briefly and then, like the proverbial ships in the night, pass and in almost no time at all any sign of that brief interaction has been wiped away traceless. But I'd always remembered Edna and wondered what became of her. She was part of my first foray into detection, even providing me with a clue, and I felt an obligation towards her. So as I stood there, panting, perspiring and hopping mad, I thought, Next time I'll be ready! I'll be looking out for you, chum, and I'll know you! Edna knew you, too . . . and she was scared.

I'd have been scared, too, if I'd had any sense. But like I was telling you, bad situations draw me fatally towards them.

Chapter Two

The unexpected meeting with Edna had reminded me of what I had so recently left behind. I've travelled very little in a spatial sense, hardly ever leaving London. That in itself, I suppose, is a bit odd these days. But on the other hand I have done quite a bit of spiritual travelling as I've drifted from reasonable normality (if the patched together world of Grandma and Dad could have been considered that) into homelessness and back again.

For most 'normal' people the world of the homeless and kinless is a foreign land yet they only have to step out of their front doors to spot its inhabitants. If they wanted to see them, that is, and most people choose not to. They throw a cloak of invisibility over them and hurry on by.

This curiously distorted 'other' world follows a weird logic. It operates by its own rules, sets out its own patterns and sometimes even keeps its own clock. Whole communities grow up and thrive in derelict properties with eviction hanging over them like the sword of Damocles, impermanence a way of life. Those who really have nowhere else to lay their heads but the street often choose to sleep by day when the thoroughfare is full of busy unheeding passers-by and pollution-spilling traffic. At night, when myriad dangers emerge from the shadows or spill from clubs and bars in drunken hostility onto damp flagstones glistening in the lamplight, the homeless prowl the streets in constant watchful wakefulness.

People in the 'normal' world should never kid themselves that it isn't easy to slip through the porous boundaries into the world of the dispossessed. Sometimes, if you are very lucky or exceptionally determined, you can make the journey in the other direction and re-enter the lost Eden of acceptable existence, moving from rootlessness to a kind of security, however tenuous. I am one of those fortunate to have made that perilous transition. I'm never unaware of my good luck. I've never forgotten those who haven't shared it.

'I always wondered about Edna,' I said to Ganesh that evening. 'You know, where she came from, why she was living in that churchyard.'

'Did you?' replied Ganesh, turning up his jacket collar against the stiff breeze whistling along the Chalk Farm Road. The wind wasn't cold, if anything it was warm and the air muggy, but it carried on it a cloud of dust and small pieces of debris that whirled around us like an urban sandstorm.

'Yes, didn't you?'

'No,' said Ganesh.

'Come on, Gan, you must have done.'

'You might not have noticed,' said Ganesh huffily, 'but back in the Rotherhithe days I spent my entire time selling spuds and onions for my dad. Just like now I spend my life running round on my Uncle Hari's behalf. Am I appreciated? Am I, heck!'

I recognised the signs of a family dispute hovering in the background. 'You've quarrelled with Hari,' I said.

'You can't quarrel with my uncle,' said Ganesh with scarcely suppressed fury. 'It's impossible. To quarrel with a person you have to get some reaction out of them, right? They listen to you and then they yell at you. You listen to them and you yell at them, right? That's quarrelling.'

'OK,' I said doubtfully.

'But I can't quarrel with Hari because he *never listens in the first place*!' Ganesh's voice rose to a shout. 'I put my point of view, politely. He ignores it. I repeat it. He says, why am I standing there chattering when there's work to be done? I ask, again very politely, can I have a little of his attention to discuss something? Oh, he is far too busy. Speak to him later, when the shop's closed. Only, later, when we're upstairs in the flat, it's something else he's got to take care of.'

'What's the problem?' I asked sympathetically.

Ganesh stopped in his tracks and wheeled round to face me. 'What's the problem? You're as bad as Hari. Isn't what I've been describing problem enough?'

'Yes, what I meant was, what is the problem you want to discuss with him and he won't discuss?'

'You wouldn't understand. It's a family matter,' said Ganesh stiffly.

'You know,' I told him, 'you won't like me saying this but in your own way, you're just like Hari.'

At this, Ganesh fell into a prolonged offended silence until we reached Potato Heaven.

All right, I know. It's an awful name and both Gan and I tried to talk Jimmie out of it but without luck. Jimmie said it would attract the punters and perhaps he was right, because it was always busy these days and Jimmie was generally wreathed in smiles instead of cigarette smoke. He still puffed away doggedly but at least he managed now to keep the fumes out of the eating area.

When we first knew Reekie Jimmie, as he was affectionately known to all, he ran a baked spud café which made not the slightest concession to customer preferences, pleasant décor, healthy eating or anything else. Then Jimmie decided to go upmarket and went into business with an Italian guy and opened a snazzy pizza parlour. I worked there for a while as a waitress (while rehearsing for a role in a never-to-be-forgotten production of *The Hound of the Baskervilles*.) There had been just a little problem with the pizza place and the law. But the cops decided Jimmie had been a hapless dupe, he just wasn't bright enough for crime, and allowed him to go back to his first love: potatoes.

'You know where you are with tatties, right, hen?' he explained to me.

But just as living in a hostel had done something for Edna, running the pizza parlour had done something for Jimmie. He had acquired Style. He'd realised that surroundings do matter. So he'd kept on the pizza restaurant premises, complete with the beautiful tiled picture of Vesuvius on the wall, but gone back to spuds, only now they came with Bolognese filling (mince) and Milanese (ham) and one called Four Cheeses (mousetrap). See what I mean?

When Ganesh and I were settled in a corner with our potatoes, Bolognese for me and Four Cheeses for Ganesh because he's vegetarian, I returned to the subject of Edna. It seemed safer than trying to talk to Gan about his problems with his uncle. Anyway, Edna was what I wanted to talk about.

'She was really scared when she saw the young guy watching her,' I said. I'd told him all about it, even how the watcher had given me the slip.

'How can you tell?' asked Ganesh frowning. He wasn't frowning at anything I'd said but because long rubbery strings of cheese dangled from his fork and he couldn't break them. The more he twiddled the fork, trying to wrap them round the tines, the longer and thinner the strings became. He picked up his knife and chopped at them but they flattened beneath the blade

'What is this stuff?' he demanded in exasperation.

At that moment the strings of cheese parted and he managed to get them into a manageable forkful.

'How can you tell how Edna's feeling?' he went on when he'd swallowed it with an expression of distaste. 'She's not like other people. Her expressions aren't like other people's. She never liked strangers. She didn't like having you stop her in the street. I expect just the crowd round her spooked her.'

'It was him,' I said firmly. 'He frightened her. If he was innocent, why did he run?'

'He didn't actually run, you said.' Ganesh can be annoyingly pedantic.

'So he walked very fast! He deliberately gave me the slip. He did it very professionally, too. He's done it a few times, I reckon, given people the slip. He knew exactly what to do.'

'If I didn't know you and you were obviously following me, *I'd* give you the slip,' argued Ganesh. 'That's your trouble, see? You're always so set on doing just what you want – and generally that means the first thing to come into your head – that you never stop to consider how it looks to other people. I know you. I accept that you act like a lunatic sometimes. I don't like it but I've learned to live with it. Other people just think you're weird.' He abandoned the cheese which had set like plastic now it had cooled, and stared at me thoughtfully. 'Especially,' he said, 'with that funny-coloured hair.'

I was feeling sensitive about my hair at that moment and I thought it tactless of him to mention it. The rest of what he'd said I generally went along with. I am aware other people sometimes find me strange. But the way I see it, that's their problem. The hair colour was mine.

'The label on the box said the rinse was dark auburn,' I defended myself feebly.

'That,' said Ganesh, jabbing his fork at me, 'isn't dark auburn. It's crimson. You look like your head's on fire.'

'OK, I'll buy another rinse and do something about it. Only I can't do anything about it now, can I? What about Edna?'

'What about her?'

'Gan!' I couldn't help my voice rising. 'What are we going to *do*?'

'Nothing. Especially "we" are going to do nothing. I have no problem with any of this. It's your overactive imagination and that drama training you had. Everything's a big production with you. Everything is villains and plots and dark deeds and you, of course, cast as the heroine putting all that right.'

I was opening my mouth and trying to get a word of protest in but he wouldn't let me and steamrollered on.

'*You* don't know anything's wrong. *You* thought she looked frightened but with Edna that might mean anything. *You* thought the guy over the road was watching. All right, then, perhaps he was. It's not illegal. It's not even odd. When I'm waiting about for you I watch people going past. The guy was hanging about for whatever reason and watching you talk to a bag lady was probably as interesting as anything else, beats staring into space.'

'But – but – but . . .' from me, in vain.

Ganesh, who would have done well on a drama course himself even though he would have been inclined to nineteenth-century melodrama, raised a hand like an old-time traffic cop. 'Then, *then* you chose to chase after him and he decided reasonably enough to shake you off. What is *more* . . .'

He glared at me because I had taken refuge in a pantomime of elaborate yawns and hand movements before the mouth.

'Even if there was the slightest chance you were even partly right, you couldn't check it out. If you found Edna again and asked her about it, she wouldn't remember, or she wouldn't tell you or she'd tell you something quite untrue. She doesn't know fact from fiction.'

Give Ganesh enough rope and he runs on that bit too far. He'd played into my hands. I put down my fork and pointed a triumphant forefinger at him. 'That's where you're wrong, Ganesh, and if you think back to the Rotherhithe days, you'll agree. Anything Edna ever said was true. It might come out sounding a bit odd. But she never invented anything. She told me after Terry was murdered that she'd seen someone hanging round the house and she was right, wasn't she? She could even describe him after a fashion. Edna doesn't miss anything. She might not choose to talk about it, but that doesn't mean she hasn't noticed. She told me today she'd been engaged to be married once and I believe her.'

Ganesh hooted with laughter, very rudely, I thought and said so.

He subsided. 'All right. The old woman isn't nearly as daft as she makes out. She probably was quite respectable long ago. Something made her flip. She dropped out and never dropped back in again. It happens all the time.' Ganesh frowned again and added wistfully, 'Only it couldn't happen to me.'

'Why not?'

'Because my family would come after me and find me and drag

me back to sell spuds or newspapers or whatever they're into at the time. There's no escaping *them*!' He eyed me again. 'You, on the other hand, might end up just like Edna.'

'Well, thanks a bundle. I'll do my best not to. I am going to find out what's going on, though, with your help or without it.'

'First you've got to find Edna again,' Ganesh pointed out.

'All right, I will!'

'No, no! I didn't mean that, not literally. I meant, you won't find her again,' he back-pedalled hastily.

'What do you bet I can't find her?' I was beginning to sound stroppy, I knew, but Gan has that effect on me.

He said gloomily, 'Fran, you're going to get into trouble again. Leave it alone.'

'According to you, there's no trouble to get into! If you're right, and the bloke watching wasn't interested in Edna after all, then I'm not getting into anything.'

Ganesh considered this argument and grudgingly admitted it made sense. 'After all,' he said, 'what possible interest could Edna be to anyone?'

'There you are,' I agreed, even though it sounded as though I had accepted what he'd said and I hadn't. I knew someone *was* interested in Edna.

I had hoped Ganesh would let it go at that but he was in lecturing mode. He couldn't get Hari to listen to him so he was obliging me to do it.

'The problem is,' he began again, very unfairly I thought, 'as soon as you start poking your nose in, there's trouble all over the place. You sort of attract it. You make things happen. You're a – a catalyst, that's the word!'

That really got my goat. 'If everyone was like you,' I snapped, 'no one would do anything! They'd all stand by and let awful things happen. Incidentally, I don't poke my nose in; I am a public-spirited citizen. What should I do when I see something I feel is dodgy, run away?'

'It wouldn't be a bad idea,' said Ganesh.

There was a silence. 'You wouldn't,' I said at last. Because he wouldn't, not if he thought someone needed help.

Ganesh pushed away the remains of the cheese-filled spud. He brushed back his hair which he'd regrown after cutting it for the play. It was now well past ear-lobe length. I wondered if that was what Hari had been nagging at him about.

'Fran, listen to me for once, will you? It's great to help someone if you can. But if you can't help and you're just meddling, it makes things worse. That's what you need to remember: there's helping and there's interfering and the line between the two is very fine.'

If he'd left it there, I would have shut up. But he overstepped the mark again and went on to say, 'And as far as Edna is concerned, you're onto a loser.'

'Someone has to help the losers,' I told him. 'I'm not running away from Edna just because she's wandering the streets wearing three layers of cast-offs and woolly hats in warm weather.'

'Don't say I didn't warn you,' was all I got in reply.

'OK, I'll consider myself warned, all right!' I growled at him.

I had told Ganesh I would find Edna and I would. I set about it first thing the very next morning. It would be no good hanging round the Tube station because she might not walk that way again for weeks. If she was scared of the man in white, she probably wouldn't. But I knew she was living in a hostel. So the obvious thing to do was to visit all the hostels in the area and ask for her.

I hadn't told Ganesh I meant to do this. It was a pretty sure thing that whatever I proposed doing, Ganesh would have objected and found a dozen reasons why a) I shouldn't do it and b) it wouldn't work if I did. He was only running true to form in all his doom-mongering, although I can't say his argument hadn't given me a moment's pause for thought. Perhaps I was imagining things and meddling? No, I decided, it might be a good idea to run from this particular little problem, but I wasn't going to do it. But when did I ever make a sensible decision?

Perhaps it's something to do with never taking Ganesh's advice.

Numerous hostels for the homeless or mentally afflicted exist in the capital. If Edna had been wandering around all day, she could have walked quite a distance from her hostel. I was aware that it need not be a local one. But I still thought it most likely she was living in the general area. Anyway, I had to start somewhere. To begin near to home and cast ever-increasing circles made the most sense.

What reason could I give anyone for asking about her, supposing I found the right place? I didn't know her surname. Perhaps her real first name wasn't even Edna.

As it happened I was again without work, either acting or any other sort. Usually, when there's nothing else on offer, I help out at the newsagent's but they hadn't needed me lately. Perhaps it wasn't because he'd refused to cut his hair but because business was so slow that Ganesh and his uncle had quarrelled. Hari gets tetchy when receipts are down. Then, when he's tetchy, he nags Ganesh about his hair. I ought to do something about my hair, too. The red colour was awful. But now I had business in hand and it would have to wait.

So I went about my task in a businesslike way. I contacted local Social Services and talked to a nice woman wearing a pink Marks and Spencer's cardigan. She worked in a cluttered office surrounded by files and pictures of cats. I told her I was a social studies student, researching the economic effects of the increase in the ageing population, with comparisons drawn over a cross-section of socio-demographic groups, projected rise in per capita outlay and falling birth rate. I wasn't quite sure what that meant and hoped she didn't ask. I got the key phrases from an article in a magazine in the local library, wrote them down and joined them up. As part of my research, I explained, I needed to investigate the provision of hostel care.

I didn't consider any of this telling lies; I considered it being creative. Besides, not all of what I told her was untrue.

'I've been homeless myself,' I said with perfect honesty. 'Luckily those days are behind me. My particular area of interest is housing the elderly homeless and those who might be considered as having mental problems. Not serious problems but low-level ones.'

'Touched?' suggested the woman kindly.

'That's it. It's a neglected category and that's why I've chosen it. People prefer to write about dysfunctional families or . . .'

I glanced at the cat photos. 'Or feral animals in a city environment. A friend of mine is writing about urban foxes. But we all grow old, don't we? And not all of us fit into society.'

The woman's face darkened and I feared I'd made a tactless remark. Perhaps she had just passed a landmark birthday date. But it turned out something else had caused her displeasure.

'One of my kitties was killed by a fox,' she said. 'Right in my back garden.'

I commiserated.

She cheered up. 'Well, let's see what we can do for you,' she said.

She eventually gave me a list of hostels, along with a load of other stuff, and wished me luck in my studies.

'Come back and see us when you've graduated,' were her closing words. 'We desperately need suitable people to come forward for training in social work. Have you thought of being a social worker? There are lots of opportunities and you seem just the type of young person we're looking to recruit. If you want to talk about it as a career option at any time, come and see me.'

I resolved not to tell Ganesh any of this because he would have asked me if I had felt absolutely no twinges of conscience. To which the reply would have been, no, I didn't.

I left clutching my list of hostels and set out. I took my dog, Bonnie, with me. I was going to be gone for the best part of the day and I don't like leaving her shut in for so long. She frets.

It was a warm day and not long before both Bonnie and I were hot and footsore and fed up. I began to think I should have listened to Ganesh. I was wasting my time. Not only that but the places I called at were unutterably depressing and, in some cases, frightening. I dodged nutters, druggies and alkies. When I wasn't scared by what I found I was angry and frustrated. I could never be a social worker, I realised, because I could never cultivate the necessary objectivity. I would care too much about each and every one and consequently probably mess up. Today only obstinacy (and not wanting to have to admit to Ganesh that he was right) made me carry on. As is often the case, just when I was about to give up I struck pay dirt.

It was a small place, run by some charity, and located in a run-down Victorian house which had once been a beautiful home. It was not unlike the house in which I had a flat. A few trees struggled to survive in the quiet road outside and one grew directly opposite the front door and spread its branches across the pavement. It wasn't yet autumn but leaves were just starting to turn colour and a few to drift down. Some lay scattered across the unswept steps leading up to the door. Among them, sitting on the top step, huddled against an ornate cast-iron boot scraper, sat a young woman with long tangled hair, wearing mismatched odds and ends of clothing. She was weeping silently.

She wasn't the first mentally ill person I'd come across in my trawl that day, but it was still awful to watch. If she'd sobbed loudly and rocked herself in grief I could have handled it better. But this silent weeping like a stone figure in a Victorian cemetery was completely unnerving. I edged round the girl and rang the doorbell.

After a few moments I heard footsteps and the door opened just wide enough for someone to peer out. They learn to be cautious in these places, I guess. I was relieved to see – as far as I *could* see him – that the man who'd answered the bell looked normal.

'We're full,' he said but in a kindly way.

'I'm not looking for a bed,' I replied.

He opened the door a little wider. 'That's all right, then. We couldn't take you, no matter what the circumstances.'

I wondered if the weeping girl had been similarly rejected and that was the cause of her grief. I indicated her surreptitiously and whispered to him, 'Is she all right?'

It was a stupid question because obviously she wasn't but I didn't quite know what else to say. The man appeared to be unaware of her although how he could be, when she sat there on his top step, I couldn't imagine.

'Sandra?' he replied. 'Yes, yes, don't worry. She's a bit sad this morning, aren't you, Sandy?'

He stooped and patted the girl's shoulder. She swayed a little to and fro and then carried on weeping as before, only now making a snuffling noise. If anything, it was worse.

'Don't worry,' the man said to me. 'We're keeping an eye on her. Was that why you rang? You were worried about Sandra?'

'No,' I confessed, 'about somebody else. Can I come in? I won't take up much of your time and I'd really appreciate it.'

'One of our residents?' he asked more sharply.

'I don't know,' I said. 'That's one of the things I'm trying to find out.'

'We don't give out information on residents.'

'I'm not asking for information.'

'You said you were,' he pointed out, not unreasonably.

'Please,' I begged, 'can I come in and explain? It will take five minutes and I'll pick up the dog.' I scooped Bonnie up into my arms as I spoke. She had been sitting by the weeping girl, watching her with interest. The girl appeared as oblivious of Bonnie as of me and the conversation going on over her head.

The guardian stared down thoughtfully at Sandra and I think it was more on her account than on mine that he made his decision. He opened the door wide enough for me to squeeze through and stood back.

I accepted the silent invitation and nipped through into the hall before he changed his mind. A long gloomy corridor stretched out before us. The hall floor was tiled in cream, burgundy red and black in a startling geometric pattern which was probably original to the house and had suffered in the one hundred and fifty-odd years since it had been put down. It was chipped, cracked and scuffed but clean enough. The stairs, to my right, were carpeted in dull cord carpet and the banisters almost black. The landing above was plunged in darkness. The doors leading off the hall were impressively panelled but varnished dark brown. Why on earth didn't they paint them white or a bright colour and cheer the whole area up? No wonder Sandra out there on the steps wept. If you got up in the morning feeling a bit low, by the time you got down to the hall you must feel suicidal. And Edna was right. The whole place did smell of baked beans.

A door opened to our left and a rather tough-looking young woman in jeans and a well-worn denim jacket stepped out of what appeared to be an office and glared at me.

'OK, Simon?'

'OK, Nikki,' he replied.

I wished she'd been called something else, because I've a sister somewhere called Nicola. But that's another story.

To me, Simon said, 'Come into the office.'

We followed Nikki and found ourselves in a surprisingly comfortable room. 'Office' to me suggests desks and computer terminals, stacks of files and so on. It's an impersonal environment although people do, like the woman at Social Services with her cat pictures, try and personalise their surroundings. This room had a computer on a little desk in a corner and Nikki had returned to it and sat with her back to us. But the rest of the room was furnished with battered but comfortable armchairs set in a circle before a fireplace which had once been rather splendid. The grate had an iron hood and patterned glazed tiles surrounding it, most of them now cracked. The fire bed itself was filled with large dusty pine cones painted gold and silver and I suspected they had been there since the previous Christmas. Clearly the hearth wasn't in use for its intended purpose. An elderly white painted monster of a radiator under the window now served to warm the place in cold weather. But the hearth provided a home for an electric kettle which was plugged into a socket on the wall beside it.

'You can put the dog down,' said Nikki from her computer without looking round.

I set down Bonnie who began to sniff around in a rather familiar way. She doesn't have the best manners. But I felt that here it didn't matter. It was a nice room, designed to make the frightened and bewildered people who came there relax. I felt better about Sandra out there on the steps. If Nikki and Simon were looking after her, her situation wasn't as bad as it first looked.

'Coffee?' enquired Simon.

'No thanks,' I said. Then, more honestly, 'I'd love a cup, to tell you the truth.'

He smiled. He wasn't bad-looking now I had a chance to study him. I supposed him in his thirties. He needed a decent haircut but then, so did I. Nikki was probably about the same age. Her haircut was similar to his and I wondered if they cut one another's hair. Neither of them was a snappy dresser. Simon wore jeans and a faded badly washed T-shirt stretched out of any shape. But his shoes were leather and although well worn looked as if originally they had been expensive. He went to switch on the kettle in the hearth. 'Nikki?'

'Yeah, sure, ta,' she said, still rattling her keyboard.

Simon took down mugs from a row of them along the mantelpiece and made us all coffee from a jar of cheap own-brand powder, adding coffee whitener powder from another jar. The result bore no resemblance to coffee as my grandma would have made it and would have horrified her. But it was hot and drinkable and I was glad of it.

'Right,' said Simon, seating himself opposite me. 'Let's hear it.'

I sipped my coffee, burned my tongue, and put the mug down hastily by my feet. I'd already decided I owed Nikki and Simon the truth, or as much of it as I was prepared to tell them. This wasn't just because they were nice people, but because they were experienced in hearing yarns of all sorts and would pretty soon suss out if I was making it all up.

'A couple of years ago,' I began, 'I lived in Rotherhithe in a squat. I don't live in squats now. I've got a flat. That is, a charity found a place for me in one of their converted houses. The rent's dead cheap.' I named the charity and Simon nodded.

'So you're one of theirs,' he said amiably and seemed to relax himself. He knew of the charity, probably knew some of its workers and could, if necessary, check on me. I wonder if he would.

I wasn't sure I liked being spoken of as if I was some sort of waif and stray collected up from the gutter but, in a manner of speaking, it wasn't that far off the mark. Things had been looking grim when the offer of the flat had come through.

The keyboard had stopped rattling. Nikki was sipping her coffee. She either had an asbestos tongue or she was listening. I guessed both.

I went on to explain about Edna living in the churchyard and how we had all been moved on and I'd not seen her since until very recently when I'd bumped into her in Camden High Street.

'She told me she was living in a hostel,' I said. 'I meant to ask her which one but she decided to cut short the conversation and scurried off. She always did that. It wasn't because of anything I'd said. It's just Edna's way.'

Simon nodded and my heart rose. Edna was here. He knew her and her mannerisms.

'I want to be sure she's all right,' I said. 'She still talks about the cats she looked after in the churchyard and how they were taken away. I don't want to think she's living somewhere rough now. She's too old.' I stopped but neither of them said anything. 'I don't know her surname,' I finished lamely.

Nikki had swivelled round on her chair and was watching us, her mug cupped in her hands. I picked up my mug from the carpet for something to do and because the coffee was now cool enough to drink. Bonnie had settled before the hearth and was staring intently at the gold and silver pine cones, ears pricked. There were probably spiders in there. She chases a big spider that comes out in the evening and scuttles across my carpet. The spider plays dead; Bonnie loses interest and wanders away. When she's gone, the spider comes back to life and resumes its nightly hunt. This means the average house spider is more intelligent than my dog.

Simon turned his head and exchanged glances with Nikki. She gave an almost imperceptible nod. He turned back to me.

'We don't normally give out information about our residents to enquirers,' he said, 'as I was telling you earlier. People are not always frank about their reasons for seeking someone out and the person concerned might not want to be found. It's particularly tricky with youngsters, although we don't deal here with too many young people. We're a small charity, not unlike the one which housed you. It means we can know our residents rather better as individuals than in bigger organisations. We like to think we live here as a family.' He must have seen something in my face because he gave a wry smile. 'You're thinking it must be a pretty dysfunctional kind of family. But we like to think we're not more dysfunctional than many families in the more conventional sense.'

I thought of my family. We'd been pretty dysfunctional. I nodded. But I was feeling a little guilty because I hadn't told Simon and Nikki about the man in white who was my real reason for trying to track down Edna. But what was there to tell? Ganesh had said I was imagining the man's interest in Edna. Who could be interested in an old bag lady? Ganesh was probably right, again.

'We think that, in this case, it's all right to make an exception – up to a point. We think we probably have your friend here. We do have an older lady by the name of Edna Walters. She's somewhat uncommunicative and that means we know very little about her. She says she can't remember her date of birth. However, we have managed to establish that she's in her sixties.'

Tactlessly I blurted, 'Blimey, is that all?' I'd always imagined her to be about eighty.

'Her lifestyle has aged her,' said Simon simply. 'Social Services had quite a time chasing her through the system and even now they can't be sure they have tracked down the right Edna Walters. I think she is the same person as the one you know because our Edna Walters was at one time living rough in Rotherhithe as you describe.'

I was beginning to feel the system was swallowing me. I opened my mouth to say that whichever Edna Social Services reckoned they had identified, I knew her to be the one who had been my sort-of neighbour, but Simon swept on before I could speak.

'She isn't here at the moment. She's out for most of the day. We don't know where she goes. She comes back at night, though, in time for our evening meal. I can't tell you more. Perhaps I shouldn't have told you that much. But it's answered your question and I hope it's put your worries about her to rest. It might not be a good idea if you made contact with her directly.'

'Why not?' I asked bluntly.

He looked embarrassed. 'We've worked hard to gain her trust. Each time she leaves the house we're not sure she'll return. So far, she has.' When I said nothing he added emphatically, 'Edna likes to be left alone. If you know her, you'll understand. I've answered your original question. You have no need to be worried she's sleeping rough.'

He was right, of course. I stood and Bonnie jumped up from her place by the pine cones. 'Thanks for telling me,' I said. 'Now I know she's here with you I know she's all right. I appreciate your telling me about it all. It's awkward for you, I understand that. Thanks for the coffee.'

As we approached the front door on the hall side I asked, pointing at the door panels, 'Are you sure it's all right for Sandra to sit out there crying like that?'

'She'll come in when she feels like it,' he said. 'We do check she takes her medication although that's not always easy.'

Sandra still huddled forlornly on the step but had stopped weeping. Simon stooped and touched her shoulder. 'Coming inside, Sandy? How about a coffee?'

She gave no sign of having heard.

'When you're ready,' he said to her. He nodded brightly at me and shut the door.

I walked carefully past Sandra and out onto the pavement. They were good people and Edna was in safe hands. I was glad I'd found out where she lived. I'd be able to tell Ganesh. Perhaps I'd been mistaken about the man in the baseball cap. It could be that everything was all right.

I set off down the road feeling quite cheerful with Bonnie pattering alongside. Then I saw him, standing on the corner, seconds before he saw me. He was still dressed all in white or some very pale colour and, as before, he turned and made off round the corner the moment he realised I'd spotted him. That's why he waited about on corners: it gave him a choice of escape routes.

'Not this time, sunshine!' I muttered grimly. 'This time you're not getting away from me!'

Chapter Three

I ran across the road and round the corner he had turned. Another long residential street stretched out before me, lined with houses much like the one I'd left. To my dismay the pavements were empty of pedestrians; no sign of the man in the baseball cap at all. He had simply vanished. I couldn't believe it. I stood there open-mouthed.

But there were two people in the street, house-painters in emulsion-stained white overalls, who stood in the roadway loading ladders and buckets into the rear of a van.

I hurried down to them. 'Hi!'

They stopped work and surveyed me. One was short with curly fair hair and the other tall with lank shoulder-length dark hair. Tom and Jerry, or Jerry and Tom, if you want to be a stickler for accuracy.

'Hullo, love,' Jerry returned my greeting.

'Sorry to bother you,' I said, 'I thought I saw a friend of mine turn the corner into this street so I ran after him, but I don't see him. Have you noticed anyone? He's young and wears a white baseball cap and T-shirt.'

They exchanged glances and shook their heads in unison.

'Sorry, sweetheart,' said Tom.

'We've been working in there.' Jerry nodded his curly head towards the house behind us. I looked. The front door was open and I could see through it that the whole place was untenanted and obviously undergoing renovation.

'Three flats,' went on Jerry. 'Three hundred grand apiece at least. Wouldya believe it?'

'Yes,' I said. 'Well, at least they'll be freshly done up.'

'Yeah,' said Tom. 'New bathrooms, new kitchens. Don't know about the wiring. You want to watch the wiring in these old places.'

'Floorboards,' said Jerry cryptically.

'Yeah, floorboards, too,' agreed his mate.

We'd spent enough time on interior decorating. 'Look,' I said. 'I know you've been busy and not paying attention to anything but work but are you sure you weren't aware of anyone going past? Even if you didn't see him exactly, you might have heard him or just sensed someone was there.'

They shook their heads.

'Sorry,' Tom.

'Will one of us do?' offered Jerry.

I thanked him and said perhaps some other time. We parted the best of friends.

I made my way back to home turf a prey to turbulent emotions like the heroine of the Victorian melodrama Ganesh liked to cast me as. I wanted to tear my hair, short though it is, and beat my breast. (I'm somewhat deficient in that department, too. I'd never get a job modelling those lace and wire confections designed to lift and separate.) All I could do was scowl at innocent passers-by. They quickened their step in alarm. Understandably people do sometimes find me strange.

I *had* seen him, dammit! There's nothing wrong with my eyesight. I don't indulge in banned substances. I hadn't been hallucinating. He'd been there and he'd seen me. I knew him and he knew me. Once again, he'd proved too quick and too clever for me. Before, this had only been about Edna. Now it was getting personal. This guy was running rings round me. It was a matter of honour. I will track you down, mate, I promised. You won't make me look like a blundering idiot. I will prove to Ganesh that you exist as some sort of genuine threat to Edna.

I called at the newsagent's. On the way in I passed a man coming out and holding the early edition of the *Evening Standard*, but otherwise inside it was customer-free. Hari stood disconsolately by his till.

'Ah, Francesca, my dear,' he greeted me with the air of an undertaker. He leaned forwards and whispered, 'Where are they?'

'Who?' I asked foolishly

He swept a hand around his shop. 'The customers! Where are they? Where are the children? School is out, isn't it? Why are they not here buying drinks and snacks and trying to pinch things, eh?'

'Half term?' I suggested.

He shook his head. 'It is worse, Francesca. I have a rival.' He pointed somewhere behind me and down the road. 'Supermarket!' he hissed. 'Isn't it enough for them they sell food and washing powder? No, they sell newspapers and magazines, crisps and Coke and chewing gum. They have a kiosk by the door. The children go there. They wander round the shop floor and it is easier to pinch things, isn't it, from a supermarket?'

Hari seemed to have a very poor opinion of local youth. I supposed it was based on experience.

'Here I watch them!' he added grimly.

The lack of welcome the young customers had got here might have contributed to their taking their trade elsewhere but it wouldn't be tactful to say so. 'Where's Ganesh?' I asked.

'In the stockroom,' said Hari. 'We should be so busy at this time he should be needed here, watching those children.'

If I was a school kid, I'd stay clear of Hari's shop.

'It is unfair competition, isn't it?' wailed Hari.

Ganesh was in the dark dusty stockroom armed with a clipboard and pencil and counting boxes of confectionery. He looked up sharply when I came in and then relaxed when he saw who it was.

'Is he still moaning?' he asked without any prior greeting.

'About the supermarket taking his trade? Yes.'

'Of course customers have moved there,' said Ganesh crossly. 'He's such a miserable git. He's paranoid, that's what. He follows them round the shop. I've told him not to do it. You've got to be pleasant, make them feel welcome, that they're individuals. Tell 'em it's nice to see them again. Ask them how they are. It's called customer relations. My uncle,' said Ganesh, 'lacks communication and interpersonal skills.'

'Have you been reading those business studies books again?' I asked him.

Perhaps the difficulties with Hari had inspired Ganesh to broaden his horizons; though I doubted they would result in his actually moving on. However, he had recently been compiling an impressive collection of non-fiction books. Some were the usual self-help sort: train your memory; improve your diet; get super-fit with simple exercises; transform your wardrobe and by this means your life. Some offered to plug the gaps in your education: the business studies; computer programming (Ganesh doesn't own a computer); present-tense Latin and so on. ('Why present-tense Latin, Gan?' 'So that I can read inscriptions, you know, in old churches and that.' 'But for that you need past-tense Latin, Gan.') Some were reference books should you feel like checking out anything. There wasn't a decent paperback among them.

'I don't need a book to tell me Hari's problem. I live with him!' snarled Ganesh now.

'I've got problems, too,' I told him. 'Stop worrying about Hari and put your mind to something constructive. That's probably in your business studies book. Don't waste time on negative energy.'

Ganesh put down the clipboard but kept the pencil so that he could jab it dramatically at my chest.

'You've been getting into trouble. I knew it. What have you done?'

'I went looking for Edna. I told you I would.'

'Did you find her?'

I shook my head. 'Not exactly. I found the hostel where she's living. The people there are pretty good.'

'So, nothing to worry about.' He looked relieved. He had been concened I was going to get into some scrape. It was quite a shame to destroy his rising optimism.

'Well, Gan, there is.' I explained to him about the second appearance of the man in the baseball cap and how he'd disappeared so mysteriously.

'He's pretty good at giving people the slip. He thinks quickly on his feet and uses whatever is to hand, like plunging into the street market. I reckon I've worked out what he did this time. He knew I was after him and if he was still in the street, I'd see him. Those two decorators were carrying stuff out of the house and they'd left the front door open. I reckon he nipped in there behind their backs, waited until I'd left and then slipped out again. They didn't see him go in and if they saw him coming out, it wouldn't matter. He'd spin them a yarn about me being an ex-girlfriend he was trying to dodge. *Or* he might have told them that first and asked if he could dash inside out of sight. They wouldn't question it and they lied to me when I turned up immediately afterwards. Blokes stick together over things like that.'

'And,' asked Ganesh in that quiet dangerous way, 'did you ask the decorators, *both* in *white* clothing, if either of them had walked down to the corner of the street a few minutes earlier for any reason and stood about where you might have seen him? Looking for a mate who was supposed to meet them there, for example?'

'Ganesh! I did not see a man in a white overall! I saw that guy in the white baseball cap and white T-shirt and pants! He likes to dress in white.'

'You're getting obsessed, Fran,' said Ganesh seriously. 'You're getting like Hari. You've got this fellow on the brain. You didn't see him. You saw a house-painter.'

'Yes, I did see him! I know what I saw. I'm not blind and I'm not daft.'

'Why should he be there?'

I expelled my breath in a long hiss, seeking self-control. 'Because he's doing what I was doing, trying to find Edna.'

'What for?'

Almost dancing with frustration, I clenched my fist and shook it at him. '*I don't know why!*'

'Negative energy!' said Ganesh smugly.

I stormed out, Bonnie at my heels, and left him to count his confectionery stock.

I realised when I got out onto the pavement that I was very hungry and it wasn't just being in the storeroom surrounded by snacks. It was almost four o'clock. All I'd had to eat since cornflakes for breakfast was a Mars bar munched as I trudged round the hostels. I slowed my step by the busy little supermarket which was the cause of Hari's troubles. But on the point of going in and buying one of those chilled meals in little trays I changed my mind. It would feel like disloyalty to Hari and Ganesh, even though I wasn't going in there to use the newspaper kiosk. I walked on and got home to discover my fridge was empty. My store cupboard (a bit of a misnomer that) only held a packet of dried chicken soup and half a packet of cream crackers which had gone soft, plus a tin of dog food claiming to be made of beef and nourishing marrowbone jelly. I made the soup and drank it while nibbling the crackers and very unpleasant it all was. Bonnie tucked into the beef, doing rather better than me. I would have to go out and buy something to eat later.

I looked at my wristwatch. It was gone five now, nearly half past. Bonnie had settled down and gone to sleep, tired by her long walk. If I went now and walked quickly I might just reach Susie Duke's office before she closed up for the day. I would explain the mystery of Edna to Susie, get her opinion and, on the way out, pick up a kebab.

'I'm going out,' I explained to Bonnie. 'But I won't be long. Be a good dog.'

She opened one brown eye to make sure I wasn't going to drag her along with me just when she'd got settled. She made no effort to follow me.

The Duke Detective Agency (confidential enquiry agents) run by my good friend Susie Duke was located at that moment above a Turkish takeaway outlet in a busy parade of little shops. Odours of grilled meat permeated upwards through the floor, but it had its advantages as a location, so Susie assured me when she moved the business in there. It was easily reached, it wasn't her home address (always dodgy to give that to punters) and at lunchtime she could nip downstairs and buy a kebab as I was planning to do for my supper.

It was a tall old building. In addition to the Duke Detective Agency directly above the kebab shop there was another business, a tattoo parlour, above Susie. The Agency and the tattoo parlour were reached from the same staircase which was accessed from the street through a door next to the kebab place. The street door was unlocked during working hours to allow visitors to climb the stairs and seek a solution to their problems either by consulting a private investigator or, if they preferred, getting themselves a whole new set of tattoos.

You met some really odd-looking people coming down the stairs from the parlour. I mean, they often looked fairly odd when they passed you going up: they looked amazingly weird when they passed you going down after Michael the tattooist had done his work. Michael wasn't a man who contented himself with 'I Love Sheryl' or 'Hammers For Ever' with a representation of West Ham's coat of arms. Michael talked people into apocalyptic visions worthy of Hieronymus Bosch. Flames crawled up their arms and legs. Fantastic creatures played among them and rode serpents with bulging eyes, straight from a Snakes and Ladders board game. Occult symbols spattered the lot like strange confetti thrown down at a wedding.

The parlour's clients, on the other hand, probably considered those who visited the detective agency equally peculiar.

If the two sets of customers shared anything, it was the apprehension on their faces as they arrived and the expression of mixed relief and doubt when they left. They were relieved they'd got it over with and beginning to wonder if they'd done the right thing. Either way realisation was dawning on them that it was irreversible.

The door on the first floor giving access to the Agency bore a neat little notice with the name of the business and the hours the office was open. If you passed through this door, you found yourself in the reception area. Because the whole office area was really just one big room, this reception area had been created by subdivision. A half-glazed partition screened new arrivals from the inner sanctum which was Susie's consulting room, to borrow a phrase from the medical world.

The furnishings in Susie's room were pretty basic: a desk, a chair and a filing cabinet. I don't know where Susie got that desk from. You can buy computer stations, nice modern ones, quite cheap from those discount warehouses. Susie's desk looked like something from a government department clear-out in the swinging sixties, cheap lacquered pine with burn and ink marks, scratches and doodles all over it. Possibly it had come with the office, understandably abandoned by the previous tenant. Her little laptop computer usually stood open on the top but I don't think Susie trusted much information to the computer. Most of it was in the filing cabinet which was battleship grey of old-fashioned design and looked as if it might have come along with the desk from the same ministry somewhere in the depths of Whitehall.

I occasionally work for Susie on odd jobs but generally the sort of thing she does isn't my cup of tea. Checking people's credit and delivering summonses or lurking about trying to catch husbands/wives/partners and others who are two-timing their better halves isn't for me. Besides, Susie had found an 'operative', as she liked to call him, who was more suited to that kind of thing: Les Hooper.

I was hoping Les would be out on the trail when I got there and I'd find Susie alone. She is usually in the office at the end of the day to check the answerphone, put away sensitive material in the lockable file cabinet and catch up on any paperwork. I wasn't keen on Les, for no really good reason other than instinct and a desire to protect Susie from landing herself with a problem. Susie is a nice woman who has a tendency to take up with unattractive men. Her late husband, Rennie Duke, had been one such and Les Hooper was another. Not that, as far as I knew, her relationship with Les was anything other than professional, but 'mighty oaks from little acorns grow', as Sister Mary Joseph used to tell us. This was to explain how our childish fibs would lead us down the slippery path to becoming wastrels and criminals in adult life. Being a child of imagination and always ready to be sidetracked from the subject by some observation of my own, I always associated the acorns of the saying with the bunions which distorted Sister Mary Joseph's lace-up brogues. Perhaps I was just easily confused at the age of six.

My instinct about Les was equally tenuously connected with a distant memory of Eddie Kelly. Eddie lived at the end of our street when I was about ten years old. He was a big fellow, running to seed and untidy, and without any known means of earning a living. He and his wife (whose name no one knew) 'kept themselves to themselves' as people then said. If you met Eddie in the street he'd give you a broad nicotine-yellow smile and greet you but then quickly pass on. Few people returned his smile. He wasn't liked.

Mrs Kelly, of the unknown first name, was a thin nervous woman with unkempt blond hair dragged back into a ponytail secured with an elastic band. She never spoke to anyone. We'd see her scurrying from her house to the shops and back again. Sometimes no one saw her for a week or more but we knew she was there because washing appeared on the line in the overgrown back garden. Eddie wasn't the sort of man who washed out his own smalls. Mrs Eddie must have put the wash out after dark because we never saw her do it. She often wore large sunglasses, even in winter, and inappropriately large amounts of colourful make-up at other times. It never did quite disguise the purplish areas beneath.

Susie is an attractive woman. Perhaps Mrs Kelly had looked like Susie when she was younger and hadn't yet taken up with Eddie. Susie runs her own little business. She would be a bit of a catch for someone like Les whom I had marked down as a perennial loser, quite apart from his reminding me of Kelly. So I hoped that Susie would eventually wake up to his deficiencies and give him the boot. I wouldn't like to think of Susie hiding away and putting on sunglasses on rainy days to go to the shops.

I was out of luck. Business must be slow. Susie and Les were sitting in the two rickety chairs drinking tea and chatting like a couple of old biddies on a park bench. This intimacy boded ill.

'Hullo, Fran, love!' cried Susie, jumping up to give me a welcoming hug.

Les raised his tea mug in salute and growled, 'Hello, darling.'

He called everyone 'darling' so it didn't signify affection, as Susie's greeting had. I didn't want affection from Les and I never like being called 'darling'.

'Hullo, Les,' I said. 'Nothing happening?' Meaning, isn't there something you could be doing somewhere else?

'Very quiet,' said Susie, answering for him. 'Real dead. Where are all the clients?'

'The Patels have the same problem at the newsagent's,' I told her.

'Yeah, well,' said Susie philosophically. 'Want a cuppa?'

Les rose ponderously to his feet and offered me his chair while

Susie re-boiled the electric kettle. This unexpected gallantry made me suspicious. He knew I had little time for him. He'd have to do more than offer me a seat to change my mind.

In lieu of his chair, he propped himself against the desk. He was a big man, like Eddie, and in the small room he loomed even larger. He wore a scuffed leather jacket and he needed a shave. His shoes were dirty. My grandma told me to avoid young men who didn't clean their shoes. This omission denoted sloppy thinking and a grubby lifestyle generally. It was certain they would never 'get on'.

Les was middle-aged, still didn't know what shoe polish was, and had obviously never 'got on', so my grandma was right. To me he looked like an ex-con and I had a horrible suspicion that's what he was. I asked Susie once but she avoided the question though she did say something about poachers turning gamekeepers.

'He knows people,' she had added mysteriously. 'He's got contacts. He's useful.'

'Just make sure he or one of his crooked mates doesn't try and use you!' I'd warned her.

'I wasn't born yesterday!' Susie had replied chippily.

She had on her business suit today, snug-fitting, black, very short skirt. With it she wore black tights and high heels. This generally meant she had been calling on some client or someone else she wanted to impress. Her blond hair frothed in a cloud round her head and her white blouse revealed plenty of cleavage. If the client was a man, he'd be impressed, all right.

'Had you come to see if I had any work for you, Fran?' she asked. 'Or is this social? I hope it's social, 'cos I've got no work for you. I had to go to the bank this morning and explain about my cash-flow problem. Clients are as rare as hen's teeth, aren't they,

Les? I mean, I haven't even got any work for Les here. That's why we're sitting here chewing the fat.'

Les uttered a gargling sound through the bottom of his tea mug.

So the business suit had been to impress the bank. I hoped it had done the trick. I debated whether to tell Susie about Edna. I'd rather Les hadn't been there because he wouldn't understand my interest in an old bag lady. But, as I'd come, I thought I might as well tell them of my adventures.

They listened politely. I couldn't tell what Les was thinking but he appeared to pay close attention. Susie hung on every word.

'Weird,' she said, when I stopped speaking. 'You are absolutely sure the man you saw opposite the hostel was the same as the one you saw on the corner of Parkway and Camden High Street?'

'I am absolutely certain. Ganesh reckons I saw a house-painter in white overalls but white overalls look nothing like a T-shirt, baseball cap and long shorts. This man, whoever he is, isn't the sort you forget. He looks as though he's been in the dark for ages and just come out into the light. It's made him long and pale like a stick of celery.'

Les put his mug to his lips although he must have long finished his tea. He seemed to realise it was empty and put it down on the desk.

'What about the old lady?' he asked hoarsely. 'Any use asking her?'

'None at all,' I said firmly. 'You can't have a normal conversation with Edna.'

'Give it a miss!' advised Les. 'Waste of time. Well, I gotta be going. Gimme a bell when you need me, Suze.'

He slouched out and the atmosphere changed.

'Right!' said Susie brightly. 'You free? Let me get cleared up here and we'll go out and eat. Give us a chance to have a natter and catch up.'

After some debate we settled for a steak house and when we had ourselves nicely parked in a corner and had ordered, I opened the conversation with the question I always asked her these days.

'When are you going to get rid of him?'

'You mean Les, don't you?' mumbled Susie, playing for time.

'Of course I mean Les! I mean, just look at him. I'm not surprised you haven't got any clients. One look at him would put off anyone.'

'Oh, he doesn't deal with the clients,' she assured me earnestly. 'I do all of that. I want to know exactly what they want and ask them for information I need to have and settle the fee, all that kind of thing. I couldn't leave it to Les. He's not got an office sort of brain.'

'Agreed. I imagine he has the brain of a not particularly gifted orang-utan.'

'Just 'cos you don't like the poor bloke,' said Susie reproachfully.

The waiter brought our wine and hung about eyeing Susie's cleavage, tilting the bottle and leaning over the table for a better look. We thanked him, removed the bottle from his grasp and sent him on his way.

'Too right I don't like him,' I said when we were alone again. 'Don't trust him; wouldn't walk down a dark street with him; wouldn't lend him money; wouldn't introduce him to anyone I knew.'

'Les is all right,' she insisted, 'and he's brilliant at tailing anyone. He blends in with the surroundings.'

I opened my mouth to ask what kind of surroundings these

might be. But I gave up the subject for the time being, anyway. She knew my opinion.

She realised I was willing to change the topic of conversation and cheered up. 'I went round old man Patel's shop the other day, as it happened. I needed to get a look at the day's papers so I thought I'd take him my business. I bought six of them, all different, you know. I was looking for a trial report I've got an interest in. Hari, he's called, isn't he? Ganesh's uncle?'

I nodded. 'Did he recognise you?'

'Oh yes, he knew I was your friend. He was very nice to me. I thought he looked a bit glum, though. Ganesh wasn't there. I think his uncle had sent him off somewhere on some business.'

'Ganesh is being a bit awkward at the moment,' I told her. 'Hari gets at him so Ganesh nags at me. He doesn't want me trying to find out what's behind this business with Edna.'

'*If* anything's behind it. You've got to admit it, Fran, the old lady doesn't sound the sort anyone would want to spend time following about.'

The steaks arrived and put an end to conversation for a few minutes. 'I believe someone is following her, even so. What do you think I should do next, Susie?' I asked at last. 'You're the expert.'

She put down her knife and fork. 'How are *you* at tailing someone?'

'Reasonable, I think.'

'Then you do what your bloke in white is doing. That way, you find out what his game is. You follow your old lady round the town for a day; see where she goes and what she does. See if this man in white shows up again, or anyone else. You know where she lives. You know she goes out all day. So if you're waiting nearby early in the morning, you should see her leave and off you go. Nothing to it.' She stared at me thoughtfully. 'You need a wig. That bright red hair is a dead giveaway. But I've got a whole lot of wigs. Come home with me after we finish here and pick one out.'

She did have a selection of wigs, a whole shelf of them in the top of her wardrobe. I tried them all on and settled for a black bob which I fancied made me look like a twenties flapper.

'Wear different clothes. Don't wear anything the bloke in white has seen before. Don't make the same mistake he made. He's got a fashion hang-up for white and it meant you recognised him second time around. Wear something neutral, jeans and a dark top.'

'Will do,' I promised as we walked to her front door.

'And wear trainers,' was her parting advice, called after me. 'Don't wear those clumping great boots you like so much. You can't run in those. Wear trainers in case you have to make a fast getaway.'

I stopped in the doorway to turn back and say, 'Thanks, Susie. Thanks for taking me seriously. You don't think I'm imagining all this, do you?'

She hesitated. 'Look, Fran, in the end it doesn't matter what I think, does it? I wasn't there and didn't see what you saw. I don't know the old bag lady like you do. What matters is that you believe you saw something fishy and you want to sort it out.' She grinned. 'I keep telling you, Fran. When it comes to detective work, you're a natural. You've got the instinct, see? And you've got the bug. You can't leave it alone. You've gotta know.'

Susie understood. Ganesh, for all his loyal support over a long friendship, didn't. Yet neither of them could fathom my yearning to act.

'Yeah,' I said. 'I've got to know.'

Chapter Four

'What have you got on your head?' asked Ganesh in gloomy resignation as if my appearance was the outward sign of a long-anticipated deterioration in my mental state, a step on the road to becoming Edna.

If I was to be out most of the day I couldn't take Bonnie with me. I particularly couldn't take her with me if I wanted to be inconspicuous. Hari and Ganesh open the shop at crack of dawn to take in the newspaper deliveries, so I'd taken her round there and asked if she could stay in their storeroom until I came to pick her up. Dogs aren't normally allowed in the shop but Hari imagines Bonnie is a good watchdog and he doesn't mind her in the storeroom. She has a little bed in there and even Ganesh doesn't grumble too much. Ganesh isn't a dog person, and he isn't a dog's favourite either. They all bark or growl at him. Bonnie puts up with him; they have an agreement to ignore one another. But someone had to feed her.

I had carefully arranged Susie's black wig over my red hair before I left home because it's the sort of job you need a mirror for. I thought it looked pretty good. It also gave me a chance to get my own back.

'You didn't like my red hair,' I told Ganesh, 'so I borrowed this from Susie until I can get my own colour changed.'

He sniffed and said nothing, looking a bit nonplussed. He had grumbled about my red hair, after all.

'Here you are,' I went on. 'Here's her lunch.' I handed him a small tin of pet food.

'What's in it?' muttered Ganesh, trying to read the tiny print on the tin in the storeroom's poor light. 'These things always stink.'

'It's chicken.'

'I'm a vegetarian; I shouldn't have to handle this stuff.'

'So use a long spoon. I'm not asking you to eat it, for goodness' sake!'

Ganesh put the tin on a shelf. 'What are you going to do all day? Or would I rather not know?'

'I'm spending the day tailing Edna, just to see where she goes and if anyone speaks to her or if anyone else is doing as I am, following her.'

'The mysterious guy in white, right? That's the real reason for the Addams Family get-up. You don't give a toss what I think of your hair. You're in disguise. You're imagining all this, you know, and that wig won't fool anyone for very long.'

'So, if I'm imagining it, it can't do me any harm. Keep an eye on her water bowl, too, will you? She seems to get thirsty these days. Perhaps I ought to take her to the vet. It might be a symptom of something.'

Hari yelled at Ganesh that he needed him and could he stop gossiping and come pretty damn quick.

I nipped out quickly too. I had to be outside Edna's hostel concealed somewhere before she left.

It was fortunate that there were so many trees in the road as I was able to station myself behind one with a fat trunk and lurk. If anyone in any of the houses noticed me they might wonder what

I was doing. But one advantage of hanging around at that early hour was that everyone was busy getting ready to go to work or on the school run so no one had time to stare around them. There were quite a few school kids in this street, I discovered. The air resounded to cries of 'Do hurry up, Clarissa!' or the like, and 4x4s rattled past almost in a convoy. I wondered how these obviously well-heeled types liked having the hostel in their midst. Not much, I guessed.

Several people came and went at the hostel. It was quite busy. I saw Simon at the door a few times, but no sign of Nikki. I had to keep a lookout for her, in case she lived elsewhere and would arrive shortly and spot me. In the same way, I had to watch out for the man in white. I was glad Sandra hadn't yet taken up her wailing position on the steps. She really freaked me out, to be honest.

A little after nine thirty, Edna came out of the front door and wobbled off down the road. I waited until she got to the corner and set off in pursuit, keeping to the other side of the street. When I reached the corner I could see her quite a way ahead of me. She moved faster than the impression she gave. I glanced round. No one else seemed interested either in me or in her.

Following Edna was intriguing and boring by turns. If she came across a cat sitting on someone's wall she would stop and talk to it for ages. The cat would rub its head against her and, if I was near enough, I'd hear it chirrup in reply. It would be a regular old conversation. If she passed a wheelie bin she would stop, open the lid and rummage inside. Occasionally she found something she thought useful and then she added it to a growing collection of items in a crumpled supermarket carrier bag she had produced from her pocket. Joy glowed in her face when she found a rosebud lying on the pavement outside a florist shop, snapped off from some expensive bouquet. She picked it up, smoothed its crumpled petals with a gentle forefinger and held it to her nose before she fixed it carefully in the buttonhole of her baggy old coat. Nothing was missed.

What she did not do was stop and rest. In someone of her age that was remarkable and bore witness to how fit she was, despite appearances. She was accustomed to be on the move and I had to keep moving too.

Eventually we found ourselves proceeding up the Finchley Road past rows of respectable suburban houses and a kindergarten. I couldn't imagine what had brought Edna out here. Suddenly the bobbing figure ahead of me veered to the right and turned up a side road. Now where was she off to? I saw a little sign and realised with quite a shock that she appeared to be heading for Golders Green crematorium.

But I was wrong. She ignored the massive red-brick complex of the crematorium and its chapels on the right and dodged across the road and through the equally impressive gates of the Jewish cemetery facing it.

What now? I followed uneasily at a distance. There was another red-brick building ahead of us. Edna trotted round the side of that. I followed discreetly after a pause. To my right was a vast area of graves surrounded by neatly raked gravel. A gardener or maintenance man worked in the distance but there was no sign of Edna. Then I looked to the left and my eye was attracted by a movement. I just caught a glimpse of her squat form heading down a path through an older grassed area of graves and elaborate headstones, so I tiptoed in her wake.

There she was. She had found a stone seat a little way down the path, with a background of rose trees, and taken up residence on it. It must be a familiar spot to her.

This really shouldn't have surprised me. When I first knew her, she lived in a cemetery. She liked them. They were quiet dignified places where few visitors came and no chance passers-by. There no one bothered her. The company of the dead didn't rattle her at all. For a living presence there were usually birds and butterflies and small mammals, all the friends she wanted or needed. She looked as if she was going to be there for a while so I retraced my steps to the red-brick building and saw another behind it which inspection informed me was a toilet block. I decided to take a comfort break. I didn't know how much longer I was going to be out and about before I got the chance to take another.

When I came out again, Edna was still on her stone bench. She had taken some kind of food from the plastic bag and was turning it in her fingers. It was one of her gleanings from a wheelie bin. I supposed her picnic wouldn't poison her. People throw out perfectly good grub. But she made no attempt to eat it though still fiddling with it. A row of small birds had lined up in anticipation on a headstone. She nodded at them amiably. I had been wrong. The picnic was being prepared for them. From time to time, she would stop destroying the bread crusts to turn up her wrinkled face to the sunshine and close her eyes, enjoying its warmth. A smile would then spread over her cheeks, full of the purest contentment. She was at peace with herself and the world and, watching her, I felt at peace too.

But if I just stood there she'd see me, sooner or later. I knew how sharp her eyes were. I'd have to wait somewhere nearby. I withdrew discreetly to find a spot. I went outside the gates and walked up and down past the crem. But though I kept an eye on the cemetery gates, Edna didn't emerge through them. I crossed to the crematorium side and entered the complex, where I found a kind of walled courtyard with memorials attached to the brick.

Many of them were to show-business personalities and I walked slowly round, reading them.

When I returned to the cemetery on the other side of the road, the whole area was empty. Edna had gone.

I thought at first she had just moved and was sitting on the ground some distance from her first location. I began to stroll round the graves, nonchalantly, playing it cool, and then more intently, throwing aside any pretence I wasn't hunting. She had just dematerialised, or so it seemed. It was quite spooky, as if the ground had indeed swallowed her up. Only a little pile of carefully crumbled bread on the path before the stone bench showed that she had been there at all. It was being approached by cautious sparrows.

Had she spotted me earlier and waited until I'd temporarily withdrawn to make good her escape? She was a wily old bird. There was a movement somewhere to my left. I stepped behind a large headstone and peered down the rows.

There he was – and doing as I had been doing. A lanky white clad figure in the trademark baseball or tennis cap, he was casting up and down the rows of burials like a patient hound. How on earth had he got here? Why was he so much better at this sort of thing than me? And what, above all, did he want? This time I meant to find out. He wouldn't give me the slip. There was no one to help him out as the house painters had done. This time I had him.

I left my shelter when his back was turned and softly approached him across the grass. He wasn't aware of me until I was just a couple of metres away and then he sensed my presence and whirled round in panic. He didn't know whether I was a spectral apparition, a mugger or a site employee about to demand what he was doing.

He saw at once I wasn't any of these, but the black wig threw him for a few moments before he recognised me. There was no doubt that he did so. He even raised a bony forefinger and pointed it at me. With his white clothing and headstone surrounds the gesture was spooky.

Ganesh had been right about the wig being a poor disguise. But having placed me, recognition served to unnerve the man almost as much as his previous confusion. A ludicrous expression of dismay crossed his face, replacing the initial panic. He seemed to debate whether to run and then changed his mind and just stood there, looking at me warily and waiting for me to make the next move.

'Hi!' I said conversationally. 'Now, I wonder what you're doing. No, please, don't tell me you're visiting a grave. Edna's given us both the slip and I think it's time you and I had a real old heart-to-heart. How did you know she was here?'

He spoke then and his voice was thin and rather weedy like the rest of him. 'You followed her,' he said. 'I followed you. It was easy. You never looked round once. You were too scared you'd lose her. You just kept going and I just kept following. Mind you, I didn't know it was *you*, I thought it might be someone else. I followed, anyway.'

It wasn't just that he was better than me at this. It was that I was a blundering amateur. He'd been hanging around the hostel the previous day and I'd seen him. So this time, he'd made sure no one saw him. He learned from his mistakes. I didn't.

I must have looked my discomfort because his features twisted maliciously and his pale eyes glittered with unkind amusement.

'All right,' I said, 'my mistake. We still need to have that talk.'

He shook his head. 'My business is my own. You mind yours.'

'And you'll mind mine, too, it seems!' I snapped back. 'You

followed me. OK, you were using me to follow Edna, but you still owe me an explanation. Who are you? What's your interest in her?'

'What's yours?' he countered.

'She's an old friend from way back. We used to be neighbours of a sort.'

That grabbed his attention. His manner changed entirely, shedding the hostility. He really perked up. 'Did you? Then perhaps we do need to talk.'

'First you tell me your interest in her.' If he now wanted to speak to me, that shifted the balance of power. I could insist on a few answers.

'It's my job,' he said unwillingly, realising he had to give me something.

'What do you mean?' I scowled at him. 'You don't look as if you're with the social and you don't look like a charity worker.'

He was quite insulted at the suggestion he might be either of these respectable callings. 'Do me a favour!' he spluttered. 'I'm a private detective.'

We made our way back down the Finchley Road in an unfriendly silence. Here at the busy junction with the Golders Green Road, we found ourselves seats in a diner belonging to a popular chain. Now he was seated across the table from me I could study him properly and I realised he wasn't nearly as young as he first appeared. His clothing was teenage-style and he wasn't carrying any middle-aged weight but he still had to be around thirty-eight to forty. Odd-looking bloke, truth to tell. He had a skin marked with old acne scars and that curious paleness, viewed closer to hand, was probably due to some defect of pigmentation. He wasn't an albino but the paleness was permanent. In the sunshine, if he sat out in its full glare for too long, he'd probably turn as scarlet as a cooked lobster but he'd never get nicely tanned. The peaked cap was, I guessed, worn to protect him from too much sun and its painful results. His face was narrow with a long jawbone and a very small mouth.

It occurred to me that with his white clothes and my black wig, and seated opposite one another, we must look like chess pieces set out on a board. Perhaps the analogy was an apt one. We were both waiting for one of us to make a move. I pulled off the wig, put it on my lap and ran my fingers through my own hair. He'd been studying me with the same frankness I'd shown towards him. When I took off the wig a new look of assessment entered his eyes, as if making up his mind whether I looked better with it or without.

'Skip the comment,' I said.

The waitress came up and took our order. I first asked just for coffee but my companion ordered fish and chips. Well, why not? I thought. It was now lunchtime and all that walking had made me hungry. I told the waitress I'd have the same.

'I always eat when I can,' my companion informed me with a nod of the baseball cap which he still hadn't removed. I wondered how much hair he had beneath it. 'Professional habit,' he went on. 'I never know what may turn up to prevent me eating for the rest of the day, especially if I'm tailing someone.'

'Yes, all right,' I told him. 'You don't have to overdo it.'

'Who goes first?' he returned. 'You or me? Only I have to protect the privacy of my client. I can't give you a name or any information. It's privileged.'

'No, it's not,' I said. 'You're not a priest and you're not a lawyer. I've only your word for it you're a private eye.'

He extracted a battered business card from one of the pockets of his long shorts and handed it across the table. It told me his name was Duane Gardner and he was an 'Enquiry Agent'. The address was in Teddington on the edge of London.

'If I wanted,' I said, 'I could produce a dozen cards like this on a computer.'

'Phone the number,' he said simply. 'I work on my own but I'm in business with my girlfriend. You might get the answerphone or you'll get my girlfriend. But the answer machine and Lottie will both tell you the same thing. She does the office work. I do the footslogging. We're private detectives. That's what I – we – do.'

I could have replied, 'So do I from time to time,' if I'd been so inclined. But I decided there was no need for him to know that I, too, had done a bit of detecting, at least not just now. I'd already told him I was a friend of Edna's and if I changed my story at all, he'd be suspicious and that would be the end of our conversation. Nor would he believe if I was any kind of detective, professional or otherwise, that I hadn't been hired by someone. From being a possible source of information, I'd turn into a rival.

'I do have to be discreet,' he said earnestly. 'I'm not a lawyer but I've done work for solicitors and they have to trust me. My professional reputation matters. People don't go to private enquiry agencies if they want their names and business blabbed around everywhere. But now you know who I am, so who are you?'

Fair enough. I owed him my name and gave it to him. He frowned as the coffee arrived, ahead of the food. Duane stirred his cappuccino and appeared to be running my name through some sort of index in his head. It must have come up a blank.

'Where and when did you live next door to Edna?' he asked.

'I didn't say I lived next door to her. I said we were neighbours of a sort and so we were. It was in Rotherhithe getting on for a couple of years ago. I lived in a squat in Jubilee Road. It's been pulled down now, all the houses were, and developers moved in. Edna wasn't a squatter. She lived in a little disused burial ground at the end of the road. We all, everyone who lived round there, knew her well. The burial ground went under the bulldozers too. I don't know what they do about the graves when that happens.'

I'd set him thinking and he answered me in an absent-minded way. 'If it's abandoned, been no burials there for ages, they dig out a grave and see if anything's left. If there's nothing, they just carry on. If there's something, they have to let the archaeologists have a look. Any coffins will be reburied somewhere else if they've still got remains in 'em. Really old burials have generally just mouldered away.'

'Dust to dust,' I said.

'That's about it. Depends on the soil and the coffin itself. A lead coffin, that and anything in it'll keep pretty well. Wooden ones just rot. If it's peaty soil then things get preserved. They've dug really interesting bodies out of peat bogs. You know, pre-historic but look like someone dumped them in there yesterday.'

'You sound like you spend a lot of time in cemeteries,' I said, putting a stop to this macabre lecture.

'Yeah, I do sometimes,' he said.

The happiest days of his life, probably. 'Why is Edna scared of you?' I asked.

'She's not, as far as I know,' he defended himself.

'Come off it.'

'I told you, confidentiality—'

I put a stop to his excuses there and then. 'Edna's not your client. The person who hired you is. I accept you can't tell me about *him*, whoever he or she is. But, if you like, Edna is *my* interest. When she saw you watching her from across the road –

while I was talking to her outside Camden Town Tube station – she really flipped out.'

'Yeah, nuisance, that,' he muttered. He sipped at his coffee.

'So, tell me why.'

'Means I can't get to talk to her easily. I want to talk to her on my client's behalf.'

'Aha!' I exclaimed in triumph. 'So your client asked you to find her.'

He glowered at me. 'I'm not saying. Confidential.'

'Is he a solicitor?' I asked. I was beginning to see where this might be leading, just possibly. 'Is it about a will?'

'Confidential,' he repeated.

'So why is she scared? You can tell me that.'

'Guess I frightened her. My mistake. I thought she hadn't spotted me but she had. I had tried to chat to her once before, just nicely. Crazy old crone took off like a bat out of hell. I didn't do anything to scare her, I swear.'

'Depends what you said to her. Did you let her know someone had asked you to find her?'

'Confidential.'

I tried to flush out some information. 'Suppose,' I suggested, 'I went to the police and told them about this?'

He grinned at me then. 'Tell them what? What do they care about an old bag lady? I'm a legit enquiry agent. They can check me out. I'm just doing a job.'

'And I'm just making it my job to look out for Edna and make sure you don't frighten the living daylights out of her,' I said.

'Spend your time any way you want to,' he returned insolently and grinned at me with his little mouth. It made his whole face look really strange, like one of those Halloween masks.

Our food arrived. We tackled it in silence. Both of us, I guessed, were planning our next conversational gambit.

I wasn't going to get any more out of him, so much was clear. Nor was he going to get anything out of me. I did have his card. I might as well eat up and go. Edna would be well away from here by now. If nothing else, the time spent with Duane in this café meant she'd had time to put distance between us.

But one thing was still bothering me. I had kept an eye out for him at the hostel and I hadn't seen him. 'Where did you pick us up? I mean, if you were following me, exactly where did you pick me up?'

'Outside that hostel where she lives, where do you think?'

'I looked for you,' I said defiantly.

'Yeah,' was the irritating reply. 'I know you did. You were rubbernecking around the place thinking I was behind every tree. I got there first, see. You've got to be up early in this business. I saw you arrive. You had to be waiting for her to leave, just like I was. I let you set off after her and Bob's your uncle.' He sounded really chirpy.

Duane wasn't bad as a private detective, I realised. He'd located Edna, in itself not easy, and he'd found out where she lived. He'd run rings round me again today. One thing I still wanted to know.

'I kept my eyes open while I was waiting outside the hostel. I didn't spot you. Perhaps you were there but *where* the hell were you?'

He made again that funny mask-like grimace again. 'I was under cover, like a birdwatcher in a hide. I was in the back of a parked van. I'll be honest. I saw, when you arrived and took up position, that it was someone on the same errand I was, but I didn't know it was *you* because of that Morticia wig. It didn't make any difference. You were following the old girl, so you had an interest. Actually, I was quite relieved, back there in the cemetery, to see that it was you. Otherwise that would have meant two other people were targeting the old lady, three of us all told, and that would have made life real complicated.'

'Your decorator mates,' I said crossly. 'They let you hide in that empty house yesterday when I ran after you, and they let you hide in their van today. I hope it cost you.'

'Cost the client,' he said serenely. 'Day-to-day expenses.'

That, more than the card or anything else, convinced me he was a real private detective.

He had an idea of his own in mind. He leaned across the table. 'My client is generous with expenses. The old lady probably won't talk to me. But if you're her friend, she'll talk to you. What do you say? I could put you on the payroll for this job. It'd be a nice little earner.'

'I don't sell my friends' confidences,' I said, getting to my feet.

'You'd find out a bit more about all this,' he coaxed.

'I'll find out,' I promised him. 'Only I'll do it my own way. Oh, since you are on expenses, as you say, you can pay for both our meals. Bill the client.'

I had the satisfaction of knowing, as I left, that he didn't look very happy.

I went back to the newsagent's, collected Bonnie and arranged to meet Ganesh outside at twenty past eight that evening. They close up at eight. Then I went home with Bonnie and sat in front of the television watching some made-for-TV American detective series. All the women in it were glamorous and most of the men had body-builder physiques except for a distinguished-looking couple of oldies with silver hair who looked like moonlighting senators.

In half an hour neatly they had solved a crime which had been baffling the sheriff's office, the Homicide department of the local cops, the DA's office, the FBI and probably the CIA. At no time did anyone appear in this line-up remotely resembling a bag lady, an out-of-work young female actor, a stressed-out newsagent or a tennis-hatted private eye who looked like an alien.

Usually watching this kind of thing helps me relax and solve whatever problem is facing me at the time. I think it disconnects my mind from reality long enough to gain distance so that when I come back to my own world I can see it more clearly. This time it didn't really work. I had a feeling that, sooner or later, I was going to have to tackle Edna herself. If a private detective has been hired to find you, you generally know why. The trouble was, she wouldn't tell me. I wouldn't have worried so much if she hadn't looked so frightened outside the Tube station. She saw Duane – or whoever was behind him – as a threat. Because that's another thing she probably knew: who had hired him.

I was outside the shop at eight, hanging about on the pavement. Ganesh came out at half past, glowering. He took my arm and propelled me along the street at a fast clip.

'What's up?' I protested. 'Oy, let go of me! I'll fall over.'

'He'll call me back. He'll find something else for me to do.'

'Ganesh!' I said, coming to a halt once we were round the corner and detaching myself from his grip. 'You've got to sort this out with Hari. He's worried, that's why he's being so difficult.'

'He was always difficult,' argued Ganesh.

'Be fair. He's not so bad. He's trying to make a living. That supermarket has taken his trade.'

Ganesh sighed. 'I know, I know. Let's go and eat. I can't face another one of Jimmie's spuds.'

We ended up in an Italian place eating pasta arrabiata and

mixed salad. I told Ganesh about my experience following Edna and how I'd been followed by Duane Gardner.

'So you see,' I said smugly, 'I wasn't imagining things.'

Ganesh hesitated but then said magnanimously, 'OK, you were right and I was wrong. It seems pretty odd, though. Who'd want to find Edna?'

'I don't know but I'll find out. Duane will go on watching her. He'll try and talk to her again. I don't know what's happening but someone has to stop it.'

As usual, he played devil's advocate. 'It sounds like meddling and if you really don't have any idea what's behind it, you ought to leave well alone. Whoever has hired this character Gardner won't like you sticking your nose in. Have you still got that agency card on you?'

I took out the business card and handed it across the table. Ganesh squinted at it in the guttering light of the candle in a wine bottle which was attempting to look as if it was there to give atmosphere. I suspected an excuse to save on the electricity bill rather than a prop to encourage romantic moments. It caused customers to peer at their food and companions as if either one might be a mistake.

'Right, Gardner,' Ganesh muttered, handing the card back. 'Although I could print off a dozen cards like that saying I represented Patel's detective agency.'

'That's more or less what I told him. He told me to check out the number.'

Ganesh leaned back in his chair with a faraway look on his face. 'You reckon it would be a good business, Fran? Investigations undertaken, strict confidence assured?'

'Not if your Uncle Hari had anything to do with it.'

'True,' said Ganesh, shaking his head sadly. 'He'd want to vet all the clients and none of them would come up to his standards. But it's an idea. I know you're not keen on us going into a dry-cleaning business . . .'

'Gan! This is not the time to discuss your daft idea about us opening a dry-cleaner's. And a detective agency, no, it's too complicated. I like doing things my own way, on my own, picking the cases I want to look into. I don't want to be like Susie taking all kind of seedy jobs.'

'I suppose so,' mumbled Ganesh.

'Edna!' I said firmly. 'We are talking about her and what I'm going to do.'

'Do nothing,' he told me, 'because you don't know what the set-up is. Whoever is looking for her must have a strong motive. If you interfere you might not be doing her a favour, as you seem to think.'

'A strong motive doesn't mean it's in Edna's interest. We don't know it.' There was a pause while we both mulled it over. 'Perhaps I was right when I asked Gardner if it was about a will,' I said wistfully. 'Hey, Gan, perhaps someone has died and left her millions.'

'Not likely, is it?' Ganesh said in that dampening way. 'She's so old, anyone older than her with millions to leave would have to be ancient and have younger heirs.'

'In fact she's not that old, not nearly as old as I imagined. She's in her sixties.'

He thought about it for a few moments and I waited because Ganesh can come up with some interesting ideas.

'All right, she could be someone's wife. Perhaps they split years ago and now the old chap wants to put his affairs in order, because he's ancient even if she isn't . . .' Ganesh was growing enthusiastic with his scenario. 'And make his will and so he wants to know if she's alive so he can fix a divorce. You know, make sure she doesn't turn up and contest it.'

'Funny you should say that,' I mused, 'because she told me she thought she had been engaged to be married once. But she couldn't remember to whom.'

Ganesh put down his fork. 'What's the worst thing that can happen, Fran? This Duane Gardner finds Edna again and talks to her. He won't get any sense out of her, any more than you did.'

'She needs protecting.'

'She's got protection of a sort. She lives in that hostel.'

'Yes,' I said. 'And the people there ought to know about this.'

'What,' asked Ganesh, 'makes you think they don't already?'

'That's another thing I'm going to find out,' I told him.

Chapter Five

I returned to the hostel the following day. Mindful of what had happened on my previous visit, I waited until I saw Edna leave and hung around long enough to make sure Duane Gardner wasn't following her. But Duane wasn't around in the street nor, as far as I'd been able to establish, was he anywhere else, hidden away. What's more, this time I had taken the precaution of first checking out the house being renovated.

I had found Tom and Jerry still at work there in their paint-splashed overalls. They bid me a cheery 'Hullo, darling!' as I negotiated ladders and pots in the hall and made sure not to lean against any painted surfaces. Everywhere smelled of damp plaster. Before I could return their greeting my ears echoed to a cavernous clang which made me jump and my head ring. This racket originated with a shaven-headed youth busy in what looked as if it might be intended to become a kitchen or bathroom. He was banging pipes with a hammer and pretending to be a plumber.

'Duane Gardner,' I said to them all briskly, as soon as the noise level let me. I meant to let them all know I was standing no nonsense. 'He's tall and spindly, wears white clothes and a tennis cap. You two let him hide in your van the other day.' I pointed at

Tom and Jerry who looked bashful and sniggered like a pair of school kids.

'Well,' I went on, 'is he here?'

'No, love, honest,' they said earnestly in unison.

'You can look round the house if you want,' said Jerry.

The plumber made a last deafening assault on the pipes and wandered out to join us in the hall. 'Whaddya want 'im fer?' he enquired. He wore a skull earring and jeans cut off at the knees. Instead of revealing pale bare legs like those Duane displayed, the shins and calves of the plumber were tattooed on every available inch of skin. It looked as if he wore particularly exotic stockings. I thought I recognised the hand of Michael in the fantastic nature of the artwork.

'Do you know Duane?' I countered. 'Or have you seen him?'

'Nah. Just want ter know why you want 'im.'

'None of your business!' I told him.

'Please yerself,' he said, unoffended, and returned to his pipes.

'I'd like to look in your van,' I said to Jerry.

He looked as if he'd like to argue but there was a glint in my eye which changed his mind.

We went outside and he opened the back door of the white van and stood by silently while I inspected a heap of tins and rope and bits of wood.

'Satisfied?' he asked when I stood back.

'Yes, thank you.' I was still being brisk but polite with it.

'He in trouble or something?' asked Jerry.

'What do you think?' I asked him.

'I think he's in trouble with *you*,' he replied.

'Got it in one,' I said. 'And if you hide him again, so will you be.'

'Blimey,' said Jerry in respectful tones, 'I wouldn't want that. I gotta feel sorry for the poor bloke, though.'

Let them all stick together. If they helped out Duane again they still wouldn't tell me if I asked, but they'd act so guilty I'd know it. I'd have given a lot to know where Duane was, though. He'd probably gone to make a report to whoever was hiring him. I wondered, as I crossed the road to the hostel, whether in that report Duane would mention me.

Again there was no weeping Sandra on the hostel's steps today, thank goodness. I rang the bell and Simon appeared.

'Oh, hi,' he said recognising me.

He didn't look guilty but he did look uncomfortable. My arrival does sometimes affect people like that. He knew I was going to ask questions. In my experience this provokes two sorts of reaction. There are people who won't talk and those who won't stop. I suspected Simon was one of the former but there was no harm in trying.

'We need to have a word,' I said, 'about Edna.'

'Well, we don't discuss—' he began.

'You are responsible for her,' I interrupted him. 'She lives here in your care. There is something you should know. Can I come in?'

He pushed his spectacles up the bridge of his nose with an index finger and nodded.

Nikki was still sitting in front of the computer in the untidy little office cum sitting room. She, too, greeted me with a laconic, 'Hi!'

Simon began to make the coffee without asking me this time. I sat down in the chair uninvited. It didn't seem presumptuous. They seemed to have accepted I was part of the scenery now, even if only on a temporary basis.

'Where's your dog?' asked Nikki, swivelling round on her chair and accepting her mug of coffee from Simon. 'Ta, Sim.'

'I left her with a friend.'

This morning I'd left her with Erwin the drummer who has the other ground-floor flat in the converted house where I live. Erwin works nights and sleeps days. But between professional gigs he sits around a lot. He's happy to walk Bonnie and Bonnie likes him. It may have something to do with the fact that, quite often, she comes back with the smell of marijuana in her fur, a spaced-out dog.

'What's all this about Edna?' Simon asked, settling himself in a facing chair.

'Someone is following her,' I said. 'Not me, I mean, but a private detective called Duane Gardner. He's about thirty-eight at my guess but from a distance looks younger. He wears a lot of white and a baseball or tennis-type cap. Has he been here?'

They shook their heads. I believed them. I wouldn't believe Tom or Jerry or the hammer-wielding plumber but this pair, I was ready to bet, were painfully honest. That was why my arrival had made Simon look so flustered. He didn't want to talk but he couldn't bring himself to lie.

'Are you sure about this?' asked Simon, now even more worried.

'I've spoken to him. He won't tell me the name of his client or why he wants to find Edna but, as far as I can make out, that's what Duane has been hired to do, find her and more.'

'More?' Nikki asked sharply.

I nodded. 'He has found her, right? But he's still following her. He admitted to me he tried to talk to her but she scuttled away. Edna is scared of him. I think she probably knows what all this is about but she wouldn't say. I think she may be in need of some protection. You, at least, should know about it, in case he does turn up here.'

'We don't discuss . . .' Simon began but tailed off miserably. They were, after all, discussing her with me.

Nikki, her mind ahead of her co-worker's, asked, 'You talked of protection. What kind of harm do you think would come to her if this bloke Gardner got her cornered?'

'I don't know. He might try and persuade her to go with him, whether she wanted to or not. He acts on the orders of his client. Because I don't know who that is, or what he or she wants, I can't guess what Duane might do. But Edna doesn't want him around. I'm one hundred per cent sure of that.'

'We can inform her social worker,' said Nikki. She glanced at Simon. 'Perhaps we should, Sim.'

Much good that would do, I thought but didn't say. But then, I didn't know what anyone could do. Edna couldn't be locked up just to protect her from Gardner. She wasn't a danger to anyone or even to herself, left alone. She wasn't likely to get herself lost, wandering about, because she knew the streets better than the average London taxi driver.

Besides, to keep Edna in any kind of controlled environment would be to kill her. She was like those cats she had befriended in Rotherhithe: a feral creature. I thought of her sitting in the cemetery with her face upturned to the sun's rays and the look of joy and peace on it. Contentment is rare and a fragile thing. Someone was trying to destroy Edna's small world of happiness.

I stood up. 'I just wanted to warn you,' I said, 'so that you can look out for him. Thanks for taking me seriously. It is serious, but Edna being Edna, people don't care.'

Simon said stiffly, 'We care!'

'I know you do. That's why I'm here. Thanks for the coffee. If she doesn't come back at night here, even once, you should do more than tell the social worker. You should tell the police.'

Nikki said sharply, 'We try to keep the police away from our residents. They are sensitive people and very easily upset.'

I took it she meant the residents of the hostel were nervous souls and not the boys in blue, although I had to admit that in my experience the police did get upset at the drop of a hat over nothing. However, not in the way Nikki meant.

'Report her missing, right?' I insisted. 'And if the cops won't take you seriously, ask to speak to Inspector Janice Morgan and when you do speak to her, tell her Fran Varady gave you her name. Inspector Morgan, got it?'

I left them muttering together and looking very concerned; but I felt better because someone other than me was taking an interest in all this. If Duane turned up now at the hostel, he'd get very short shrift. But Duane was cunning. He wouldn't break cover by going to the hostel. They'd ask too many questions and, even as charity workers, they represented inquisitive officialdom.

But what could I do now? Where could I go? Really I needed to find Duane Gardner, because only he could lead me to his employer. I could phone his office or go there. But that would be to walk into a situation without having taken any precautions. I needed to know more about him first. He probably wouldn't be at his office, anyway. I'd find Lottie, the girlfriend who acted as general dogsbody, and she'd warn Duane I was sniffing around. I could phone him and ask to meet but I wouldn't learn any more from a second talk with him than I had at the first.

He was a private detective! I stopped in the street and struck my forehead with the palm of my hand. Idiot, Fran! Susie was a private detective. She hadn't recognised him when I'd described him but she hadn't then been aware he was in the same line of business as she was. She might not know him by sight but she might know of his one-man agency. I turned my steps in the direction of the Turkish fast food outlet and the Duke Detective Agency's office above it. It was lunchtime, anyway, and I was hungry. After I'd talked to Susie, I'd go down and buy a kebab.

* * *

It was all go in the food outlet: smoke and steam and yelling Turkish voices. Knives flashed as an unidentifiable joint on a pole was shredded, customers pushed in and out, a powerful aroma of cooked meat and spices rolled out into the street. I went up to the agency's office.

The building was old and the staircase probably original. The treads were narrow and creaked underfoot. I passed a door which I knew led into a washroom area with a loo, hand basin and broken hand-dryer. 'Staff Only' announced a label importantly in order to deny admission to any passer-by caught short. The first-floor door with 'Duke Investigations' emblazoned on it stood ajar. That was unusual because Susie like to hear the jangle of the bell as it opened so that she knew someone was there. I stood there for a moment listening for voices from within but there was no sound although I could hear a creak of floorboards above and a distant murmur of conversation. It was punctuated by the muffled squawk as someone exclaimed, '*Ow!*' Michael was plying his trade.

I pushed the agency door open a fraction more and called out, 'Susie? It's Fran.'

There was no reply. She might be in the loo, or have nipped out for something, but she wouldn't leave the door open. I felt uneasy and gave it a hefty shove that sent it flying wide with a protesting crack of the hinges.

The outer office, as I have explained, was just a tiny area separated from the main office by a partition and right now it was empty. Two wooden chairs of the old-fashioned kitchen type stood there for clients to wait on, should there be a rush of business. I don't suppose anyone had sat on them for quite a while. The only light in there came through the glazed panel in the partition, via the window in the main office. I couldn't see any movement through the frosted pane. I tapped at the door into the inner sanctum and called out again. No reply.

I really didn't like this. But I was probably just being jumpy for no good reason. Any second now a tap of heels would herald Susie running up the staircase from the loo and she'd appear behind me. I opened the connecting door and walked in.

Susie wasn't there. But Duane Gardner was. At first I thought my eyes or my imagination must be playing tricks. But unfortunately he was real and shake my head or rub my eyes or just try denying the evidence before me though I might, he wouldn't go away. He was sitting on the floor with his back propped against the far wall and his legs splayed in front of him, for all the world like a wooden puppet with broken strings. He wore his trademark baggy long shorts with the pockets and his white cotton T-shirt. The white baseball hat had fallen off and now I could see his hair was very fair and fine and clipped close to his skull. His eyes were open and stared at me. His small mouth formed a circle of surprise. I'd wanted to find him and now I had, but far, far too late for us to talk. I knew, with sinking heart, that he was dead; that this was only the outer husk of poor Duane. In that sense he wasn't really there. The person had gone, departed on that final journey.

My legs trembled and I sank down on to the chair placed for a visiting client before that scarred old ministry desk of Susie's. Even now I can see the entire little office in my mind's eye, every piece of rickety furniture, the steel-grey filing cabinet, the cobweb draped across the corner of the unwashed window-pane. Outside, on the window ledge, was a scruffy dark grey London pigeon with scaly feet and a wary yellow eye. It seemed to be looking in; perhaps it was. It could probably see me and hoped I'd open the window and scatter some breadcrumbs on the ledge. But to have an audience of any kind at that moment was an unacceptable intrusion into a scene that should have been private. For death ought to be a private matter, in my view. We all fancy ourselves surrounded by our nearest and dearest as we shuffle off the mortal coil but I know, from my dad's death and later my grandma's, that even if your loved ones are there, you are already cut off from them by a gradually thickening pane of glass, like that pane in the window. You can no longer reach across to them nor they to you. It is the most private moment of your entire existence, that time when you come to quit it.

I could no longer reach out to Duane in any real sense. Physically I could have touched him, had I wished, but it would have been meaningless. He could neither have known nor responded. Yet had I arrived here, what? Half an hour ago? Perhaps even less? If I had, even now, at this very moment he and I would have been chatting or having some sort of conversation even if only an argument. He would probably have been accusing me of not telling him I was a professional and I would have been denying that I was any such thing. Duane, in that imaginary never-to-be held conversation, was jeering at me, demanding 'Oh, yeah? Right, then, what are you doing here?'

What the hell *was* I doing here? Why did it have to be me? And what was *he* doing here? That's what I would probably have retaliated, had I arrived earlier and we faced one another now exchanging insults. The question now rephrased itself as 'what was he doing here – *like that*?'

All this passed through my head in a mere couple of seconds. I heard my own voice uttering a low moan of distress. Initially it wasn't a cry of fear, in shock though I was. I felt confusion and above all pity. I hadn't liked him but he was a relatively young man and apart from outwitting me, he'd not done me any harm.

Not until now. Now, whatever he'd been involved with, I was involved with it too. He had been a good detective. He'd tracked me down in some way and learned I worked occasionally for Susie. He'd come here in order to find me, confront me or leave a message for me. It could only mean trouble for me of some sort. Now at last I began to be afraid.

I begged quietly and uselessly, 'Please, Duane, don't do this to me.'

He was beyond obliging me. The small round open mouth seemed almost to be about to tell me what had led to this, but the communication had been terminally interrupted. He would have looked surprised had the film of death not already been dulling his gaze. His expression seemed to say, 'This can't be happening to me. It's a big mistake. You want someone else.'

Then, as I watched, the muscles of his jaw twitched as if he would speak, after all, and his mouth stretched in a ghastly yawn. I nearly jumped out of my skin and thought for a second or two that I was wrong, he wasn't dead. I called to him, 'Duane?'

But his mouth, at the widest extent of the yawn, froze and remained open in a horrid rictus. It was the involuntary contraction of the muscles in the first signs of approaching rigor.

There was a sudden clatter of footsteps behind me. I whirled round and dashed out into the reception area just in time to intercept Susie. She had on that black business suit and carried a battered document case.

'Hullo, Fran!' she greeted me. 'How long have you been here? I've just been stood up by a potential client and I'm bloody fed up. I reckon I've been given the right old run-around. Let's stick the kettle on.'

Chapter Six

She made to enter the office but I barred her path. 'Wait, Susie, don't go in there. There's something I've got to tell you first.'

Her gaze sharpened. 'What's up?'

I indicated the connecting door. 'There's a visitor in there, a dead one.'

Susie stared at me. 'What do you mean, a dead one?'

'I'm not likely,' I said, my voice breaking and sounding, to my own ears, as sharp as chalk scraping on a blackboard, 'to make a mistake over something like that.'

'Let me see!' She pushed me aside and opening the door, strode through it. 'Crikey . . .' I heard her gasp. Then, 'Bloody hell!'

I didn't want to return to the inner office but I edged inside it to stand behind Susie and look over her shoulder.

She had more presence of mind than I did. She turned her head towards me. 'Have you rung an ambulance?'

'No. Well, look, it's too late for that.'

'I'm not a bloody doctor and neither are you!' She was refusing to accept the evidence of her eyes. She walked over to the slumped form, crouched down and stretched out her hand to his shoulder. 'Oy, mate? Can you hear me?'

'No, he can't,' I said. 'He's a goner, Susie. Face it.'

She gave a little squeak, snatched her hand away from him and jumped to her feet, scuttling back to stand beside me.

'Who is he?' she whispered.

I told her. 'It's the guy I told you about, all in white, who was tailing Edna. It turned out he was a private detective by the name of Duane Gardner. You ever heard of him, Susie?'

'Gardner? No, but the detection business is getting crowded these days. He didn't work from an office round here, that's all I can say.'

'He has – had – his office in Teddington.'

The fringes of the metropolitan area counted as the darkest unknown territory in Susie's book.

'Teddington? Right out there? Upmarket area that, isn't it? Blimey, I wouldn't know him, would I? What was he doing here and how did he get in?' Her forehead crinkled in a frown. 'What did he want?'

I shook my head. 'He must have been looking for me.'

Susie moved towards the desk and the phone.

'Perhaps you ought not to touch that,' I said as she stretched out her hand.

She froze, let her hand drop and turned to me. 'This isn't a crime scene, Fran. Look, there's no blood. He's just dropped in his tracks. Best way to go, really. You don't have time to know what's happening.'

'I don't care,' I snapped, 'use your mobile!'

'All right, then.' She retrieved the document case that she'd left by the door, dug out a mobile phone and rang the police on that.

'We wait,' she said, as she put the phone away. 'But I'm not waiting in here – with him. We can sit out there in the reception.'

I looked round the office. 'Before we do, and before the cops get here, does everything look all right to you?'

She glanced round. 'Yeah, sure, all of it. Fran, what's up with you?'

'Shock, I guess,' I said. 'Like you say, he probably had a heart attack or something sudden like that.'

We went back to the reception and sat down side by side on the kitchen chairs. Susie, moments before such a trim sprightly figure, looked pale and cold. She shivered. Her shoulders slumped. Even her blond curls seemed to have lost their springiness.

'I could do with a cup of tea,' she muttered. 'But the kettle is in there.' She jerked her thumb over her shoulder. 'Anyway, I suppose you don't want me to touch that, either.' She rallied a little and sat up straighter to look me full in the face. 'It's not foul play, Fran. It's life playing one of its sick jokes.'

Usually I'd agree with her about life's often misplaced sense of humour, but general unease prompted me to ask, 'What time did you go out, Susie?'

'Out of the office or out to work? I haven't been in the office this morning till now. I had a call to make first, business, or I thought it was.' Susie's voice took on a grim tone. 'I've been all the way out to Richmond and for nothing. Some woman made the appointment over the phone and sounded kosher. She'd met a new bloke and he was really keen but she thought some of the stories he was spinning sounded a bit unconvincing, so wanted me to check him out. Straightforward stuff but plenty of legwork and surveillance and day-to-day expenses so out I went to meet her in some upmarket pub calling itself a wine bar, only she never showed.'

'Did you try and get in contact with her?'

'Of course I did! I rang the number she gave me and

some other woman, not the same one for sure, it was a different voice – she said she didn't know anyone of that name. I know when I've been given the run-around and believe me I am not pleased!'

'I do believe it,' I told her morosely, 'and I also believe it sounds as though we've been set up, both of us.'

She looked startled and then thoughtful. 'Someone got me out of the office so that they could fix to meet whatsit, Gardner, here? And then croak him? Leave him here for one of us to fall over when we got back? Why? I mean, why *here*?'

'Because it drops me right in it, doesn't it?' I muttered. 'You'll have to get your story about your trip to Richmond absolutely straight, remember all you can about this woman who contacted you. The police will ask.'

She sniffed but having a story to get clear had concentrated her mind and temporarily wiped out the image of Duane. She took on a more businesslike air. 'Oh, right. Well, normally, I'd look in the office first, before I went to meet anyone, to check if there were any messages or post. But Richmond is a long way out and I thought it better to go there direct from home.'

'Was Les coming in today?'

She shook her head. 'I told him not to bother for a week or so. I'd phone him if I needed him. Like I said, we've had no work to speak of. That's why I grabbed the offer to go out to Richmond. I didn't ask enough questions. I just thought she sounded as if she had the money to pay for an in-depth search.'

'So, did you lock the outer door when you left last night?'

'Of course I did!' Susie was getting her normal confidence back. 'Even if I hadn't Michael would've locked up the street door downstairs when he left. He's got a lot of expensive equipment up there. He wouldn't want to come in the morning and find it ripped out, or some crackhead dosing up or old wino sleeping it off in there. If you're in any kind of business around here security is like breathing: you do it automatically and you don't forget. Look, we don't know why that poor stiff in there came here, unless it was to find *you*.'

Susie gave me a stern look as if I'd set it all up on purpose. 'Perhaps this Richmond business has nothing to do with it. There could be someone else out there giving me the run-around for the fun of it. It could be someone I've investigated, someone who was into things he didn't want my client knowing and I found out and told the client all about. He or she could be getting his or her own back. People get vengeful when they're found out. It's not unknown for them to blame the private investigator. It's like shooting the messenger. I mean, we're only the hired help, right? But people can get nasty. I know that finding him like that was really horrible for you but well, like I say, whoever got me out to Richmond could have had some other reason. I got enemies, too, you know.'

'The door was open when I got here,' I interrupted her.

She pushed out her lower lip in thought. 'Les does have a key. There's only the two of us. One of us can't always be here to let the other one in. So I gave him a key, only to the door, mind, and the loo. He doesn't have the key that unlocks the filing cabinet. He doesn't need that. Anyway . . .'

Anyway, Les wasn't the sort of person whom you allowed access to sensitive files. She didn't need to say it.

'I hope,' I said, 'that Les has an alibi, too.'

'I told you, Fran, Les has got no reason to come in today.'

A heavier thump of feet on the stairs heralded two very young coppers who appeared one behind the other and squeezed into the small area, making it very crowded.

'Where is he?' asked one of them.

'In there,' said Susie.

They went into the office and I heard one of them say. 'He's a stiff, all right. Better call the doc to certify death.'

One of them came back to us and asked, 'A Mrs Duke phoned in. Which one of you is that?'

Susie raised her hand wordlessly in admission.

He took out a notebook. 'Do you know his name?'

'Duane Gardner,' I said. 'I've got his address if you want it.' I took out the crumpled business card and handed it over.

The copper looked at it and then at me. 'Private detective?'

I shrugged. He raised his eyebrows and wrote Gardner's address and telephone number in his book, before handing the card back to me.

'You know his next of kin? Was he married?'

'He has a girlfriend. He runs – ran – his business with her but I've never met her. I only know her name is Lottie.'

The constable heaved a sigh. 'This is a detective agency, too,' he said with a touch of disapproval in his voice. 'It says so, on the door there.' He jabbed his pen at the outer door.

'That's right.' Susie bridled. 'Although, as a matter of fact, on the door what it actually says is "confidential enquiry agents". I run it. I'm Susie – Susanna – Duke.'

'That right?' The copper nearly grinned at her then remembered in the nick of time that this was a serious occasion. 'So, the deceased gentleman was here on business, was he?'

'No. I didn't know he was here. I was out visiting a client. I don't even know how he got in here.'

The constable was beginning to look suspicious. 'So, who found him? You?'

'I did,' I spoke up. 'My name is Francesca Varady.'

He wrote that down. 'Do you work here too?'

'Occasionally,' I said. 'Freelance.'

'Were you here when he collapsed?'

'No. I called in to see Susie, only she wasn't here, as it turned out. The door was open and I looked into the office and saw Duane on the floor. Then Susie came back.'

'From Richmond,' said Susie. 'I went to meet a client. She didn't show. I was stood up. I chatted to a barman while I waited. He'll probably remember me.'

Barmen did remember Susie.

'Natural causes by the look of it. How was his health?' asked the copper.

'No idea,' said Susie. 'I didn't know him, never met him.'

He looked enquiringly at me. I said, 'I only knew him slightly. I met him a couple of times. I don't know any personal details about him.'

'What was he doing here, then?'

'We don't know!' Susie and I chimed together. Then we looked at one another.

The copper was studying us both. 'Oh, right,' he said and wrote something down.

More feet on the stairway and Susie's neighbour appeared, wearing a sweaty T-shirt and jeans under a grubby apron. He had a luxuriant moustache and flashing dark eyes.

'What is wrong? Why you cops here?'

'Who are you?' asked the constable.

'I run food bar, downstairs. You park your police car outside. That's bad for business. Customers think you are visiting me. I like if you move car.'

'Did you see anyone enter these premises earlier, sir?'

The food bar proprietor waved a hand the back of which was

plentifully covered with black hairs. 'This is separate entrance. Anyway, it's lunchtime. We're busy. What you think?'

'All right, sir.'

The other copper came out of the office, closing the door quickly behind him before the visitor could see past him and glimpse the grotesque figure inside. 'Doc's on his way.'

'What is wrong? Someone ill? Mr Les ill?' The cook brightened with interest. Then he scowled and wagged a hairy finger at us. 'He not eat anything from my shop give him belly trouble. No one ever get belly trouble from my shop! I had council inspector come just last week and he said he wish all fast food bars like mine.'

'It's all right, sir, nothing for you to worry about. Perhaps you ought to get back to your customers.'

'I told you, they don't like police car. It keep them away. You going to move it?'

'All in good time, sir.'

'Can't make bloody living, what?' sulked the cook. 'I am honest man. I call cops when someone break into my house six months ago, steal beautiful big new, top-of-range telly. They don't turn up for four whole hours and stay five minutes! Tell me contact my house insurance. Now I got cops all over place and bloody car outside.' He got in a last shot. 'Like London bus, what they say? First you wait and none come, then all come at once.' He stormed out and stamped away down the staircase.

'Can't please them all,' said the copper with the notebook, snapping it shut.

The next one up the stairs was the police surgeon, an elderly man exhibiting no interest whatever in the surroundings or the grim casualty awaiting him. They led him to the inner office and Duane, stiffening there on the floor while we all argued outside.

There was a silence during which Susie and I looked at one another uneasily, imagining the examination of the body. Then some discussion broke out.

They all came back and the police surgeon left. The second copper looked from one to the other of us.

'Either of you two girls remove anything from the scene?'

'No,' I snapped, 'and it would be polite to call us "ladies".'

'All right, then,' he retorted sarcastically, 'either of you two *ladies* happen to pick up anything from the floor, say?'

We both told him we hadn't.

'And you say neither of you two was here when he collapsed?'

'I told you,' I said, 'I found him like that. Mrs Duke arrived later.'

'The Turks downstairs saw me go past their place on my way in,' said Susie suddenly, not liking the way this was going.

But it drew his attention. He chewed his lip and asked, 'Mind if I have a look in your briefcase, madam?'

'Yes,' said Susie. 'I do and you won't, not unless you give me a bloody good reason.'

'I've got a reason,' he countered, 'if I suspect that despite what you say, you may have removed something from the scene.'

He'd picked the wrong opponent. Eyes blazing, she stepped up to him. The top of her blond curls only reached halfway up his chest but he took a pace back.

'This is my office. I don't know what that guy is doing here or why he chose this place to drop dead. That's it. I never saw him before in my life. That's the extent of my involvement. Got it? If you want anything more out of me, then you arrest me, OK? Only you'd better be able to back it up or you're in big trouble. Or, if you prefer, I'll call my solicitor now and if you want to ask me anything more, you do it in his presence.

Oh, and if you want to search anything, you get a warrant.'

The guardians of the law exchanged glances again. The one who had been talking to Susie turned to me.

'You found him, you say. Have you got a bag, backpack, anything like that?'

'No,' I said.

'What do you carry your stuff in, then?'

'My pockets,' I told him. 'I haven't got any stuff: no mobile, no credit cards, no make-up, no car keys. I carry loose cash, house keys and a couple of paper hankies. That's it.'

'Blimey,' he said, 'I wish my wife was like you.'

But that was the end of the quiz session. The first officer took over again.

'OK,' he said. 'We'll get him removed.'

'Will there be a postmortem?' I asked.

'That's up to the coroner. It's his body.' His gaze flickered curiously over me. 'We'd like to know how the deceased entered the premises.'

'So would I!' muttered Susie.

He walked back to the main door and rattled the handle before stooping and peering at the lock. 'You want to get this changed. Kid could open this one with a credit card.'

A streetwise kid: somehow that seemed to describe Duane nicely. Not that he was young, but he dressed it and there had been something of an Artful Dodger about him. A pity he hadn't been able to dodge whatever had happened to him here.

They removed Duane's body efficiently and took him away in a little white van with no windows. The Turks had all come out of their kebab house and stood watching solemnly as it threaded its way into the traffic and was lost to view. The owner enquired again if it was Mr Les who had died and appeared happy it wasn't. Les must be a good customer. Then, with a collective shaking of heads, they returned to work.

Susie and I went back to the office and she sighed. 'How am I going to be able to work in here from now on, Fran? I'll be imagining him, there on the floor. Every time I look up from the desk, I'll see him staring back at me. I had a job finding this place. Rents round here for office space, well, you wouldn't credit what they are. I don't want to work from home. It's risky. But I'll have to look for somewhere else. I've got all my cards printed up and everything. It's going to cost me. And then there's that bloody lock. I'll have to get it changed today and tell the landlord.'

'Who is the landlord? Wouldn't he have a key?'

'Some property company is landlord. Yeah, they probably have got one. But they wouldn't hand over a key to anyone other than me. If they have, they're in deep trouble. Still, they must hold spare keys to all the properties. A tenant might do a moonlight flit, go off without paying the rent or a forwarding address. They'd need to get in. But there's no way your mate Gardner would have been able to get it from them, is there?'

'He wasn't a mate,' I said dully.

She stopped worrying about relocating and turned to stare at me. 'I didn't mean a proper mate like your pal Ganesh. I just meant someone you know.'

'I didn't even know him. I just met him; our paths crossed. Come on, Susie, let's go over to the pub. I'll buy you a brandy. You look like you need a drop. I know I do.'

She came to pat my arm sympathetically. 'I'm really sorry this happened to you, Fran.'

'Call it my luck.'

But my luck hadn't been out; Duane's had.

We turned back towards the exit but I lingered, sure there must be something here to tell us exactly what had happened.

'What's the matter with you?' asked Susie impatiently. 'Are you expecting to find an explanation all nicely written out and put on the desk for us to find? Look, he didn't have time to write us a note, poor bloke. He didn't have time to call an ambulance or get downstairs to the kebab place to ask them for help or anything.'

'All right, all right, I'm coming!' I said. 'But this is only the beginning of it, Susie. The cops won't believe neither of us know why he was here. Why did they think we'd removed something from the scene? What?'

She shook her head. 'Cops are like that . . .'

'You are sure nothing was moved or missing from the room?'

'I told you! Everything was fine – except for him on the floor. Give over, Fran.'

'How can it be fine? If neither of us let him in, nor even Les, then he broke in. That's going to take some explanation. What was he after? He probably came to find me, saw the office was empty, and decided to snoop about to see if there was anything concerning Edna here. He'd found out who I was – and I really *would* like to know how he did that! Once he knew I worked for you occasionally, he must have felt sure I was following Edna for the same reason he was: someone was paying me. When we talked I didn't admit it. He thought I'd pulled a fast one on him. He reckoned he was entitled to know what I was up to. The cops will be back asking more questions and I don't want to tell them about Edna. They'll pester her and she'd be terrified.'

'You don't have to,' she said, suddenly brisk. 'Let his girlfriend, that Lottie you mentioned, do that. She runs the business with him. It's a professional matter. Anyway, you don't know he was here about Edna. It's a fair guess but only a guess. My wild-goose chase out to Richmond still could have nothing to do with it. Maybe Gardner just fancied you and wanted to chat you up.'

'Do me a favour. He was here about Edna,' I said. 'And I reckon so was someone else.'

Chapter Seven

Ganesh hit the roof.

'What did I tell you? Didn't I say you ought to leave it alone?'

'I didn't invite him round to Susie's office,' I argued. 'I don't even know how he knew he might find me there. I didn't tell him I worked for her occasionally.'

We were sitting in my flat that evening, nursing glasses of some cheap wine I'd picked up on the way home. I got it at the supermarket causing all Hari's woes. Any guilt I might have felt at taking them my business was overcome by the facts that a) I had other things on my mind and b) Hari didn't sell alcohol, anyway.

'This is horrible,' said Ganesh now, thoughtfully.

'Yeah, you should've seen him. He looked sort of surprised. It was creepy.'

'I meant the wine. The Gardner business too, of course.'

'Thanks for the sympathy. The wine was the cheapest they had, special consignment.' I tasted it. 'Yuk, my grandma always told me you get what you pay for.'

Ganesh leaned back on the sofa and Bonnie rolled an eye at him, just checking.

'Gardner asked someone about you,' Ganesh went on slowly. 'He must have done. Otherwise, how would he have known he might find you at Susie's? I understand he was curious about you. He might have suspected you were working for a rival firm, targeting Edna and trying to get to her first, before he did. That's the most likely thing. So he asked around and whom did he ask?'

Ganesh never mixes up 'who' and 'whom'. He's got a pedantic side to him but also, when he gets the time, he writes poetry and takes a lot of trouble over it.

'He probably talked it over with his girlfriend, Lottie. She runs the business with him.'

'Then you need to talk to her, Fran. Find out how he tracked you down. She probably knows. Although perhaps you ought to wait a bit; see if the cops make a move.'

Right on cue the doorbell rang. We looked at one another. Ganesh went to peer from my window. I live in a flat to the left of the front door in the converted house and because the window is a bay, it's possible to look through the side pane and see who is standing in the small porch outside. This is often useful.

'It looks like that woman inspector you get on so well with,' he hissed. 'Morgan, isn't it?'

'Tell me that's a bad joke,' I begged.

'No way, she's outside your door . . .' Ganesh broke off to smile politely and wave at the unseen person outside. 'And she's spotted me now so you can't pretend you're out. If I'm here, you're here, right?'

At least it was Morgan and not Sergeant Parry. I wouldn't agree with Ganesh that I get along well with her, but I'd rather have to talk to her than Wayne Parry. He has a ginger moustache, suspicious eyes, rotten sense of humour and, worst of all, he fancies me.

'Hullo, Fran,' Janice Morgan said cheerfully when I opened the door to her. 'Can I come in for a chat?'

Grandma Varady used to say some people had no dress sense. She used to do home sewing for people, like wedding dresses and outfits for women who couldn't buy anything to fit them, so she had an interest in such things. In a way, she bequeathed it to me. I don't mean I'm turned out like a West End shop window dummy. I mean, I notice clothes.

Grandma used to get hold of glossy magazines and cut out some of the fashion shots to give her inspiration. I don't think it ever occurred to her that she was pinching some designer's work. I think she had pinched the magazines, too, from visits to the doctor's or dentist's waiting room. They were too expensive to buy and the ones that came in the house were always out of date and well thumbed, smelling faintly of antiseptic. But again, I don't think she thought of that as in any way wrong because in her view the original owners of the magazines had put them in the public domain by leaving them in waiting rooms, up for grabs.

If Grandma could see me now I suppose she would have been pretty critical of my wardrobe and got out her old treadle machine straight away, running me up something snazzier. However, even if I don't go along with high fashion, I do make an effort at least to have some style of my own and Grandma would have approved of that. But Morgan would have had Grandma incoherent with frustration.

Morgan's approach to clothes appeared to be to go out of her way to pick all the dullest fabrics, colours and styles on offer. If she had been making a statement by this I would have understood and even cheered her on. But I reckoned it was based on a wish not to stand out. All right, a plain-clothes officer has to be discreet. I'll buy that. But she was heading for anonymity and in my book that was plain unhealthy. This was a nice-looking woman with a respectable income and no one but herself to spend it on. Yet today she was wearing a baggy charcoal-grey pinstripe suit and a white shirt and flat black loafers. Perhaps the outfit was meant to look professional but to me it just looked uninspired. It wasn't brightened by any jewellery, not even a pair of simple clip earrings, or a coloured scarf. She didn't wear her wedding ring any longer as the divorce from Tom was well behind her. Her mousy hair was chopped off in an unflattering long bob just skimming her shoulders in a straggly way and it needed a colour rinse or highlights. She hadn't bothered with make-up although with a bit of lipstick and eyebrow pencil she'd look really pretty good. Perhaps I ought to volunteer her name to one of those make-over shows on telly. Or hey, who's talking? Perhaps someone should volunteer my name.

Bonnie gave a little bark as she entered the flat and pattered towards her. But after a sniff at her lightweight support stockings, my dog turned away and settled down again. She kept her eyes on the new arrival, though. Bonnie has a strong instinct for the police in any guise.

'She remembers you,' I said. 'Want a glass of wine?'

'That would be very pleasant,' said Morgan, smiling brightly at Ganesh. 'Nice to see you again, Mr Patel.'

'Likewise,' said Ganesh. 'I thought—'

I glared at him and he shut up. I knew he had been going to say that he thought the police didn't drink on duty.

Morgan had guessed it. 'This is an informal call,' she said. 'I'm in my own time.' She lifted the glass. 'Cheers!' She sipped and winced. 'I saw a report about a fatality discovered in Mrs Duke's office earlier today,' she went on.

She replaced the wine glass on my newly acquired occasional table. The table is square and weighty and supported by a carved elephant. One of Ganesh's aunts had been about to throw it out and he rescued it for me.

'The report said the body was discovered by you, Fran, so I thought I'd pop round and have a word about it. I'm sorry you had a nasty shock.' She sounded sympathetic and it was probably genuine. The police are trained in dispensing sympathy in cases of sudden death, but Morgan knew me well enough to realise how shaken I was and to have some personal concern.

'Yes, it was nasty,' I said. 'And I don't know that I want to talk about it.'

'It helps to talk,' she assured me. 'Don't you think so, Mr Patel?'

'Depends to whom she's talking,' retorted Ganesh, getting his 'whom' right again, even in the stress of the moment. 'If she's talking to a friend, like me, that's fine. If she's talking to the police, even if the officer in question is off duty, it's not so good. Put it this way, you lot are never off duty. Would you have called to see Fran this evening if she hadn't stumbled on a dead body earlier?'

'No,' Morgan admitted. 'But I thought she'd rather chat to me here in the comfort of her own home than down at the station.'

'If you've seen the report of the incident,' I said, 'then you'll have read what I told the two officers who attended the scene. I've nothing to add.'

I've dealt with the police a few times now and I've got to know the rules.

'Oh, Fran,' she said sorrowfully. 'This is me. How long have we known one another? You always know more than you tell us.'

'She's got nothing to add!' Ganesh said crossly. 'You have no grounds for what you say.'

'Rubbish,' said Morgan amiably to him. 'Now, Fran, why don't you tell me how you come to be acquainted with Duane Gardner?'

I saw Ganesh give an imperceptible shake of the head but chose to ignore it. Morgan was right, of course; I had to tell her all about my meetings with Duane. I had to tell her about Edna. It might be the best thing to do for Edna's sake. If the police took an interest in what was happening around her, whoever had hired Duane might be scared off. Besides, they couldn't deny that something was going on around Edna, not now with Duane down at the morgue.

But I had a question of my own first. 'Can you tell me what he died of? He wasn't old. He didn't look too healthy, I suppose, and might have been sick. Has a postmortem been done?'

'It will probably be done in the morning,' Morgan told us. She eyed her wine glass and wisely decided against taking another sip. 'The attending doctor who was called at the time noticed fresh puncture marks on his arm. Did you know Gardner was an addict?'

So that was what all those questions from the two coppers at the scene had been about. They'd been pretty casual about it before the doctor turned up, but once he had pointed out the marks to them, they wanted to know if Duane had been shooting up in the office either on his own or in company and if so, where the syringe was. They thought either Susie or I had removed it. I'd been too horrified by the general scene to take a close look at the body or I might have noticed the tell-tale puncture marks myself.

'I have no idea,' I told Morgan. 'If he was a user then his girlfriend would know. She runs the business with him and her name is Lottie. I don't know anything else about her and I've never met her. But I suggest you ask her.'

'Her name is Lottie Forester,' Morgan told me. 'She tells us Gardner had a habit some years ago, but he went through rehab and he'd been clean for some time. She denies he'd slipped back into old ways. But he might have hidden it from her.'

'If she was living with him, she'd have known,' I argued.

I spoke absently. My mind was running on well ahead of the point the conversation had reached. Morgan was waiting patiently. She could see I was reasoning it out. But I remained puzzled. I'd sat near to Duane in that Golders Green coffee shop eating fish and chips for about three-quarters of an hour. He'd worn a sleeveless top and I'd had ample opportunity to spot the signs if there had been any to see. Regular needle users make such a mess of their arms I could hardly have missed.

'There's something you're not telling me,' I said. 'I know the postmortem hasn't been carried out yet, but there has to be something else about the body that brought you round here to see me so fast. What about signs of violence? I didn't see any, but then, I wasn't looking.'

Yet I had been suspicious and asked Susie if she noticed anything odd or different in the office – a corpse on the floor aside. There was no way I could accept Duane had just dropped down dead there for me to find. I know coincidences do happen, but this hadn't been one.

Morgan said slowly, 'Although there has been no proper autopsy yet, a preliminary examination of the body has found a bruise on the back of his head.'

'Shit,' I said.

'Of course,' she went on, 'he might have acquired that when he fell. He was found sitting with his back against the wall, I understand. You didn't move him, either you or Mrs Duke, before the police arrived?'

'Neither of us even touched him. Susie was going to shake his shoulder because she thought he might just be unconscious but she changed her mind.'

'So he might have fallen backwards.' Ganesh had been following all this with furrowed brow and now broke in. 'And as he fell he struck his head against the wall behind him, then just slithered down to a seated position.'

'Yes, indeed he might have done that,' agreed Morgan in a way which told us she didn't believe it happened that way for a minute.

'Are you saying, or hang on . . .' I paused to rephrase it. 'I know you are not saying this, but is there a possibility he was coshed and then someone jabbed a needle full of heroin or some other substance in his arm?'

The postmortem would tell if a fatal overdose or a contaminated substance had killed Duane. If it had, and he wasn't on drugs himself, then someone else administered it to him. Normally he'd have resisted unless, of course, he couldn't for whatever reason. The most obvious would be that someone had knocked him out first.

Ganesh muttered something and was so distressed he took another deep swig of his wine and didn't even blink.

'We'll know in the morning,' said Morgan soothingly. 'Now, are you going to talk to me, Fran?'

'Oh, all right,' I said.

Morgan fished a small tape recorder from her pocket and put it on the elephant table amid the glasses.

'Oy!' snapped Ganesh. 'What about this being an informal call?'

'It's all right,' I said wearily. 'Switch it on. If they've got it all on tape then perhaps they won't keep coming back and asking me the same daft questions all over and over again, Gan.'

'Just watch what you say!' he ordered.

'I know!' I said irritably.

'Yes, and I know you. It's all that business about being an actor. Stick you in front of a mike or in front of that tape recorder there and you react like you're on stage. Cut out the dramatic flourishes, right? You're not auditioning for a part.'

Morgan switched on her little gadget and it began to whirr softly. 'Interview with Francesca Varady,' she informed the room. She glanced at her wristwatch and added the time and for good measure, the location.

I explained about seeing Edna and remembering her from the Rotherhithe days, about her running away from Duane and my attempt to follow him. I told her about the hostel and Simon and Nikki, about following Edna to Golders Green and meeting up with Duane Gardner again in the cemetery there.

'I didn't make any arrangements to meet him again.' I finished. 'I didn't tell him of my connection with Susie's agency. He shouldn't have known anything about it. I had the shock of my life when I walked into Susie Duke's office and found him.' I hesitated and then repeated, 'I only *found* him. I hadn't arranged to meet him there. I told you, he shouldn't even have known I could be reached through the agency.'

'Yet you are assuming,' Morgan pointed out, 'that he *had* gone there to find you.'

Ganesh joined in at that point to say, 'Fran might be assuming that, but I'm not. Gardner was in the detection business and might have had half a dozen reasons to visit a colleague in the same line of work. He may have gone there to find Susie Duke because he wanted her help in some professional matter. That Fran turned up was just bad luck.'

'You seem to have a lot of bad luck of that sort, Fran,' observed Morgan, giving me a funny look.

'I don't ask for it!' I snapped.

'Perhaps you do, Fran,' she argued reasonably and to my annoyance I could see, from the corner of my eye, Ganesh nodding agreement. 'You take too much interest in what's going on around, could that be it?'

'I'm a concerned citizen,' I told her. 'We're always being told to keep our eyes open for anything dodgy, aren't we?'

She nodded, 'Of course, and if you should see anything, you *report it straight away to the police*, right?' She had that minatory gleam in her eye that I knew so well of old.

'Yeah, yeah,' I said, 'as if you'd have been interested in Edna.'

'It's always worth trying me,' she replied. 'I have a lot of respect for your intelligence, Fran.'

Before I could recover from the shock of this unexpected endorsement, she added:

'But I often don't think much of your judgement. Before you do anything else, Fran, think!'

She got up to leave at that point, abandoning her wine. 'Here,' she said, holding out a scrap of card. 'You can reach me on this number, should you think of anything.'

'See?' said Ganesh smugly when Morgan had left. 'I'm not the only one warning you. Do like she says, will you, in future? Think before you get into things!'

'I'm thinking,' I promised him. 'I'm thinking.'

I was too; I was thinking what I could do next about this business. I wasn't going to let it drop and to do her justice, Morgan hadn't asked me to do so outright. She'd known I wouldn't and although she'd never admit it, I had come up with some pretty useful information in the past. If I read the signs right, then she was prepared to turn a blind eye to my activities over the next week or so, provided I didn't tread too heavily on police toes.

Or, at least, that's how I chose to read it.

I couldn't do anything until Ganesh had also left and by that time it was too late to phone anyone. I had to wait until morning. I chose breakfast-time because I guessed that Duane and Lottie probably ran the business from their home address. I wanted to catch her before she went out for the day. There was a chance I'd only get a recorded reply but I was in luck.

'Yes?' That was all she said. She didn't give the name of the business. In the circumstances she didn't need professional enquiries just now. 'Is that Lottie Forester?' I asked.

A pause. 'Yes,' the girl repeated. Her voice sounded young and guarded. She'd been dealing with the police. Perhaps now she thought I might be a reporter from a local rag. If a private investigator is murdered, the greenest cub reporter sniffs a good story. It wouldn't surprise me if she hadn't had a reporter or two knocking at the door already and, if not, she certainly would do soon.

'My name is Fran Varady,' I said. 'Did Duane mention me to you at all?'

'Yes.' The reply hadn't changed but her tone had, gaining a note of hostility. Was she going to blame me for what had happened to her boyfriend?

'I'd like to come and see you,' I said. 'I think we need to talk, Lottie. I realise it's a bad time and I'm really sorry about what's happened, but it's not going to get better for a while. This can't wait that long. We both want to know the same thing, you and I, don't we? We want to know who killed Duane.'

I thought I might get the standard affirmative reply but instead she said crisply, 'Come this morning. Can you get here by half past ten?'

'Make it eleven to be sure,' I said. 'I've got to find you.'

'We're in the *A–Z*,' was the terse reply. 'You can get a suburban train out of Waterloo. Get off at Fulwell station. We're near the golf course.' She hung up.

It occurred to me, as I did so, that I was intending to call on someone in mourning and almost certainly in deep shock. To describe my proposed action as tactless was an understatement. But I didn't have time on my side. The police might already have told Lottie not to talk to anyone. I wasn't just anyone: I was the person who had found the body. But if she had time to think about it, and time to recover some composure, she might clam up on me and I'd get nothing.

I thought wryly that perhaps I'd missed out on a career with the brasher end of the tabloid press world. Their reporters work on the same principle. Get in quick or you'll get no story. I felt ashamed but still determined. 'Bonnie,' I addressed her aloud and she cocked an attentive ear, 'Susie thinks I'm a natural for the detection business but really, I'm not. I'm too sensitive.'

'Like how . . .' Ganesh's voice seemed to echo in my ear in an unpleasantly sarcastic tone.

'I'm misunderstood,' I told Bonnie.

This time even Bonnie's expression seemed to say, 'Oh, yeah?'

She wasn't at all as I'd expected although, to be honest, I wasn't sure what I'd thought she'd be like, other than understandably distressed. From her voice she'd sounded young and educated. On the other hand, from my brief acquaintance with Duane I'd imagined his partner would be someone a bit freaky like him. You have to be fairly tough to deal with the day-to-day seediness of life seen from the private detective's viewpoint. Susie used blond curls and a bouncy personality as a weapon. But Susie wasn't Duane's type. I imagined someone in unisex clothing, with cropped hair and smoker's complexion. Yes, that would be more in Duane's line.

When she opened the door to my ring I found myself looking at a young woman not a great deal older than I was, certainly no more than twenty-six or -seven. She was very pretty, contrary to all my expectations. Poor Duane had been no hunk. But this girl was almost beautiful and if her eyes hadn't been reddened from weeping and shadowed underneath from lack of sleep, she would have been stunning.

She put me in mind of a Botticelli painting, with long abundant reddish hair which kinked naturally and if cut short would have curled. Her face was oval and her greyish-green eyes thickly lashed. She was slim and wore a full cotton skirt in three contrastingly patterned tiers, gipsy-style. With it was teamed a figure-hugging black top with three-quarter length sleeves and a deep V-neck. Her tiny feet were shod in tightly-fitting pointed black fashion boots with very high heels. It was almost as if she stood on tip-toe and the resulting effect reminded me of pictures I'd seen of women with bound feet in old China.

I wore clean jeans and a top and because I had my *A–Z* booklet together with a notepad with me, I also had a little black leather backpack, contrary to my usual habit. So far so good, plain but professional (I hoped), but I did wish I'd had time to do something about the colour of my hair, its crude red dye contrasting unfavourably with Lottie's natural auburn curls.

I'd found the house easily enough. It was a thirties-built detached suburban villa with a double-bay frontage and garage to the side reached by a weed-pocked gravel drive. It was only a short walk away from a golf course which turned out to be a private one. In this part of the world a house like this would cost a fair bit of money. People with that kind of income don't swing a golf club with any old Tom, Dick or Harry.

I had stared up at the frontage. Although it could do with some paint and TLC, it didn't appear to be divided into flats or to have suffered the even worse fate of being turned into student bedsits. You can tell such places by the mismatched curtains and rooms obviously in some use other than that originally intended; bottles of washing-up liquid propped on bedroom windowsills. There were no battered bikes in the neglected forecourt and no name cards by an array of bell-pushes. The absence of all that surprised me. I wouldn't have thought Duane and Lottie could have afforded to rent the whole place, unless the detection business was doing exceptionally well in this nook of suburbia. As to having a mortgage on it, that didn't bear thinking of. A pair of city high-flyers with no dependants might manage it but not a youngish couple of hand-to-mouth amateur 'tecs.

'You're Fran?' She pushed a selection of Indian bangles up her left arm with her right hand as she spoke. It was a gesture full of ill-suppressed tension. Her voice was sullen and her gaze hostile.

I'd been worrying about this moment. Sobbing women are out of my competence. This girl was hopping wild, raging against life's – and death's – unfairness. I could have told her about that; but realising I was gawping at her, I hastened to identify myself and thank her for agreeing to see me.

'I nearly didn't,' was the blunt reply. 'Do you think, at a time like this, I want to talk to nosy strangers? I'm only seeing you because I want to know what swine did that to Duane. He mentioned you to me. He said you were a ruddy nuisance. Perhaps that's all you are but you'd better come in.' She gestured inwards.

I followed her inside and she shut the door behind us. The hall was long and narrow with a parquet floor in need of a good polish. There was a majolica jardinière, I guessed Victorian replica and probably worth quite a bit, if those TV antiques programmes were anything to go by. The plant in it was a straggling fern of neglected appearance. It hadn't been watered in a while, its thin leaves browning, and someone had stubbed out a cigarette in the compost. It was an unloved plant unworthy of the jardinière. I wondered if it had been inherited. Plants are sometimes passed on when property changes hands. A steep staircase faced us running up to a mezzanine landing furnished with a similar potted plant on a stand. I can take or leave healthy houseplants but expiring houseplants are definitely out.

I glanced round quickly, my curiosity more than usually intrigued. Also in the hall was an old-fashioned hatstand with some outdoor clothing hanging on it, an oval mirror with a heavy carved frame and a couple of nice watercolours of the bridges of Paris with Notre Dame showing in one of them. On a table with barley-twist legs stood a blue and white porcelain bowl that looked old to me, older than the Victorian pot plant holders. What appeared to be car keys rested in it. Everything was rather dusty but it was good stuff: not, however, quite the sort of things I'd have imagined a young couple buying. I wondered how they'd come by it all and whether either Lottie or Duane had any idea how much some of this might be worth.

Lottie was marching ahead of me down the hall, gipsy skirt swinging from side to side, the high heels of the boots clattering on the parquet and scoring further dents and scratches on it. She ignored a door to the left which must lead into a front parlour and opened another door halfway between that and a further door at the rear of the hall leading into what must be a room at the back of the house. Spacious accommodation downstairs doubtless matched by corresponding roominess upstairs. That was a lot of area for just Duane and Lottie to rattle round in.

The room beyond the opened door was small and had been fitted out as an office. It all looked very efficient and I was impressed. A fireplace with a black-lacquered hood and aquamarine tiled surround was the only sign that this had once been part of a domestic setting, probably what used to be called a breakfast room. Now it housed a modern computer station, a fax machine, a typist's chair, two black-leather swivel chairs and a low pine table. The contrast between this obviously fairly recently renovated room and the state of the rest of the place I'd seen so far was striking. It underlined the shabbiness of Susie's office and Whitehall throw-out furniture.

Lottie gestured to me to take one of the swivel chairs, her Indian bangles chinking softly. I slipped off the backpack and sat down. She took the opposite one and rested her hands on the arms. She began to twist to and fro on the central spindle, all the time assessing me with no attempt at disguise. It was difficult to read in her face what she was making of me. The green eyes were as bright and expressionless as a cat's. Her full well-formed lips were nicely lipsticked in a flattering mauve shade. Possibly keeping her physical appearance together helped her keep her mental state from disintegration.

'Nice place,' I ventured at last because her silent scrutiny was beginning to unsettle me. 'Are you sole tenants?'

She shrugged. 'It's my house. I own it.'

Now I was impressed and must have looked it.

'My gran died and left it to me!' she said impatiently. 'Duane and I were already together and she wanted us to have a proper place to live.'

That explained the old-fashioned furnishings out in the hall and the withered potted plants. Lottie and Duane had moved in and kept all of Gran's furniture except in this room. Granny had been well off. Lottie looked and sounded privately educated. (I was too but I don't sound it.) I wondered if her full name was Charlotte and also if she'd keep the business going now she didn't have Duane to do the legwork. Susie had kept her business going without the late Rennie but I couldn't imagine the girl in front of me trawling grubby pubs and hanging out on street corners keeping observation.

'What happened to Duane?' she charged suddenly, eyes like green ice.

'I don't know,' I said. 'But I want to. How long were you two together?'

For the first time the grey-green eyes evaded mine. She didn't want me to see her pain. 'Nearly six years. He was a bloody good detective, you know.' Her voice shook slightly.

'Yes, I do know,' I told her. 'Lottie, did he go to the Duke Detective Agency looking for me? If he did, how did he know he might find me there? Or at least, that they could tell him where to find me? I didn't tell him about it.'

'I told you,' Lottie said impatiently. 'He was a *good* detective. He didn't buy that story of yours about knowing the old lady ages ago in Rotherhithe. Someone had to be paying you to find her, and that meant you had to work out of some agency. So he asked around. He drew a blank at first but eventually someone told him you worked out of a place in Camden.'

'I asked about *him*,' I retorted, 'but nobody knew him. I'm surprised he found someone who knew *me*. Who was it?'

She gave a mocking little smile. 'Confidential,' she said.

Now, where had I heard that before? I didn't bother to argue with her about my reasons for taking an interest in Edna. She wouldn't believe me; especially since she and Duane had found I'd a connection, however tenuous, with the Duke Detective Agency.

'Someone was and probably still is paying you and Duane to find Edna and more,' I said. 'Who's your client? What does he want with Edna?'

She opened her mouth but I forestalled her.

'Don't say confidential, all right? This business has got Duane killed. Unless he had a heart condition or something like that. Did he?'

She shook her head. The tip of her tongue ran over her lower lip. She wasn't as in command as she appeared. How could she be? She'd had a terrible shock and lost not only her business partner but boyfriend of six years. She must be a little older than she looked, perhaps twenty-eight or -nine. I'd placed Duane in his thirties. She was doing pretty well dealing with the situation, all things considered. She might still crack at any moment. I felt cruel at harassing her at such a sensitive time but circumstances didn't leave me any option, as I'd told myself before setting out.

'Lottie,' I said, 'I don't know what kind of work your agency handles. But I bet it hasn't involved dealing with murderers before now, right?'

She blanched. 'Who says he was murdered?'

'As far as I know, no one yet. But it has to be on the cards, Lottie, so let's assume, as a basis for our immediate future plans, that his investigations got him killed.'

'The police—' she began but broke off.

'The police, or one of them, came to see me,' I said. 'Duane had hypodermic marks on his arm and a bruise on the back of his head. You told the police he wasn't into drugs.'

'He was when we met,' she admitted. 'Nothing serious, but enough. I made him give it up. He hadn't touched anything for years. We've got a business here. You can't mess with drugs and run a business.'

'Fair enough. I'm sorry,' I added. 'I know all this blunt talk is painful. But nothing is going to make the situation better and, let's face it, you and I are still alive and we want to stay that way.'

She swivelled back and forth on the chair for a moment. 'The police told me there will be a postmortem, probably this morning. I don't know if they'll phone me when they've got a result or come round here. They said I should wait and see what the autopsy shows up.'

She looked and still sounded obstinate. 'They haven't called it murder.'

'They have to wait and make sure. I don't,' I said. 'And while you're waiting for the cops to show up with a printed autopsy report,' I went on, 'our killer is planning his next move. Lottie, you could be in real danger. Whatever Duane knew, the killer will assume you know it, too. You do realise that, don't you? Are you living here alone now?'

'I've got security,' she said.

I'd noticed the blue box of a burglar alarm on the front of the house as I'd walked towards the front door.

'The killer's good at getting into places,' I said. 'He got through a locked door into the Duke Agency, unless Duane was the one who knew all the tricks with a plastic card. *Had* Duane gone there to find me?'

She nodded. 'He reckoned you'd been holding out on him. He thought we might pool our resources. The way things were going, our enquiries had to collide with yours and we were going to be falling over one another at every turn.'

'Are you prepared to tell me the name of your client?' I expected to hear 'confidential', but if she was rattled enough, she might give it away.

'I couldn't tell you that,' she said quickly, 'unless the client agreed. I have not yet spoken with the client.'

'What, not at all?' I gasped. 'You'll have to tell him what's happened! Anyway, the police will want to speak to him.'

'Telling the police is different to telling you,' she pointed out reasonably enough. 'Will you tell me the name of *your* client?'

'I can't,' I said. I couldn't because I hadn't got a client but she wouldn't believe that any more than Duane had.

'Then it's stalemate,' she said calmly.

I sighed. 'Look, Lottie, at least ask the police to move you to a safe location.'

'I can go and stay with my mum and dad, if it comes to that.'

'If you think the killer can't find where your parents live and won't check it out when he finds you're not here, you're nuts,' I said unkindly.

'I'll discuss it with the police,' she said coldly.

I wasn't going to get anywhere down that path. I tried another. 'Edna's an old bag lady, or was,' I said. 'She was living on the streets for years and now she's safe, warm and cared for after a fashion in a hostel. I don't know why anyone would want to find her. But in particular I don't know why anything about her should be such a threat that someone would be prepared to kill to prevent it being known.'

I broke off suddenly and thought, Shit! It's not this girl the killer will come after next, it's Edna!

I scrambled to my feet. 'I've got your card,' I said. 'Here's one of the Duke Agency's. I'm not always there but you can leave a message for me any time. If you change your mind about talking to me, call that number. And remember what I said about asking the cops to move you to a safe location.'

I was on the move myself as I spoke, struggling to pull the straps of the backpack over my shoulders. I stepped out into the hall and made for the front door. I had to get back into London and to the hostel and check on Edna and then I had to get hold of Morgan and impress on her that she had to make sure Edna was moved somewhere safe. The trouble there would be that Edna would almost certainly refuse to cooperate.

My sudden decision to go had startled Lottie and wrong-footed her. She had jumped from her swivel chair and followed me.

'What's up?' she demanded sharply. 'What have you thought of?'

'Confidential!' I snarled, striding towards the front door.

I heard her high heels clicking along behind me. 'Wait!' she called.

I stopped, not because of her sudden wish to talk to me but because through the frosted glazed panels of the front door a large dark shape had loomed up and stood there, exuding silent menace. Lottie had another visitor.

We both froze, huddled together like a couple of scared puppies. 'Who is it?' whispered Lottie, not sounding so confident now.

'I don't know, do I?' I muttered back. 'Copper?'

The bell gave a sudden loud buzz which made us both jump.

Lottie pushed past me and up to the door. 'Who is it?' she shouted at the glass panels and the sinister shape.

'Only me, gal!' came a rough male voice which sounded very familiar. I frowned.

Lottie relaxed and put her hand to the latch. 'It's all right,' she said to me over her shoulder. She opened the door. 'You gave us a fright, Les. You ought to have said you were coming over.'

'Yes, Les,' I said brightly from behind her, 'you really should let people know what you're up to.'

I'd never seen a grown man look so shame-faced and awkward. 'Oh, 'ullo, Fran,' he growled, 'fancy meeting you here.'

'Yes, just fancy.' I turned back to Lottie. 'So this is how you found out about me occasionally working for the Duke Agency? I think I'd like to talk to Mr Hooper. I can do it here and now or I'll sit on your doorstep until he's finished his social call, which?'

'You'd better both come back to the office,' she said. 'Bloody hell, Les, why didn't you telephone first?'

Chapter Eight

The little office which had been snug with just me and Lottie in it became, as did Susie's little office, uncomfortably crowded with Les's burly frame squashed into one of the swivel chairs. It was Les's way that he dominated any area not by personality, in which he was lacking, but by sheer bulk and miasma. He exuded a faint air of nicotine, sweat and dogs. I wondered if he owned a dog or just hung around with people who did. Did I smell of Bonnie? I hoped not. I had showered before I came out and I doubted Les had. He hadn't even shaved very well. He looked very much as if he'd like to light up a cigarette right now but didn't dare. At any rate, put Les in the middle of an empty Wembley stadium and he'd still manage to overpower the place.

I'd retaken my previous seat and Lottie perched on the typist's stool by the computer. She was looking from Les to me and back again with a kind of dispassionate interest, as if we were zoo animals and might, if she watched long enough, do something justifying her attention but it wasn't guaranteed.

I decided to get the ball rolling. 'OK, Les,' I began. 'When I described to you and Susie the person I'd seen watching Edna, you recognised him as Duane Gardner but you didn't say so.'

'No point in blowing Duane's cover,' Les croaked, giving Lottie an apprehensive glance tinged with appeal. 'I didn't know what he was up to but I reckoned it must be in the line of business.'

'In a line of business you work for Susie Duke,' I snapped.

But here he rallied and had a counter-argument. 'I'm freelance, ain't I? I don't work for Susie regular, no more than you do. When she needs me, she calls me. I work on the same basis for others, like Duane and Lottie here. I work for a lot of private agencies. They know they can call on me. Blimey, gal, if I only worked for Susie Duke, I'd starve.'

Lottie chimed in, confirming his claim. 'He works for us on an occasional basis. Now and again we need someone. Duane could handle most of it but sometimes he needed help.'

She broke off and frowned. Perhaps it had occurred to her that if she was going to continue in the business, she'd need the services of Les or someone like him a lot more. Using Les from time to time was one thing. Having Les around permanently was another. She gave him a speculative look and fell to chewing her lower lip thoughtfully.

'Yus, that's right,' said Les with some confidence.

I guessed he was thinking along the same lines. No wonder he was round here touching base. He foresaw a lot of work coming his way from what was now solely Lottie's agency.

'What was Duane doing in Susie's office?' I asked him bluntly.

His confidence drained away with almost comical rapidity. 'I dunno, darling. So help me, I've got no idea.' He spread out his hands to underline his statement.

'Had he gone there to meet *you*?' I had been assuming Duane had gone there to find *me*. Morgan was thinking the same. But the person Duane had known far better and longer than me was Les, his old mate and occasional fellow-sleuth. Was it Les he'd arranged to meet? Or had he in fact met him there on that fateful morning? Was I staring at Duane's killer?

From the corner of an eye I saw Lottie blink in that catlike way she had, slowly and appraisingly.

'Ah, no!' said Les quickly, leaning forward and waving a sausage-shaped and tobacco-orange finger beneath my nose to emphasise the point. 'He wouldn't have done that. If he wanted me, he'd see me down the pub. If it was urgent, he gave me a buzz on the old mobile. Nah, he wouldn't have come over to Susie's place for me. No need, see? Usually he rang me and I went to him, that is, I come here, don't I, Lottie?'

This time her endorsement of his argument was half-hearted. She was no longer paying such close attention to what he had to say but was mulling over some line of thought of her own. I guessed it was probably not a million miles away from my own. 'Mm,' she mumbled.

Les threw her a reproachful look. 'I don't know what he was doing in the office, girls, I swear.'

He was beginning to work up quite a sweat and his body odour was getting worse, gaining a hint of additional origins like fried food. The advertising people who write up those posh wines could create a good description of Les: full, mature and fruity with a hint of chippie and back-street repair garage.

'Did you lend him the key? Susie told me you hold a key to the outer door.' I leaned forward in best interrogator fashion as I asked, and fixed him with as direct a look as I could manage.

He looked alarmed, as well he might. I don't know whether the question or the body language worried him most. 'No, and don't you go putting that idea in Susie's head. She'd kill me.'

There was an awkward silence during which even Les seemed to realise that he had made a less than tactful remark.

'I never gave him the key,' he repeated at last in a more sullen tone. 'I'll swear it on a stack of Bibles.'

'Did you know he would be going there?'

'No! Leave it out, willya, Fran? It's no use giving me the old third degree. I'm sorry for what happened to Duane, honest, Lottie. He was a really good bloke. But I don't know what he was doing over at Susie's place. How the hell should I? He didn't tell me he was going there.'

He was getting rebellious and very soon would tell me in no uncertain terms that he wasn't going to sit there and let me quiz him indefinitely. I got in my last questions while I still could. 'OK, Les, did Duane tell you anything about his client or why he was tailing Edna?'

At this Lottie looked up quickly.

Les shook his head.

'But you told him I worked for Susie Duke, on and off, like you do yourself.'

Les fidgeted. 'Look, Fran, I'm being honest with you. Business is slow everywhere in the private enquiry line. Susie has no work for me no more than she has for you right now. You heard her say so yourself that day you came into the office and told us you'd seen someone watching the old lady. After that I went and called on a couple of fellows I know in the private enquiry lark just to see if I could get a job from them, but they told me the same. Any work they had on at the moment, they could handle themselves. So I thought, I'll go out to Teddington and see if Duane has anything for me. I knew from what you'd told us that he must have a job of some sort. I hadn't said anything to him straight away about you spotting him because, well, it didn't seem to matter that much. You didn't know who he was and you weren't likely to see him again. In the same way, I didn't tell you that I'd recognised him from your description. I'm discreet, see? I try to keep everyone happy,' Les added plaintively, 'and look where it gets me!'

He gazed at us beseechingly, inviting our sympathy, but he didn't get it.

'Go on,' I ordered.

He gave a wheezing smoker's sigh. 'I saw him down at the pub here, locally, the night before he – the night before you and Susie found him in the office. First I asked him if he had any jobs I could do and he said he hadn't.'

Les looked pathetic. It was awful, like a mistreated bloodhound, baggy eyes, drooping jowls and all. 'I wanted to remind him I was useful, got an ear to the ground. That's why people like Susie or Lottie here use me, because I know what's about. So I told Duane about you coming in and describing someone who sounded a lot like him and if it *had* been him, following someone around Camden Town Tube area, he ought to know he was being picked up.'

'And?' It was Lottie asking the question now, not me. Her tone was distinctly chilly.

He gave her another beseeching look. 'He bought me a pint. He said, "Cheers, Les, and thanks for the tip." That's it and all about it, I swear.' His meaty paws closed on the arms of the chair.

'Hang on!' I said. 'Did he tell you he and I had met again in the grounds of Golders Green cemetery?'

'Blimey, no! What were you doing out there?' Les looked really taken aback and goggled at me. 'Funny place to go to meet someone, ain't it?'

'It's quiet,' I said curtly.

'Can't argue wiv that,' said Les. 'Here, Fran, you don't have to be mad at me. What's wrong wiv telling him you work for Susie, off and on? It ain't a bleeding state secret, is it?'

Les spread out his huge callused hands in a gesture of innocence and gave us a look intended to inspire trust. I'd never trusted him and I wasn't about to start now. I wondered to what extent Duane had trusted him, even if he had used him from time to time. He had thanked Les for the information about me, but he'd not told Les of our meeting in the cemetery. That would have been discussing a job with him and if Les wasn't working on it with him, then that was none of Les's business. Duane's watchword had been 'confidential'.

Lottie was rather less keen on Les, I guessed, than she had been when he arrived. We both glared at him.

'I'll come back later, Lottie,' Les said in the face of our silent hostility. He struggled to his feet and she followed him out.

When she returned from the front door, I said, 'I wouldn't take him into your confidence, Lottie. Not because I'm saying he did anything to bring about Duane's death but because he's unreliable. Did you know he worked for other people?'

'Yes. We didn't think it mattered. We didn't think he'd blab our business and as far as we – as I know, he never has. He's a rough diamond but he's all right.'

As far as I was concerned the only kind of diamond Les was, was paste.

But her voice had wavered on the last statement. She suddenly looked very tired and a tad bewildered. She needed to be alone. It was time for me to go.

'Well, watch yourself, anyway,' I advised. 'Don't forget what I told you about asking the police to move you to a safe place. If they do, don't let Les know the address!'

Chapter Nine

I hurried back into London as fast as I could make it. The suburban train link was fairly frequent and it wasn't a long run, but still by the time I got to Waterloo I was in a lather of impatience.

Thoughts had been churning around my brain during the journey and of course Les featured in most of them. Although I'd told Lottie I was not accusing him of anything to do with Duane's death, I hate coincidences. It did seem awfully odd to me that the morning after Duane learned about my association with the Duke Agency from Les, the poor guy turned up dead there. Or had it just been a natural progression of events? I didn't mean Duane being murdered. That was out of any ordinary progression of any kind. I meant that as soon as Duane learned I was in the same line of business, he was off like a hare to find me and accuse me of double talk during our chat in Golders Green.

I jumped down from the train and filled my lungs with the familiar blend of engine oil, fast food, dirt and human sweat which passes for air at mainline railway stations. The loudspeaker was announcing delays just down the line at Vauxhall as I threaded my path through the crowds on the concourse. Vauxhall was barely out of Waterloo and the information boded ill for anyone thinking of taking a long journey to the south coast. Now they knew things were screwed up on the main line, would-be passengers milled about in a discontented mob. I stopped long enough at a bagel stall to pick up something for my lunch and plunged down into the Underground.

But my luck was really out. In a situation mirroring that above our heads, an announcement came that there was a signalling problem on the Northern Line which resulted in fewer Tube trains and packed platforms. Several of the would-be Tube travellers had come down from the main rail terminal above and were equipped with a variety of luggage, including a fair sprinkling of Aussie backpackers laden up like camels. I didn't fancy squeezing onto a train, when and if one came, in that crush. I moved over to the Bakerloo Line where it wasn't much better but there were more trains running. I was able to take the Underground as far as the Baker Street station. I emerged thankfully into the fresh air through the main entry in the Marylebone Road, blinking blindly like a mole, and finally focusing my gaze to find myself face to face with Sherlock Holmes. I don't mean a statue of the great detective like the one outside the Baker Street exit from the Tube station. I mean a flesh and blood one.

All right, I know it sounds like a bad joke, but someone really was dressed up as him: deerstalker, pipe, caped coat and everything. This Holmes lookalike was walking up and down smiling pleasantly at everyone, something I doubted Conan Doyle's Holmes ever did. In the stories he always struck me as a miserable old sod with a pretty high opinion of himself. He uses loyal old Watson as a target to practise his verbal and other cleverness on. If I had been Watson I'd have walked out.

The sight of him was disconcerting. Not that anyone else seemed to find it in the slightest odd except me. They passed him by with busy step and nary a glance. Cripes, was I hallucinating? I couldn't help staring and caught his eye. He beamed at me in a welcoming way. It was bad enough seeing him. I wasn't getting into some weird conversation with him and, with some relief, I hopped on the first bus heading towards North London.

The bagel rested on my stomach in an indigestible lump. I sought distraction. London buses are good at getting you places but they are often slow. You have plenty of time to sit on them, observe the world outside which is often moving at much the same pace on foot as you are in the bus, and think. I wanted to make some really good plan with regard to ensuring Edna's safety but couldn't come up with one, the main problem being Edna herself. Sherlock Holmes kept forcing himself back into my consciousness, largely because of the apparition outside the Tube.

He had been just one of the many bizarre sights on our streets, regular enough to gain a kind of normality in their strangeness. Why should anyone stare at him? He was happy. There are many people who choose to remodel a world in which they feel ill at ease into one in which they are perfectly comfortable. Why should Edna be such an oddity, after all? Why should anyone care about her? There are scientists who shut themselves away for months in a self-contained, controlled environment encapsulated in a giant glass dome. It is accepted that no one should disturb them. Why disturb Edna in her self-created eco-system? In my own way, was I disturbing her? Was Ganesh right? Ought I just to let well alone?

No! I told myself immediately. Biblical Eden had a snake in it: and a faceless threat prowled the undergrowth in Edna's private Eden Project here and now. Of that, if of nothing else, I was quite certain. But how to flush it out into the open and with the minimum disruption to Edna's life?

I thought wistfully of the world Conan Doyle had created for his great detective. That was doing detection the gentleman's way. There the old violin-scraper had sat in his comfortable rooms, with Mrs Hudson running up and down stairs with life's necessities on a tray and poor old Watson sent out to do all the legwork. Holmes himself exercised his brain but precious little else. If you have a brain like the Great Man then perhaps you don't need to do anything else. I know he occasionally bestirred himself to dress up and hide out on Dartmoor or hire a private train to take him somewhere but I have always thought that Holmes managed his detection in the way we'd all like to be able to do it, from the comfort of his armchair.

Sadly real life doesn't permit it. I don't have his brainpower or even Poirot's amazing little grey cells and I would have liked to know how either of those great detectives would have dealt with my problems. I had a nutty old lady and an unidentified threat to her which was becoming hourly more dangerous. I'd fallen over a stiff whose last wish in life had apparently been a head-to-head conference with me. Holmes hailed a hansom cab when he wanted to get anywhere. I had to battle the vagaries of London's modern transport system. Poirot had Inspector Japp grovelling before him. I had Morgan.

Lottie wouldn't tell me the name of her client so I didn't know whether the client or someone else represented the threat. It was possible the client's aim was the same as mine: to protect Edna. If so, I needed to find the client and talk to him or her.

The bus lurched onward at increased speed and deposited me reasonably close to where I wanted to go, the hostel. I completed the journey at a jog trot, despite the bagel, and arrived breathless before its front door.

Sandra wasn't sitting on the steps today; instead she opened the door to me.

'Hi,' I said, rather taken aback. 'Is Simon there, or Nikki?'

Sandra stared at me silently. Her face with its unhealthy pasty skin was surrounded with long wisps of unwashed fairish hair. Her eyes were large, pale blue and vacant. She looked completely spaced out. I didn't know whether this meant she hadn't taken her medication or had taken too much of it. At least she wasn't weeping.

'Simon?' I repeated more loudly, pointing past her in the general direction of the office. 'Nikki?'

She moved aside to allow me to pass by her, at the same time pointing silently towards the door of the office. I thought she wasn't the best person to put in charge but perhaps this was part of her rehabilitation programme.

'Thank you,' I said brightly, more to cheer up myself than her. 'Are they both in there?'

Sandra's forehead puckered and she pointed urgently at the office door again.

'All right, all right,' I said hastily, not wanting to set off the waterworks. All in all, I felt I was surrounded by strange beings, like poor Alice in Wonderland. Sandra's long thin pale grey finger waggled at the door and I obediently followed its silent bidding.

I tapped at the door and called out, 'Fran Varady here, can I come in?'

There was a rustle and bustle from the other side of the door. A chair scraped, voices murmured urgently. I realised I'd interrupted something. Sandra was not reliable as doorkeeper. I prepared to beat an apologetic retreat as footsteps approached, but the door was opened a hand's breath. A narrow vertical strip of Simon's face peered out at me. That too was unsettling.

'Sorry,' I said, 'I didn't mean to interrupt. I'll go and come back later.'

From behind him a female voice spoke, that of someone I couldn't identify. 'Perhaps I should meet her?' suggested the voice.

Simon dithered and eventually pulled open the door enough to allow me, by now completely spooked, into the room.

I didn't know by now quite what I expected. The sight was surprising enough in its way. Seated in a chair by the dusty pine-cone-infested fireplace was a sophisticated-looking woman I judged to be in her late forties, possibly just fifty. With people as well groomed as that, it's often difficult to tell. Her hair was short and expensively cut and I had to restrain an impulse to put my hand to my own thatch to smooth it. The visitor wore a wool two-piece outfit in an unobjectionable caramel colour with an expensive-looking silk scarf tied loosely round her throat. The skirt was short but she could get away with it. She looked trim and fit and still attractive although no longer exactly the pretty girl she must once have been. Her chin was just beginning to lose its crisp line. All, including neatly trimmed eyebrows and enamelled nails, had been made up discreetly with a practised hand. A jarring note was provided by outsize gold and pearl earrings. In contrast to the rest of the outfit they seemed out of place. It was as if, at the last moment, she had surveyed herself in the bedroom mirror and decided to glam up a bit before setting out.

Nikki, dressed in her usual thrown-together style and seated at her spot by the computer, observed rather than asked, 'Sandra let you in.'

'Was she not meant to?' I countered.

Simon cleared his throat and glanced briefly at his co-worker. Sandra was a resident and not to be discussed before me. Their obstinate adherence to discretion was beginning to bug me. Were they going to tell me who the woman with the pearl earrings was?

Or would she tell me herself? It was easier to find out for myself.

I marched over to her briskly and held out my hand. 'Hi,' I said cheerfully. 'I'm Fran.'

Simon and Nikki both looked horror-struck at losing the initiative. Tough. The woman blinked once and then took my hand, giving it a brief firm shake. Her skin was very soft; regular application of hand cream and not much housework, I guessed.

'I'm Jessica,' she said. Her voice was as pleasant as the rest of her but I was on the receiving end of cool grey eyes. She wasn't someone easily thrown off balance in any social situation.

OK, Jessica what? Was I not to be given any surname? Not yet, anyway, it seemed.

'I overheard you say to Simon that perhaps you ought to meet me,' I went on, ignoring Simon's increasing distress and Nikki's ferocious scowl. 'That wouldn't be because you're here asking about Edna Walters, would it? Because if you are, then I agree that you and I need to have a talk.'

'I'm terribly sorry, Jessica,' said Simon to the woman. He rubbed his thin hands together. 'This really shouldn't have happened. She ought not to have been admitted. Sandra ought . . . No, I can't blame Sandra.' He realised he was about to blame someone in his care and that wasn't in order. 'I should have locked the door.' His misery was now complete.

Unexpected support for my position came from Nikki. 'No, Sim,' she said. 'Fran's right. Jessica needs to hear from her. After all, we told her about Fran's interest in Edna.'

I continued excluding the two of them from my attention and addressed myself to Jessica.

'You know my interest in Edna. I'd really like to know yours. Are you the person who has been looking for her?'

She remained cool, poised and unfazed by my slightly hostile tone. 'I have been making enquiries about Edna but whether I'm the person you're talking of, that I can't say.'

'Because you don't *want* to or because you're acting on behalf of a principal and *can't* say?'

She wasn't my idea of another private detective but she might still be asking on behalf of someone else. I realised with dismay that I was in the situation poor Duane had found himself in when he'd discovered me. Here I was thinking I just about had my finger on the pulse, when a brand new and totally unknowable element presented itself.

She smiled. 'I get the impression, Fran, that you feel people haven't been open with you.'

'I think I've been given a real run-around,' I said bluntly. But I was calming down. She had that effect on me and in any case, if I offended her, I'd get nowhere. 'I really want to know what's going on,' I added.

'I see.' She paused and appeared to be sorting through the facts at her disposal: what I might be told and what I might not know. She did this without any attempt to hide it.

'You're quite right in thinking I'm making enquiries on behalf of someone else,' she began. 'You're very shrewd, Fran, if you don't mind my saying so. The person concerned is an elderly gentleman. He would like to know Edna's whereabouts and circumstances. He's not in a position to carry out enquiries himself. He's well over eighty and his health isn't good.'

'Are you related to him?'

'He's a friend,' she said quickly. 'He's asked me to do this for him as a favour.'

'All right,' I said, 'and in order to do him this favour have you hired a private investigation agency based in Teddington, run by Duane Gardner and Lottie Forester?'

Her smooth brow crinkled in a frown which was quickly erased. 'No,' she said simply.

'You don't know anything about them?'

'I've had no dealings of any kind with them.'

I was feeling less sure of myself. This conversation wasn't working out as I had expected. Her answers worried me. Was I being given another run-around? Was I getting neurotic? I had to assume, for the time being at least, that she was speaking the truth. Why shouldn't she be? Well, then, had someone else hired Duane and Lottie, neither the elderly gent who had asked Jessica for her help nor Jessica herself? How many people were there out there looking for Edna? For probably more years than my lifetime Edna had been of no interest to anyone. Suddenly everyone wanted her.

'You're not a lawyer, are you?' I was struck by this possibility.

She shook her well-groomed head. 'No, I teach ballet and mime.'

That certainly took my interest. To begin with, given my own theatrical interests, teachers of dance and mime were in much the same business as I was. Secondly, stagecraft is taught in various forms but they all train the student to perform in public, how to assume a character and how to control face and speech. If Jessica was lying to me, I'd have a very difficult time picking out just the moment it happened. Moments earlier I'd been prepared to believe everything she said. Now I was cautious. I thought over the answers she'd given me and realised that on the face of it they had been simplicity itself. But in fact they had also been elusive. If you are going to tell lies, as I know from experience, don't elaborate. If someone asks you a question just reply as briefly as you can. No one can accuse you of falsehood if you haven't said anything. I wondered again if Jessica was being open with me or just very clever.

In one way my curiosity was satisfied. The gold and pearl earrings were a theatrical touch. Jessica wanted to catch the eye when the curtain went up. Simon and Nikki constituted Jessica's audience and now I was part of it.

I didn't tell her of my own ambitions. Just as Duane had changed his mind about me once he knew I had a connection with the Duke Agency, so Jessica would begin to think about me the way I was now thinking about her, once she knew I'd had stage training.

Jessica had turned to Simon and Nikki. 'You had just begun to tell me, shortly before Fran arrived, that some young man had been following Edna about. Would he be this person Gardner?'

She leaned back in the rickety armchair as she spoke and crossed her legs. She probably wasn't as relaxed as she looked but she knew how to put it on. I took the opportunity to glance at her legs which, though slender, were exceptionally muscular. She was a dancer, all right.

Nikki indicated me. 'Ask her. She knows about him. Neither Sim nor I has ever seen him.'

'Yes, it was Gardner I saw tailing Edna,' I said. 'It was part of a job given to the agency he and his girlfriend run at Teddington.'

'Ah . . .' Jessica expelled a long soft breath. 'Then perhaps it's time I had a chat with Mr Gardner.'

I shook my head. 'Sorry, you won't be able to do that.'

'His agency is located in Teddington? I can find it easily enough then,' she returned.

'You'll find the house and you'll find Lottie Forester, his partner. But unfortunately Duane can't be interviewed by you or anyone else now. He's . . . he met with a fatal accident.'

'*What?*' they all three exclaimed at once.

Jessica looked shocked, quite genuinely so, I'd have sworn to that. But just for the moment, then she rallied and murmured, 'I'm very sorry to hear that.'

Simon's reaction was more physical, jumping to his feet and waving his hands desolately, his mouth opening and closing as he sought the right way to ask what had happened.

Nikki wasn't so scrupulous. 'What happened to him?' she demanded roughly. 'How can he have a bloody accident *now*?'

She was a shrewd one, too. Yes, it's shocking and sad that anyone can meet sudden death but in Duane's case, why now?

'Perhaps you'd better contact the police,' I told her. 'Inspector Janice Morgan is handling it. You can tell her I told you.'

Jessica had been sunk in thought. Despite her outer poise, she was still clearly shaken. She turned her attention to Nikki. 'I'd better do as Fran suggests. I'll go now and try and talk to this police inspector.'

She was rising to her feet and I said hastily, 'Before you go, can I have a number to contact you? I don't know if there will be any need but perhaps it would be a good idea.'

She sank down again and opened her expensive-looking handbag. 'Yes, of course. You think of everything, Fran.' (Ouch! Was that a dig at me?)

Jessica produced a notebook, scribbled on a leaf torn from it and handed it to me. 'Thank you for your time and hospitality, Simon, and you, Nikki,' she said. 'But I need to look into this so I'll go now, if you don't mind. Nice to meet you, Fran.'

The pair of them hastened to escort her off the premises. I was left contemplating a half-drunk mug of coffee, representing the 'hospitality', which now stood abandoned on the floor by her chair, a thin scum forming on the cooling surface. From the other side of the closed door I could hear a confused murmur of voices, then the slam of the front door and returning footsteps. I quickly unfolded the slip of paper Jessica had given me. On it was written an outer London number and the name 'J. Davis'. So she was Jessica Davis. As the door of the room reopened I pushed the piece of paper into my pocket to join Morgan's card already nestling there. Nikki barged in closely followed by Simon. They looked over me in a joint attack.

'What's going on, Fran?' Nikki demanded. 'And what has it got to do with Edna?'

'That's what we all want to know,' I pointed out.

'How is it going to affect our work here at the hostel?' asked Simon. 'Our residents are sensitive people with great personal difficulties.'

'To be perfectly honest with you,' I told him, 'I have no interest in your work here, only in Edna. Where is Edna?'

Simon waved a hand irritably towards the window. 'Anywhere, somewhere . . . she'll be back later.'

'I certainly hope so,' I told him. 'Duane died in unexplained circumstances. The police are looking into it. Someone has to keep an eye on Edna. She's not safe from someone's bad intentions, someone who could be violent.'

'But *no one* would hurt her!' protested Simon. 'She's harmless and her mind, well, she lives in a world of her own. She wouldn't understand what anyone wanted of her and she certainly wouldn't understand she was in any danger. If you're right, that is?' He raised his eyebrows and his expression begged me to say I was exaggerating.

'I don't know if I'm right!' I snapped at him. 'I just want all precautions taken. Can't you try and keep her in the house for a couple of days?'

'No.' Nikki shook her cropped head. 'It's impossible. Rain or shine, out she goes first thing in the morning. She's a tough old bird. The only way you'd keep her in would be if you sedated her.'

'You can't do that!' I cried in horror.

'No, no, of course we can't!' Simon assured me. 'It would need a doctor to say it was necessary and she would have to be removed to a psychiatric unit – we're trying to keep her out of one of those places! That is the purpose of this hostel. You must have realised that all of our residents, or most of them, come to us with mental problems. We're not a clinic, of course. We're not any kind of institution. Our purpose is to provide safety and support. We leave it to professionals to do the rest. Look, Nikki and I will do our best. But really, you know, though I'm sure you're sincere, I just *can't* believe she's in any danger.' He glanced at his wristwatch. 'It's five o'clock. We have our supper here at six thirty. Nikki and I prepare it so we have to get started in our kitchen soon. Sandra helps,' he added, 'under supervision, of course.'

A kitchen can be a lethal place full of sharp implements offering loads of opportunities to anyone of a distressed state of mind. I hoped they kept a close eye on Sandra.

'Edna will be back by suppertime,' Nikki took up. 'She might come back at any moment. Jessica was going to wait for her but, well, your news has well and truly put the cat among the pigeons.'

'How long,' I asked, meeting her gaze with a very direct stare of my own, 'have you known that Ms Davis was seeking out Edna on behalf of this old fellow she's pally with?'

'We didn't know anything about her until today,' Nikki told me earnestly. 'She arrived on our doorstep rather as you did. Simon and I consider ourselves good judges of character. We decided to trust you and we also decided to trust her. But we do expect our confidence in you both to be returned.'

'I can't speak for her,' I said. '*I've* been absolutely straight with you both.'

'Yes, yes,' muttered Simon, not looking too impressed by my assurance. 'Look, do you want to wait here until Edna comes in? Just to satisfy yourself she's all right.'

I hesitated. I was tempted to take up the offer but supper was an hour and a half away and Edna might not return until a few minutes before it was served. That was an hour and a half in which I might be doing something useful.

'I'll leave it to you to get in touch with the cops, right, if Edna doesn't turn up on time?'

They both nodded furiously.

Sandra had taken up her station on the front steps again. She gave no sign she recognised me as I edged past her and bid her goodbye.

Chapter Ten

There was no sign of Jessica Davis outside, which wasn't surprising as she had had plenty of time to get clear of the hostel. Still, I was rather sorry as I'd hoped she might have lingered to see if I came out. It would have given her a chance of a private word with me. I would certainly have liked a further word with her without Simon and Nikki present, but perhaps the feeling wasn't returned. She didn't want me quizzing her.

At least I'd like to have seen what kind of car she drove away in and even got its number. I guessed there had been a car. She hadn't looked ruffled enough to have battled her way there by public transport with the rest of us. A taxi could have brought her but she wouldn't have picked up one easily in this quiet residential street on leaving the hostel. I set off briskly just in case I might spot her walking ahead of me. There was always a chance.

Looking for Jessica had made me careless of looking around for anyone else. I'd fallen into the same error when, intent on following Edna, I'd failed to spot Duane. Just to show I don't learn by my mistakes, I jumped out of my skin when a shape moved out from behind a wall and a voice demanded hoarsely and urgently, 'Has she gone?'

I looked round and down. Edna had materialised from

someone's patch of front garden, holding the householder's cat in her arms. The cat appeared to have no objection. It lounged there, flicking its tail just occasionally, its amber eyes fixed on me with a contemptuous look. 'See?' it seemed to be saying. 'Fine detective you are! You wanted to find Edna and you were just about to walk right by her!'

'That woman!' repeated Edna crossly when I didn't reply at once. 'Has she gone? The dressed-up one with the earrings.'

'Yes,' I said. 'She left before me. How long have you been hiding there, Edna?'

'Don't know,' said Edna promptly, looking down at the cat. The cat looked up at her and I swear they exchanged glances of complicity.

'But you saw her arrive? That means you saw me arrive too?'

'Mm,' she mumbled.

'But you didn't see her leave?'

'I was here,' Edna gestured with her woolly-hatted head towards the dank little garden behind her. 'I kept well down.'

'Did she arrive in a car?'

'Blue one!' said Edna triumphantly.

I vaguely remembered seeing, as I'd arrived earlier, a blue car parked a little way down from the hostel facing the opposite direction from where I now stood with Edna. Jessica had probably driven off in it, continuing in that other direction and not passing Edna hiding behind her wall.

Edna looked away from the cat but her gaze didn't engage mine. 'Mutton dressed as lamb, my dear,' she muttered. 'I don't hold with it.'

'Do you mean me, Edna?'

Now she looked at me severely. 'Don't be silly, dear. That woman. What did she want?'

'Do you know her, Edna?' I asked, determined to get something out of her. 'Have you seen her before?'

'I see people all day long,' said Edna. 'What did a woman like that want visiting the hostel? They don't have people like her there. And people who are there don't have people like her visiting them. She wasn't from the social.'

'Her name,' I said, 'is Jessica Davis. That mean anything to you, Edna?'

'Jessica . . .' murmured Edna dreamily, stroking the cat. 'I like that name. It's a pretty name. Yes, Jessica, I like that.' Her manner changed abruptly. 'No, I don't know her! How should I? I can't be doing with people, only cats.'

'Edna,' I said carefully because she was so easily frightened off, 'I'd like to talk to you seriously. You know me. You know I'm your friend, don't you?'

Edna shuffled and looked sullen.

'I don't know what's going on,' I continued. 'Do you?'

She shook her head but it didn't necessarily mean a negative reply. She was probably just trying to shake the sound of my voice away.

'The man who was following you, the one who wore a white cap,' I touched my head. 'You were afraid of him.'

Her eyes flickered up at me. I'd taken her full attention now.

'You needn't be afraid of him any longer,' I said. 'He won't be following you any more.'

Edna set the cat down on the pavement. It shook itself and leapt up nimbly on to the wall.

'Where's he gone?' Edna asked.

This was progress. She wasn't denying Duane's existence or that it had worried her.

'He's gone away,' I said evasively. 'He won't be back.'

'Is he dead?' asked Edna in a conversational, casual way.

'Well, yes, he is, Edna,' I floundered.

'Oh,' she said, but it didn't seem to mean anything much to her one way or an other.

I debated how much more I might tell her safely. If I told her Jessica had been at the hostel seeking Edna herself and acting on behalf of another party also seeking her, then there was a very good chance Edna wouldn't return to the hostel that night or, indeed, ever again.

I took a leaf from her book and simply dropped the subject. 'Simon and Nikki are about to begin cooking the supper,' I said.

'Baked beans,' said Edna gloomily. 'Macaroni cheese is better. They don't eat any meat; they're vegetarians. I don't mind that because I don't like eating animals. I wished they cooked chips. But they keep telling me chips are unhealthy. She makes a pie with aubergines and tomatoes. That's not bad.'

This digression on the menu at the hostel had led to quite a lengthy speech. I decided to build it.

'Come on, Edna, I'll walk to the hostel with you.'

We proceeded back down the pavement. The cat followed up along the top of his wall until it ran out, then settled down to watch us.

'You are comfortable at the hostel, though, aren't you, Edna?'

Edna mumbled indistinctly.

'Simon and Nikki do care about you. I care about you. What we all want is for you to take care of yourself.'

'I've been doing that,' said Edna starchily, 'for forty years. Why should I suddenly be unable to take care of myself? I'm not potty. I know my way around.' She stopped and looked up at me with a perfectly lucid gaze. 'I'll tell you something, dear. You remember it. You never have any trouble as long as you're looking after yourself. It's when other people start thinking it's their business to take care of you that all the trouble starts. You mark my words.'

'Edna,' I said quite humbly, 'I'm not trying to meddle, honestly.'

'And the worst ones,' retorted Edna fiercely, 'are the ones who are doing it all out of the kindness of their hearts. If they want something to take care of, they should get a cat!'

We reached the steps and found them untenanted. Edna climbed to the front door and rang. It was opened after a moment by someone I couldn't see from where I stood. I thought it might be Sandra if she hadn't yet been called to duty in the kitchen. Edna didn't greet whoever it was, just plodded indoors without a backward glance to bid me farewell. The door shut. She was safe inside for the night.

As for me, I'd been well and truly told off. But it didn't mean I was going to stop looking out for Edna. One thing had been confirmed for me. She could be perfectly coherent if she wanted and, what was more, she was a bit of a battleaxe. All that dottiness was a shield! I fumed. It didn't alter the fact that she was still vulnerable, whether she wanted to admit it or not, the cantankerous old bat.

I set off back to my flat because I'd left Bonnie with Erwin that morning. He would probably be getting ready to go out soon if he was playing at a gig that evening.

Erwin had company. I could hear laughter, Erwin's infectious high-pitched whoop and female giggling which sounded a little familiar. I hesitated. I'd barged in on a private meeting at the hostel. It seemed I was about to do so again. I had no wish to be discreet and bust up a romantic twosome. Perhaps I ought to wait a little.

But Bonnie had already heard me. She would have been

listening for me the whole day. I heard her whimper on the other side of the door, then bark. Claws scrabbled at the wood.

The door was pulled open. 'Hi!' beamed Erwin. 'Come on in, girl!'

I trotted inside to behold Susie Duke comfortably seated on Erwin's sofa. She waved a mug at me with one hand and a funny-looking cigarette with the other.

'Hullo, Fran, love! Where've you been?'

'Out to Fulwell, Teddington way,' I said, sounding to my own ears primly disapproving, not unlike my old headmistress. 'I've been following up enquiries. I got held up on my return. Sorry to have left my dog for so long, Erwin, and thanks for taking care of her. I'll take her back now.'

'No, problem,' said Erwin happily.

'Hang on,' cried Susie, lurching to her feet. 'I came out here to find you. Don't scarper now. Thanks for the coffee, Erwin, and the . . .' She gave me a hunted look and surreptitiously ground out the spliff.

'Any time,' said Erwin, the perfect host.

'How long have you been waiting?' I asked when we got back to my room where the atmosphere seemed in contrast rather boring.

'Not long, honest.' She transferred herself to my sofa. 'He's a nice bloke, isn't he? He was telling me about his band, how hard it is to get people to hire them. It's nearly as difficult to make a living as a musician as it is being a private investigator, by the sound of things. How did you make out at Teddington?'

I resisted the temptation to reply that I hadn't made out as well as she had with Erwin. Instead I gave her a summary of my visit to Lottie. When I told her about Les, Susie became more serious.

'Well, that tells us how Duane found out about you sometimes working for me. Thing is,' Susie's brow puckered, 'how did Duane get into the office? You reckon Les did lend him the keys?'

'If he did, then they would still have been on Duane when I found him,' I replied, 'unless the killer took them. I wish I'd had the nerve to search his pockets before the cops turned up.'

'I don't like that idea much,' said Susie slowly. 'I don't want anyone, let alone a killer, running round London with my office keys. Well, I have to get the lock changed anyway. I won't give Les the new keys, that's for sure. I think it's unlikely he lent them to Gardner but well, better safe than sorry, eh? He won't be surprised if I don't give him the new keys, not in the circumstances.'

'Did you know he worked for other agencies?' I asked her.

She nodded. 'Lots of people use him. I know you don't like him much, Fran, but Les is good at what he does. I've never thought he was likely to talk out of turn, tell anyone else what I was doing. He never told me what anyone else who used him was looking into. You're cross because he didn't speak up and tell you he recognised Gardner from the description you gave us. But I reckon he was right to keep quiet. He didn't know what Gardner was doing but he wasn't going to blow his cover by letting us know Gardner was a PI.'

We decided by unspoken agreement to leave it at that. 'Well,' I said, 'what's brought you out to see me? Just asking how I'm getting on?'

'It's a bit more than that, Fran, love,' she said, leaning forward. 'Things are in an awful mess back at my office. Well, truth to tell, I can hardly say I've got an office at the moment! The police have sealed off the whole place and the staircase as well. No one can get in to consult me and no one can get upstairs to Michael's tattoo parlour, come to that. He's really upset and seems to think it's all my fault.'

There was a silence. 'The cops are treating it as murder, then,' I said at last.

'Looks like it, don't it?'

More silence. 'There's something else,' I said and told her about my visit to the hostel and meeting with Jessica Davis.

Susie shook her head. 'You need help on this one, Fran. I'd offer but I don't know any more about this than you've told me. It seems to me the person you ought to make common cause with is Lottie Forester.'

'I don't think she wants to see me again,' I said. 'She sort of seems to hold me responsible for Duane's death. I can't blame her, not that I had anything to do with it. I didn't invite the idiot to go tracking me down. But he did die because he was looking for me and I did find him.'

'All the same,' said Susie. 'I reckon you should give that girl out at Teddington a bell and arrange to have a chat with her. She'll want to find out who bumped off her boyfriend and she's the one who knows who hired him to follow your old bag lady.'

'Yeah, you're right, of course,' I said. 'I'll phone her tonight. I just hope she's there. I told her to ask the police for protection and if she is a material witness they may just have whisked her off somewhere nice and private already.'

But Lottie was at the Fulwell address when I phoned later that evening.

'I've got to make a living, haven't I?' she snapped when I asked whether she was planning to move out temporarily. 'I've got to be here to deal with enquiries. If clients try to reach me and can't, they won't try again. I'm in business on my own now, aren't I? I can't just hand everything over to some secretary. I haven't got one!'

'All right, all right,' I said hastily, cutting into this flow. 'Then can I come and see you?'

'Yes.' Her voice was crisp. 'We do need to talk. I've been thinking about things since you left. I want to know who did this to Duane and I'm not sitting around here just brooding about it. I want to bloody do something.'

A girl I could do business with.

The weather was treating us to a fine drizzle when I set out the next morning. The temperature had dropped several degrees. Teddington looked damp and grey; even the Fulwell golf course was bedraggled.

Lottie had taken my strictures to heart. Although she knew I was coming, when I rang the bell she replied by hanging out of an upper window to check who it was.

'Hang on a sec!' she called down.

She was all in black today, tight black pants and a top made of some flimsy material which floated about when she moved. Perhaps this signified mourning. She still wore the boots. Her manner was slightly friendlier. She had decided we had something to trade and was ready to do business. At least, I hoped I was reading the signs rightly.

I thought she'd take me back to the office but instead she led me to the far end of the hall and opened the door into a large comfortable kitchen.

'We might as well sit in here,' she said. 'We can have a coffee and it's a bit warmer. The office is cold without any heating on.'

She busied herself making our coffee while I sat and took in my surroundings. The original kitchen had been enlarged by the addition of a glazed extension. It led to a garden which must have been pretty once, in Granny's day, but was sadly neglected now. Roses rambled in wild profusion over trellis work which sagged and needed a prop and a few nails to keep it from inevitable collapse. The lawn was in need of a trim and between the patches of long grass the bright green cushions of moss were visible. Weeds sprouted between the flags of a pathway. There were a couple of large glazed pots but nothing now grew in them except more weeds. Even so, this was still a highly desirable property and if the detection business didn't prosper, Lottie could sell the place for a tidy sum and have the funds to take her time thinking what she did next.

The furniture in the kitchen was mostly pine of a style which was fashionable years ago when people living in urban areas wanted to pretend they lived in a Cotswold cottage. Every worktop was cluttered: dishes and pots, paperwork, bottles and a tiny television set. Dusty bunches of dried flowers dangled from hooks. Copper pots in need of a rub decorated the walls. There could be no greater contrast to the office I'd seen previously. That had been meticulously tidy but, professional surroundings aside, Lottie was no housekeeper.

I'd been thinking about my grandfather's studio portrait recently and now my eye was taken by a collection of what I assumed to be family photographs framed and hung in a careful display on one wall. Some looked old. One was of a stout man in very formal dress with a watch chain draped across his waistcoat. He had a square face with a bulldog expression and glared at the camera. I was rather glad I had never met him. There were a couple of wedding groups and a pretty baby sitting on a rug in a garden.

'You?' I asked, pointing at the picture, as Lottie returned with the mugs.

She looked vaguely surprised and stared at the portraits as if she'd forgotten they were there. She probably had. They had been there all her life.

'Yes,' she said.

'Who are all the others?'

Lottie walked to the collection and I followed her pointing finger. She indicated the ferocious old fellow with the watch chain first. 'My great-grandfather.'

'Oh?' I said rather feebly. There wasn't much I could say. My own grandfather's portrait had possessed a certain rakish charm. This old bloke, a generation older certainly, didn't suggest any charm.

Lottie had moved to the wedding groups. 'This later group shows my parents and the earlier one shows my grand-parents.'

'That's the grandma who left you this house? Was she your dad's mother or your mum's?'

She was looking a little resentful. She didn't like being quizzed.

'I was brought up by my grandmother,' I explained. 'She was my dad's mother.'

'Oh?' For a moment she looked mildly interested. 'Lilian was also my father's mother. She didn't like being called Grandma or Gran or any of those names. I always called her Lilian. Does any of this matter?'

I like old photos so although I didn't ask any more questions, I took a last good look. Her parents' group showed a conventional white wedding with a seventies stamp on it. The groom's hair was nearly as long as the bride's and he wore disastrous flares. The bride had on a mediaeval sort of floaty gown with full sleeves and a high round collar. Her long straight hair was garlanded with flowers. *Peace, man* . . . and all the rest of it.

I looked at the earlier wedding group as a contrast. This was a register office do. The bride wore a wasp-waisted suit with a pencil skirt. They were as thin as rakes, those nineteen-fifties women.

She had a round flattish saucer hat like the traditional Chinese coolie's. She was an attractive woman but I judged her a tough one. There was a thinness to her mouth and surely, on her wedding day, she could have raised a smile. Her husband was an unexceptional fellow with a balding dome and moustache. He looked as if he ought to have been a bank manager, whether or not he was.

I didn't know whether bride or groom had the dubious distinction of being the offspring of the scowling man with the watch chain and felt I couldn't ask any more questions.

'Those old pictures have had their day,' said Lottie now rather brusquely. 'Duane and I planned to turn everything out when we did up the house. All those old pics are for the bin along with most of the rest of the junk in this house.'

She plumped herself down on a chair opposite me across the table and pushed aside a collection of magazines and old newspapers. 'We didn't get round to it. We were always busy.' A hint of sadness touched her voice.

I thought she might later regret throwing away old family photos. Sentimentality aside, perhaps she ought to get some of the china and stuff valued before she chucked it out. I was remembering the old blue and white bowl in the hallway. But that wasn't for me to suggest.

'Private investigation business good around here?' I asked.

'We've been doing all right. I told you, Duane was a good detective.'

We sipped coffee and eyed each other speculatively.

'Look, Lottie,' I said, putting down my mug. 'We've got to work together. Just to show you I'm on the level, I'll tell you what happened to me yesterday after I left here.'

I told her about Jessica Davis. I watched her closely but

she didn't bat an eyelid. If she knew the name she was good at hiding it.

'You don't know her?' I prompted.

'All news to me,' she said. 'Never heard of the woman. Who is your client?'

'I swear I'm not working for anyone on this. Honestly, I'm looking into it all for my own satisfaction. That is, it was just for my own satisfaction but now, in view of what happened to Duane, it might be for my own preservation.'

She fiddled with her mug, turning it round and round. 'The police came to see me yesterday, early evening,' she announced baldly. 'They'd got a report from the autopsy on Duane. They think it's possible someone knocked him out and then stuck a lethal shot into his arm. I'd like to get my hands on whoever did it!' she added viciously.

'Come to that, he might like to get his hands on you,' I reminded her. 'Not that I want to scare you or anything.'

'I don't scare that easy.'

Bravado keeps the spirits up but it doesn't keep away the bad guys.

'Are you sleeping here in the house?' I asked.

She nodded. 'Absolutely, anyway . . .' She looked up and the grey-green eyes met mine calmly. 'We want whoever it was to contact me, don't we? Flush him out? Think of a goat tethered out in a jungle glade to tempt a tiger. That's me, the goat.'

'I hope the cops didn't suggest that!' I snapped.

'Of course they didn't. They want me to move out, just like you said they would. But I told them, I'm staying here.'

The moment had come. 'I have to know the name of your client,' I said. 'I have to know who asked you and Duane to track down Edna.'

'We're working together on this?' The grey-green eyes challenged me.

'We're working together. You haven't got Duane. You can't trust Les. You need me.'

'How much of a cut do you want out of our fee?'

I hadn't thought about the fact that it was a paid job to her, not just a personal matter as it was to me. 'I don't want paying,' I said. 'I want to walk down the street without looking over my shoulder all the time. You should have the entire fee. You're entitled to Duane's share.'

She cheered up. She was a businesswoman, after all.

'All right. My employer is Henry Culpeper.'

'Culpeper?' I asked. 'Is that on the level? It's not an alias?'

'No!' she retorted impatiently. 'Of course not. I check out clients. I'd be daft not to. I might end up working for any dodgy sod. His name is Henry Culpeper.'

'OK, OK.' I held up a placating hand. 'It's just that I seem to have heard the name somewhere.'

'*Culpeper's Herbal*,' said Lottie. 'It's a famous old medicine book.'

'And what does Mr Culpeper want to do, now that Duane's dead? When I last saw you, you hadn't spoken to him but I'm assuming you've spoken to him now.'

She fidgeted. 'Not directly.'

'Oy!' I protested. 'You can't hold out on your client like that! He thinks he's hiring two 'tecs, not one. Anyway, if he reads his *Evening Standard* . . . I assume he does live in London?'

She interrupted me. 'I'm not holding out on him! If you'd give me a minute to explain? I don't deal with Mr Culpeper directly. I deal with his representative. Henry Culpeper knew me when I was a kid. That's why he was happy to deal with us – through his intermediary.'

I stared at her thoughtfully until she began to fidget again and give me uneasy glances from the grey-green eyes.

'Why can't he deal with you directly?'

'He's in poor health. He asked his grandson to find a reliable private investigation agency. To be absolutely honest the grandson, Adam Ferrier, came to us, Duane and me, because he already knew me of old. He was a sort of boyfriend once, before I met Duane – nothing heavy,' she added hastily, 'just a couple of dates. Anyhow, his grandfather asked him about using a private detective. Adam said not to worry, he knew me and that I'd set up an agency with Duane. He'd take care of it. His grandfather was pretty pleased to think we'd be the investigators. The bill is being paid by old Henry but we – I report to Adam. It's simple.'

It wasn't simple; it was another layer in a concealing fog. Somewhere behind all this was someone who wanted to be kept out of it. But was it old Henry Culpeper? And how many old gentlemen were interested in Edna's whereabouts? Jessica Davis was working on behalf of an elderly man in poor health. Did Edna have a secret geriatric fan club? Lottie had denied knowing anything about Jessica. But old Henry might have more than one iron in the fire. Perhaps he hadn't been completely convinced by his grandson's recommendation of Duane and Lottie? Had he decided to take out a little insurance and consulted Jessica? But more to the point, why go to so much trouble?

'Why does Mr Culpeper want to know where Edna is? What more does he want?'

'I don't know, Duane and I didn't know, why he wants to find Edna Walters. He just does and that's our job. He would like to meet her. Duane was supposed to track her down and bring her out here, that is, persuade her to come with him and Adam would take her to his grandfather.'

'And what about Adam Ferrier, where does he live?'

'He's got a flat in Docklands but he comes over here to visit his grandfather pretty often, so does Rebecca.' Seeing my raised eyebrows, she added, 'Rebecca is his sister. She and I were at school together.'

'Well, well, well,' I said sourly. 'Isn't this just pally and girls' old-school-tie?'

'No, it's not,' she retorted crossly. 'If you want to call it anything, call it networking.'

I could have told her I went to a good school once. My father and Grandma had scrimped and saved to send me to a place with a reputation for turning out educated young ladies.

'We've not had many failures,' the headmistress finally announced regretfully, 'but sadly, Francesca, we are unable to count you among our successes. Such a pity. It could all have been so different.'

I didn't mention it. But I was getting uneasy. It's one thing to deal with a straightforward client and agency relationship. It's quite another where there are old friendships mixed in the brew. What had Duane thought about this ex-boyfriend of Lottie's who turned up with a job offer?

'I'd like to meet Adam Ferrier,' I said firmly. 'Can you fix it?'

She blinked at me in that slow appraising way she had. 'I can ask him. It's up to him if he wants to meet you.'

'I'd be obliged,' I said, 'and as soon as possible.' I got up. 'I need to go back now but you can ring me—'

I remembered that the Duke agency was currently off limits thanks to the police. 'You can't ring the agency. I'll give you the number of the payphone in the house where I live. People there are quite good about passing on messages.'

She read the details I wrote out for her, her expression full of misgiving. I thought she'd decided I was about as trustworthy as Les. She probably regretted letting me into whatever she was working on. But she didn't have Duane any longer and Les's role in all this had yet to be fully investigated. Hobson's choice. I was the horse nearest the door.

'OK,' she said. She twisted the scrap of paper in her fingers back and forth. 'I'll discuss it with my principal,' she said.

'Mr Culpeper?'

'Well, no.' She looked a little uncertain for the first time since we'd met. Perhaps it was dawning on her at last that Duane's death had left her in a curious limbo. 'I told you, I don't speak to Mr Culpeper, only to Adam. It's Adam you want to meet and you can't meet his grandfather any more than I can. He's ill, I told you.'

'Then speak to Adam,' I said.

I wasn't accepting that I couldn't meet aged Grandpa Culpeper, but that encounter would have to be arrived at without Lottie and Adam interfering, and was for the future.

'Tell Mr Ferrier,' I said, 'that we need to talk soon.'

Chapter Eleven

I made my way back into London and my flat. Bonnie was pleased to see me, bouncing around like a furry football. 'All right, take it easy, I'll take you for a walk,' I promised her. There was a note pushed under my door. It was from Ganesh.

'The police are looking for you,' it read alarmingly. 'Contact Morgan *asap*.'

I rang the shop, despite the '*asap*'. 'What do you mean; the cops are *looking* for me?'

'Where have you been?' demanded Ganesh's voice. 'Morgan wants to speak to you. She sent Parry to your flat and when you weren't there he came round here in case I knew where you were. I told him I didn't but he didn't believe me. He just stood there staring at me in that evil way of his. "Are you sure?" he kept asking, as if I was a dodgy witness.'

'Oh no,' I moaned. 'Don't say Parry is in on this.'

'He said he was just bringing the message because it was on his way. I reckon he was doing it because he hoped to find you on your own.'

'If I have any control over it, I'll never be on my own with Wayne Parry. Is he likely to turn up again?'

'How should I know? Do the cops take me into their

confidence? I told him I never know where you are. Where were you, anyway?'

'Teddington, talking to Lottie Forester. What's happened? Did Parry say why Morgan wants me?'

'There you go again!' snapped Ganesh. 'You're the one they're looking for. *You* ask them what they want. *All right, all right, I'm coming!*'

This last bit was obviously addressed to his uncle. I hung up, clipped on Bonnie's lead and walked her over to the cop shop. I assumed Ganesh's words didn't mean there was a warrant out for my arrest. But anything was possible.

Sergeant Wayne Parry, the man I most don't want to be marooned on a desert island with, was in the parking area in front of the station.

'Hullo, Fran,' he said cheerfully. 'Turned up, have you?' He smoothed the smudge of ginger hair on his upper lip that he likes to think is a moustache. 'Long time, no see. How are tricks?'

I took his greeting to mean I wasn't on the most wanted list. 'Morgan wants to see me,' I said. 'Or so I hear. Ganesh said you went to the shop.'

'Your mate got a message to you then, did he? He reckoned he didn't know where you were.' Parry gave me that knowing look coppers have off to perfection.

'He didn't. He left a note for me. Is Morgan inside?' I pointed at the building.

'Yeah, go on in.'

'Do you know what it's about?'

I didn't like appealing to him for help but I wanted to know something about the reason for Morgan's wish to see me.

'Ah, well, you've got to talk to the inspector, haven't you?' He was being awkward.

'Look, Sergeant,' I said. 'This has to do with the sudden death of Duane Gardner, am I right?'

'Nothing to do with me, sweetheart,' said Parry, ever obnoxious, 'I'm not on that case.'

I found that obscurely comforting. But I still asked, 'So why were you the one sent to my flat?'

'Shortage of personnel,' said Parry. 'I was available. No one else was.'

Morgan was in the reception area when I walked in. She was talking to the desk sergeant about something. When she saw me, she said, 'Oh, Fran, come on through!' I found myself hustled down a corridor and into a bleak little interview room which smelled faintly of vomit.

'Oy!' I said. 'If I'm being interviewed I want a solicitor.'

'You're not being interviewed,' she said. 'I just wanted to talk to you in private. It's a sort of personal thing.'

'Not to do with Duane Gardner?'

'We'll have to talk about him again but not right now. Your friend, the old lady, Edna Walters . . .' She paused.

'What's happened to Edna?' I asked sharply. Morgan looked uncharacteristically nervous.

'She was crossing the road, so witnesses say, and was nearly hit by a motorcycle.' Morgan held up her hand at the sight of my appalled expression. 'She had a lucky but narrow escape. A passer-by yelled and jumped out to drag her to safety at considerable risk to himself. The biker was probably a courier, and you know how many of those are on the streets. He didn't stop. The old lady fell as the rescuer pulled her onto the pavement. She was taken to hospital to be checked over and I understand they are keeping her in overnight.'

'I want to see her,' I said firmly. 'Like, right now. And don't tell me Edna was wandering across the road without due care and attention. She toddles round the streets all day long, crossing roads.'

Morgan shook her head. 'She's getting on, Fran. She really shouldn't be wandering around. I think she ought to be in a more secure place than that hostel, I mean, somewhere permanent.'

'You mean lock her away somewhere!' I said furiously. 'That would kill her!'

'She's likely to kill herself, Fran, if she goes on roaming around like she does. Actually I don't mean lock her away. I just think she ought to be somewhere under closer supervision. We'll talk about it later. I'll take you to the hospital. Come on.'

On our way there I suddenly thought to ask, 'Hey, how do you know about it? If it was a minor traffic incident, as you want to think, how come you're dealing with it? Have they downgraded you to traffic section or what?'

'Not yet,' retorted Morgan snappishly, 'although if I continue to have more dealings with you that might yet happen! The reason I'm involved is because you told a lady by the name of Nikki Novak that I was the person to contact if anything happened to your mate Edna.'

'Nikki at the hostel?'

'Nikki at the hostel. She was round here, banging on my desk and demanding I tell her what I knew about Edna being targeted by hostile forces, as she put it, like someone was firing Scud missiles at the old dear. I had to tell her I knew sod all, only I said it more politely. Are you going to hand out my name to all and sundry, Fran? Do you think I don't have enough work on my desk already? Am I on call for all your little problems?'

'I don't think it's a little problem – but then I don't think it's a traffic incident, just a near miss between a confused old lady crossing a road without due care and attention and a speeding motorcycle freak.'

'Has it got anything directly to do with the death of Duane Gardner?' she almost yelled.

'Yes!' I shouted back.

'Then tell me *how*, if you are so sure.'

'I can't, not yet. I will. Give me time.'

'No private sleuthing, Fran!' she warned, 'not if it's a murder case!'

'Watch that cyclist,' I advised. 'Or you'll be part of a traffic incident.'

Edna was propped up in bed. They had dressed her in a white garment that fastened down the back and taken away her hat. I'd never seen her without her hat. Without the layers of clothing she was a tiny figure. They'd also given her a haircut. Her grey locks, which had previously straggled round her face, had been trimmed into an urchin cut of a sort which made her look younger. She looked like a discarded rag doll, thrown down on the bed by a careless child.

'Hello, Edna,' I said, taking her thin mottled hand which lay on the blanket. 'How are you?'

Her eyes turned to me but didn't show sign of recognition. The lucidity with which she had harangued me on the hostel steps had been wiped away as completely as a splash of mud on a window frame, leaving only a clean and blank surface. I felt panic rise in me. I knew that however imperfect the hostel was, Edna had to be returned to it and a measure of freedom. Hospitals turn the elderly into so many case numbers. If she stayed here for long she'd drift away into that nebulous half world and she'd leave here for a residential home where all she would be doing was sitting all day with vacant eyes on a flickering television set. Just the sort of situation she'd escaped from at her own insistence once already. If she was ever to take care of herself again, she had to get out of here.

'I'm Fran,' I urged. 'You know me, Edna!'

To my huge relief some recognition flickered in her expression. Her withered mouth moved. 'Take me out of here,' she whispered.

It was heartbreaking. For all her vaunted independence, now she was asking me for something and I couldn't deliver it.

'I can't take you with me now, Edna, but I won't abandon you, either, I swear it. I'll sort something out.' I leaned over her. 'Edna, do you remember what happened? Do you remember the motorcycle?'

She rolled her cropped head from side to side on the pillow. 'He wasn't there when I started across. He came roaring at me . . . he saw me. What have they done with my clothes?' Her voice was suddenly louder, crosser, more belonging to the Edna I knew.

'I'll sort everything out, Edna,' I promised. 'Leave it to me.'

There was a rustle behind me and a nurse appeared.

'Is she badly hurt?' I asked, straightening up and moving away from the bed a little.

'Only bruises,' said the nurse. 'She's a tough one, isn't she?'

'Yes,' I said, 'she is and she wants to go home, back to the hostel where she lives.'

'Oh, someone from the hostel was already here. We'd like to keep her in and run a few tests on her, just to be sure.' The nurse gave me a kindly reassuring smile. 'Are you a relative?'

'I'm a friend,' I said. 'I don't think she has any relatives. Why have you cut her hair?'

'Well, hygiene, you know,' said the nurse conspiratorially.

'Come off it, she didn't have nits.' I was pretty sure Simon and

Nikki would have spotted something like that. 'Look,' I said, 'I'm sure you need the bed. If she's OK, not injured, and she wants to discharge herself, she can, right?'

'The young man from the hostel said he would like us to keep her overnight,' retorted the nurse, checkmating me. 'They're not a nursing home. They're not qualified to monitor her and haven't the time. Not that we have, either!' she finished tartly. 'She *is* taking up a bed and she's uncooperative.'

'Are you going to sedate her?' I asked suspiciously.

'That's for the doctor to decide.' Nurse was brisker now. Clinical decision. None of my business.

Morgan materialised at my side. 'Come on, Fran,' she said. 'They've got a coffee place here. We can talk.'

I patted Edna's hand and told her not to worry.

'We've got jelly for tea,' the nurse was saying brightly to her as I left.

'What flavour?' Edna's grumpy tones drifted after us as we quitted the ward. 'I don't like green or yellow. I only like red jelly.'

The double doors to the ward swung to and I didn't hear what kind of jelly it was to be. But I was happy to hear Edna still had the energy to declare her preferences.

The coffee shop was run by a pair of plump ladies from the League of Friends. We gathered up our beakers of watery coffee and a wrapped chocolate biscuit apiece and retired to a free table. Around us people sat quietly sipping tea or coffee. One man was doing a crossword. There were health notices of various kinds pinned to the walls and a painting of a flowering cherry orchard supposed to inspire a sense of happier days ahead, I guessed. Despite that, the atmosphere in the cafeteria was one of quiet depression.

'We've got to get her out of here, Janice!' I said urgently to

Morgan. 'She'll deteriorate fast, mentally, I mean. They'll look after her physically but turn her into a zombie.'

'She's quite safe here,' Morgan returned. 'Isn't that what you wanted? For her to be safe?' She raised her eyebrows.

'I don't believe this was an accident,' I said. 'Someone tried to run her down. She says the bike wasn't coming when she started across the road. Edna is very observant, in case you're wondering, and has excellent hearing. She doesn't make things up. She notices and she remembers.'

'All the same,' Morgan said. 'We have to be cautious about accepting her account. The man who pulled her to safety can't tell us much. He said the bike roared out of a side road without warning and he saw Edna in its path. He darted out and dragged her to the pavement. She stumbled, of course, and fell, but all the same, he saved her life.'

'Who was he?' I asked. 'I'd like to thank him.'

'I'll convey your thanks to him.'

I unwrapped my chocolate biscuit and stared at it without much enthusiasm. Suddenly what I wanted more than anything else in the world was a slice of Grandma Varady's chocolate cake. I forced the memory away.

'Someone out there means Edna harm,' I said. 'Duane Gardner and Lottie Forester were hired to look for Edna. Jessica Davis is looking for her, too.'

'Who is Jessica Davis?' Morgan asked sharply.

I blinked at her in surprise. 'Hasn't she been to see you? I thought she was on her way.'

'No one of that name has been to see me. Who is she?'

I rallied and explained. 'Lottie told me that her agency's search was initiated by an old fellow called Culpeper who apparently knew her when she was little. But she doesn't see him. He acts through his grandson, name of Ferrier. Lottie deals with him only and has done from the first. I got the impression neither she nor Duane had had any face to face meetings with Culpeper.'

Morgan was sitting looking at me in a blank way that didn't let me know how all this information was going down. It was like speaking into her little tape machine, impersonal, and it irritated me. What was this? Were we back in that interview room at the station?

I said crossly, 'You probably know all this already. Lottie must have told you. It was like drawing teeth getting her to tell me, but you're investigating officially. Duane was supposed to find Edna and take her to Culpeper. But Jessica Davis is also acting on behalf of an elderly man and surely it has to be Culpeper as well? How many old blokes can there be out there who want to see Edna after donkey's years and have the money to hire an enquiry agency? Although I get the impression he doesn't have as much confidence in Duane and Lottie's agency as Lottie or the grandson, Adam, think he does. He's played it a bit crafty and used Jessica as a sort of second-string investigator. That's how it seems to me. She isn't a professional. She's a dance teacher. But she struck me as very efficient and she seemed all set to go and see you after I spoke to you. She left in a hurry.'

From the corner of my eye I saw the matronly ladies at the coffee counter trying to look as if they weren't listening to our conversation. Morgan might have thought this cafeteria a good place to talk but I didn't. Our conversation had to be more interesting to the League of Friends volunteers than endless listening to people talking about their operations.

'Then she may well turn up,' Morgan spoke at last but seemed even more irritatingly complacent.

'Have you spoken to Ferrier or Culpeper?' I was suddenly

suspicious. Was the blank look because I was rattling off old news? If so, why didn't she say so and tell me to shut up and not waste my breath?

'I can't discuss police matters with you, Fran, and whether or not we've spoken with either of the people you mention, that's not your concern. Frankly, we're not enquiring further about the incident involving your old lady in the bed back there . . .'

Morgan indicated an area elsewhere in the hospital with a vague wave of the hand. 'As far as we're concerned, she wandered out into the road and was saved from injury or worse by the prompt action of a passer-by. The biker involved didn't stop but he was probably a courier and when he saw that the old lady had been pulled clear he was keener on keeping to his schedule than stopping to get involved. We won't find him.

'As for Culpeper's wish to trace Edna, it's not illegal either for him or anyone else to be trying to find her. They may, and probably do, have nothing but the best intentions.'

'Edna believes those are the worst sort,' I said gloomily.

Morgan eyed me. 'Fran, to be honest, I think you're on a hiding to nothing with this one. The old lady won't cooperate with you. She wouldn't cooperate with us. Oh, yes, I did try and chat to her. She acted gaga. It was only an act, of course, even I could see that, but if she chooses to behave like that, there's nothing we or you can do. She only goes along with the hostel rules in as far as she turns up for meals and stays there at night.'

She sighed. 'Well, if you choose to make it your problem, that's up to you. Our interest is in the death of Duane Gardner, which is being treated as suspicious. We would only be interested in the people employing Gardner's agency to find Edna if it had a direct bearing on the matter of his death and so far, Fran, nothing shows that it has. He died in Susie Duke's office. The inference is he was there to meet either you or Susie. So far there is nothing to show why he wanted to speak to either of you. To say it's about Edna is supposition. All right, it's plausible. But I'm a police officer and I'm not into plausible. I'm into facts.'

'OK, Janice,' I retorted. 'Let's stick to facts. Have you established yet just how the killer got into the office that morning? Did someone force the lock?'

She pursed her lips and studied me. 'There's no sign it was forced but it might have been a skilled job. Both Mrs Duke and her part-time helper deny lending their keys out to anyone. You're sure you've never held a key?'

'Never! I haven't done that much work for Susie. I never had need of an office key. The door was open when I got there that morning. I told the cops at the time.'

'Yes, you did. I'm still not convinced you don't know more about that than you're saying, Fran. I've warned you before about withholding information.'

'I've told you everything I know!' I protested, raising my voice despite myself and attracting renewed interest from the direction of the tea urns.

'At the very least, he had something he wanted to discuss with you,' Morgan ploughed on obstinately. 'You have to have some idea what that was, Fran.'

'No, I don't. Unless it concerned Edna and you don't want to look into anything concerning Edna. In my mind, she's what matters in all this. All right, so let's say Duane wanted to discuss something with me. Someone else wanted to stop him! Come on.' I was getting increasingly hot under the collar.

Morgan bit into her biscuit, showering crumbs on the table top. 'I hate these things,' she said, staring at the remains of it in her hand. 'They're too sweet and don't taste of anything else.'

'So why did you take it?'

'Not much choice, was there?'

The ladies looked offended and then concerned. They muttered together. We all have our worries. I worried about Edna, Morgan about Duane's death and the ladies about brands of biscuits. That's what it is with worries: they may be big or small and other people may find your own unimportant. But to you they are the only thing to matter at the moment.

The man at the next table folded his crossword, rose to his feet and limped away. He at least hadn't been listening or, if he had, wasn't bothered about listening any further. He presumably had his own private worry. There was no way of telling whether it was an inoperable condition or the frustration of not working out five across.

'I'm Edna's friend,' I said as quietly as I could. 'As far as I know I'm her only friend. Simon and Nikki at the hostel care, but they're professionals and Edna is just one of their residents. If she gets to be too much of a problem, they'll move her out somewhere else. In the meantime, I intend to talk to Adam Ferrier and I hope to Culpeper himself. I can give you Jessica Davis's phone number if you want to talk to her.'

'I only want to talk to her if she has information regarding the death of Duane Gardner. Do you think she has?'

I shook my head. 'I can't say. It's up to you whether you talk to her or not. But I do think you ought to speak to Susie Duke again and ask her about Les Hooper and the key he holds to the office. And while you're about it, you might try putting the frighteners on Les himself.'

'We are acquainted with Mr Hooper,' said Morgan enigmatically.

Now, why didn't that surprise me?

'I'm sorry to hear Mrs Duke is still using him to do odd jobs. We have told her she might do well to reconsider that.'

I decided to chuck my bit of information into the brew. I owed Les nothing and if the police came between him and Susie, so much the better.

'He works – worked – for Lottie and Duane sometimes, and for other private investigators, I think.'

'Regulations governing private investigation agencies are being tightened up,' Morgan told me. 'New rules won't tolerate someone like Mr Hooper.'

I didn't remind her that someone like Les was a real artist when it came to getting round the rules.

Chapter Twelve

When I got back home I discovered the payphone in the hall was as dead as a dodo. Not many tenants used it nowadays. Everyone except me has a mobile. For all I knew, the phone company might even have disconnected the thing. I went over to the newsagent's and told Ganesh and Hari about Edna. Hari never knew Edna but he was interested.

'It is a very bad business,' he said, shaking his head and looking thoroughly satisfied. Hari enjoys bad news. You know where you are with bad news, that's his motto. Good news generally carries an unseen snag with it. Sooner or later you find out what it is but until you do, it lurks there in the background, ready to jump out and surprise you. But bad news means you know the worst straightaway and you are not lulled into any sense of false optimism.

'And our house phone has given up the ghost,' I went on, 'so can I borrow your mobile, Ganesh?'

'Sure,' he said, looking worried. 'Come up to the flat.'

Once in the flat above the shop he fixed me with a glittering eye like the old mariner in the poem. 'For once I'm in complete agreement with my uncle. This is a thoroughly bad business and you've meddled in it enough. Take the mobile, by all means. I'm happier knowing you can call me here at any time. But leave all these people to sort themselves out. The police are on the case, anyway.'

'*Not* on Edna's case,' I corrected. 'They're following up Duane's murder. No one is saying the word "murder" but that's what it is – was. I'm not looking for Duane's killer. I'm trying to protect Edna.'

'You're splitting hairs, that's what you're doing,' said Ganesh, handing over the mobile phone. 'And don't lose this. You lost the last one I lent you.'

I'd dropped the previous phone in a river in Oxford, but that's another story. I promised him I'd take great care of this one.

As soon as I got out of there I rang Lottie Forester and asked her if she had managed to set up a meeting with Adam Ferrier for me. I also told her my house phone was out and gave her the number of Ganesh's mobile.

'Can you come back to my place this evening?' she asked. 'Around seven thirty?'

I was surprised but pleased that she'd set up the meeting so quickly. Rocking and rattling my way out there again in the chugging suburban train, this time uncomfortably packed with homeward-bound commuters, I tried to list all the questions I wanted to ask Ferrier, but instead found myself thinking of Duane Gardner. A phrase of Lottie's kept popping into my head.

'*Duane was a good detective.*'

If he hadn't been killed, he and Lottie would have run a profitable little business out there in Teddington. I felt sorry for Lottie, sorry for Duane.

Good detective, good detective, good detective . . . chuntered the train.

'He was a bloody good detective!' I muttered suddenly aloud, gathering a few alarmed and in some cases resigned looks. It's not unusual to find yourself opposite someone muttering to him or herself on local trains around London but I didn't want to be tagged as one of the mentally scrambled. 'Sorry . . .' I apologised to anyone who could hear me.

Alarm increased and heads went down over paperback novels or disappeared behind copies of the *Evening Standard.* Travellers who had armed themselves with neither simply closed their eyes.

I returned to my thoughts. He must have been *very* good to have found Edna as he had. But how had he found her? How had he known she was still alive and in London? She could have been anywhere in the country or given her age and circumstances have shuffled off the mortal coil years ago.

'Because,' said that other person who lives in my head and goes by my name but thinks more logically than I generally do, 'someone gave him a clue.'

'What do you mean?' I asked the other Fran, silently this time.

'Someone told him where to look. Someone knew about her.'

'All right, who?' I persisted.

'You'll have to find out, won't you?' said other Fran. 'That's something you might ask this chap Ferrier.'

'He didn't know where she was, you twit!' I informed my alter ego. 'If he had, he could have gone and got her himself. He needn't have employed Duane.'

'All right,' said the other Fran smugly, 'so someone else is out there, someone else has a finger in this pie.'

It was still light when I got off at Fulwell station but the sky glowed gold and cerise in the setting sun. By the time I left to go home again, it would be dark. A few lights were already shining inside homes as I passed by them, but Lottie's house was in darkness. A car was parked on the weed-covered drive, one of those little boxy jobs. I didn't know if it belonged to Lottie or to a visitor.

I rang the bell. There was a pause and then I did see an electric glow through the frosted glass panels of the door. Someone had opened a door at the rear of the hall. Feet tapped towards me and the front door was opened by Lottie. She'd changed into her gipsy skirt and a silky top and still wore her favourite boots. She had also tied up her hair with a sort of bandanna; hoop earrings dangled from her lobes. She looked as if she was about to invite me in to tell my fortune.

'We're in the kitchen,' she said without any preamble and not waiting to hear any greeting from me. 'Go on through.'

She stood aside to allow me to pass. 'Thanks,' I mumbled and obeyed instructions. She followed me to the kitchen door and reached past me to push it open. The full glow of electric light struck my face and made me blink.

'This is Fran,' Lottie, behind my shoulder, announced me. 'This is Adam and his sister, Becky,' she added casually to me.

I'd gathered my wits by now and accustomed my eyes to the bright light. The three of them had evidently been sitting round the kitchen table quaffing white wine and stuffing themselves with nibbles. An opened bottle and three used glasses stood witness together with a saucer of pistachio nuts and two empty crisp packets.

The young man stood up and held out his hand. His sister remained seated.

'Hullo,' he said pleasantly.

The siblings were different in build as well as sex. The boy – I suppose he was at least my age and probably more but I found myself thinking of him as a boy – was of medium height but strong and chunky and very good-looking with lots of reddish-blond curly hair and a wide, easy smile.

The girl wasn't just short but tiny. Her long fair hair fell dead straight like a mermaid's over her shoulders and down to her bust. Like me, she was pretty flat in the chest department. She wore a T-shirt with bunnies gambolling across it. It looked like a kid's garment but, given her small size, she could probably wear stuff intended for bigger kids. Yet she had a woman's face, for all the baby-blue eyes and pouting little mouth. Men probably curled up and rolled over before her.

I shook Adam's proffered hand and then held mine out to the girl. She leaned across the table, took my fingers in her limp little mitt and gave them a consolatory squeeze as if I were the bereaved, then drooped back into her chair.

Lottie had joined us. She indicated a chair to me and put a glass down in front of me. I sat. I felt very much the odd one out. It wasn't just that they were all so good-looking, or obviously well heeled, or even that they knew one another so that I was heavily disadvantaged. Friends communicate in ways outsiders don't even notice. Chiefly, though, I felt the outsider because they simply came from another world.

At my private school, during my brief stay there, I'd brushed shoulders with lots of kids like Lottie and Becky. They hadn't liked me then and I suspected that, deep down, these two girls didn't really like me now. Lottie had some sort of an excuse for her dislike. She connected Duane's death with my appearance on the scene. I didn't know what the boy thought of me. I reminded myself to call him a young man. But he looked the sort who could turn on personal charm – and turn it off again if he thought it was being wasted on an unprofitable target.

Lottie poured me a glass of the white. It was Chardonnay, I

noticed. I'm not keen on Chardonnay but this wasn't the moment to start a discussion of the fine points of different wines. It had to be better than the dreadful white plonk I'd served poor Morgan.

'Lottie tells us,' Adam Ferrier began. He sounded a trifle pompous. 'That you'll be helping her out in her business for a while, until things are settled.'

This wasn't quite what Lottie and I had agreed, but as it was obviously what she had told them, I went along with it and nodded.

He looked a little less sure. 'I suppose that's all right. I mean, when I contacted Lottie and Duane on behalf of our grandfather, I hadn't anticipated another person getting to know our private family interests. You'll understand?' It was a question.

I assured him I understood. 'I've been in this business for a little while myself,' I said. 'I'm an associate of Susie Duke who runs the Duke Detective Agency. I fully understand the need for discretion.'

There is a difference between saying you understand the need for discretion and a promise not to talk about things with other people, but I was banking on the Ferriers not picking that up. Instead, Adam had picked up something else.

He glanced nervously at Lottie, who had taken her seat at the table with us and was twirling her empty wine glass.

'The Duke Detective Agency,' he said. 'Isn't that where poor Duane . . .'

'Yes, that's right!' I said in a bright, businesslike tone.

Lottie said, without looking up at any of us, 'Fran found his body.'

The Ferriers stared at me. Adam's eyes gained a calculating expression.

Becky spoke in a curiously cultivated little-girl voice which gave me the heebie-jeebies. 'Are you investigating his death?'

'No, of course I'm not!' I said sternly, giving her a look which I hoped told her I'd appreciate it if she could try and talk like a regular adult human. 'That's for the police.'

'Are they including you in their investigations?' asked her brother more sharply.

'I gave a statement about finding him. Other than that I have no knowledge of what the police are doing. Lottie probably knows more about it than I do.' I was putting down my markers with a firm hand. I wasn't going to discuss anything with these two other than the matter of Edna. I wanted information from them. I wasn't about to give them any.

'They say they are treating his death as suspicious,' said Lottie dully. 'I really hate that word. Why can't they just come out and say murder?'

I opened my mouth to say there was a procedure in these matters but it wouldn't do to sound too knowledgeable. 'I only found him,' I repeated. 'My bad luck.'

'How awful,' breathed Becky batting her eyelids. She reminded me of one of those dolls with the long-lashed eyes that close when you put them flat, and open again, disconcertingly bright blue and glassy, when you sit them up. 'You must have been really scared.' Blink, blink.

Yuk! Help! 'Yeah, well,' I mumbled, finding myself unexpectedly stuck for a reply. 'It was sort of weird.'

'Bloody awful!' boomed Adam suddenly with unexpected energy and far too loudly so that I jumped.

So was this. I'd stumbled back into *Alice in Wonderland*, this time at the point of the Mad Hatter's Tea Party. Lottie was presiding like the Mad Hatter himself – for hat read bandanna – and Adam, who I fancied was developing an odd gleam in his eyes, was the March Hare. I sipped my wine and hoped Becky, like the dormouse, would soon fall asleep with her head resting on the saucer of pistachio nuts. She looked as if she might have as little to contribute to our conversation.

I looked round the kitchen desperately for some topic of conversation which would get us away from the image of Duane's dead body and me standing over it which was occupying all our minds just at the moment.

My gaze fell on a series of pale oblong shapes on the wall opposite my seat. I frowned.

'You've taken down the family photos,' I said to Lottie.

She was hunched over her glass of wine and cast a dismissive glance up at the area.

'I can't settle to anything,' she said. 'I just think about Duane all the time. I thought, perhaps I'd make a start on redoing this kitchen. I could paint the walls and it would take my mind off it all. I went to Homebase and got a couple of tins of emulsion.'

'What colour?' asked Becky, showing a flicker of animation.

'Sort of duck-egg blue.'

What colour jelly . . .?

I owed it to Edna not to let myself be outmanoeuvred by this trio. To be fair to them, it was that individual worry thing again. Lottie's worry wasn't what colour to paint the walls; it was who killed Duane and what this meant to her future. The Ferriers worried, I deduced, about old Mr Culpeper. But much as people try to seduce you into sharing their problems, mine was still my old ex-bag lady. I said as much and they turned to me.

Lottie was staring at me with mild interest, as if struck by a sudden thought. 'Have you got a boyfriend or partner or anything?'

'Not even an anything,' I told her. 'I've got a very good friend. We leave it at that. Why mess with an arrangement that works?'

Her expression changed and she leaned towards me with real seriousness in her face. 'That's so right,' she said. She pointed at the denuded wall. 'I've got a really nice pic of Duane. I thought I might have it enlarged and hang it there. What do you think?'

I didn't share what leapt into my mind which was an image from that film, *Friendly Persuasion*. A Quaker farmer finds himself visiting a hillbilly cabin. Above the hearth, surrounded by a wreath, is a picture of the late head of the house, a grim-looking black-bearded type. Politely the visitor points heavenward. Firmly the widow responds by jabbing the stem of her pipe downwards. I saw the film on afternoon TV not long ago. I like old films. So I couldn't help but wonder if Lottie would decorate Duane's portrait with a silk bow and evergreen leaves. No, of course she wouldn't. It was just my imagination behaving badly. I couldn't control it, though I did my best.

'Nice,' was what I actually said aloud.

Adam Ferrier was growing restless. He probably feared this was going to descend into girl talk.

'Lottie says you want to meet my grandfather.'

'Yes, I do, and as soon as possible.'

'That rather depends on his health on a given day. Some days he's able to cope with strangers and some days he finds it all too much. Give me a phone number and I'll call you.'

I gave him the number of Ganesh's mobile. 'I appreciate your grandfather has dodgy health,' I told Adam, 'but I do still need to see him asap.'

'Will do,' he said laconically.

It seemed we could only leave it at that. I had no wish to sit here with the gruesome threesome and they probably wanted to see the back of me. I stood up. 'I'll be in touch,' I said sternly to Adam, just to let him know I wouldn't be sitting around waiting for that promised call. If it didn't come, he'd have me pestering him.

He reacted with a really antagonistic look. 'I told you,' he said coldly, 'I'll arrange it when it's convenient.'

'Great,' I said and left.

You know how it is when you feel you've been dismissed? The French have a wonderful phrase about the 'wit of the staircase'. It's that clever reply you think of on your way out but unfortunately failed to think of when it was required. All the way back to North London I came up with various snappy quips to put Adam Ferrier in his place. By the time I got back home I was really frustrated.

Whether I did Ferrier a disservice or whether he realised I'd be a regular pain in the neck until he did what I wanted, he rang me late the following morning.

'My sister has been to see our grandfather and it appears he's able to meet you this afternoon. If you're free, I'll stop by and pick you up and take you there. Where do you live?'

I told him and he said, 'Then it won't be far. Just give me time to get to you.'

I remembered Lottie had told me he had a flat in Docklands. 'Fine,' I said. 'I'll be waiting.'

'Two o'clock!' he said crisply, swatting me again.

I tried to remember all the witty put-downs I'd worked out the previous evening on my way home and found I'd forgotten them all.

* * *

Adam turned up on time in a BMW. Perhaps the small car I'd seen at the house had belonged to Becky.

'Flash wheels,' I observed as I climbed in and buckled myself into the passenger seat.

'Company car,' he said briefly.

Why is it that once you are pretty well off, people start giving you things?

'Are we going back to Teddington?' I asked as we picked a way through the traffic.

'No, not that far.'

I tried again. 'Has your grandfather some particular medical problem or is his problem age-related?'

'He's recovering from surgery,' Adam said in that clipped way and didn't elaborate.

I didn't ask further. He didn't want to chat. Fair enough. When I met Grandpa I'd see for myself.

When I saw the place I gasped. It had that kind of effect on the first-time viewer. Normally I like to play it cool, but this house was really something. It was an old place, at a rough guess mid-Victorian, with weathered brickwork and elaborate stonework and carved gables. It was the kind of house that if it hadn't been so beautifully maintained might have ended up looking spooky, as if either the Munsters or the Addams families might suddenly issue forth from the front door. But this was spick and span and so were the grounds. I realised the back garden must run down to the Regent's Canal and probably had private mooring. The front drive was protected by a high electronically operated security gate. A burglar alarm stood out prominently on the façade of the house and the windows downstairs had those security grilles that concertina back and forth. You'd need to ram-raid this place to break in. Adam had been right in saying that location-wise it wasn't far from me. But in social and financial terms we might as well have travelled to the Moon.

Adam glanced at me and allowed himself a little grin.

Smug bastard! I thought. 'Nice place,' I said aloud, trying to retrieve my loss of poise, 'worth a bit.'

He didn't reply to that, just operated a remote control device. Slowly the gate slid to one side to admit us.

I knew Ferrier wasn't the sort who thought it vulgar to discuss money. People like Adam talk money all the time. He knew to the last penny what the current market value of this house was. I guessed at least a couple of million. Perhaps more? Was he hoping to inherit it? Or were he and his sister to be joint heirs? And, more to the point, was the fact that Grandpa was worth a mint a relevant factor in all this? And where the hell did a bag lady come into it?

I recalled Ganesh scoffing at my theory that all this business might be about a will. But perhaps I'd been on the right lines. Where there's money there's motive for murder.

The front door was opened as we got out of the car. A briskly efficient woman appeared, looking as though she might be part housekeeper and part nurse.

'He's feeling quite bright today,' she said to Adam and extended her smile to me, something I appreciated after Adam's attitude towards me. No one likes being treated like something the cat dragged in. 'Just go on up.'

So far, thank goodness, there had been no sign of Becky.

I followed Adam up the staircase and he led me down a corridor to a bedroom door. He tapped, opened it and put his head through the gap.

'OK, Gramps? I've got the woman private detective here, the one I told you about.'

An elderly voice murmured a reply.

The door was pushed wide open by Adam who gestured to me to enter. I walked past him and into a large, light room which had been converted from bedroom into a first-floor sitting room. There was not a great deal of furniture, just a couple of chairs, a television console and a bookcase. Nor was there any carpet. The floorboards had been sanded and stained. By the far window, looking out, sat a man who made no effect to get up and turn to see the new arrival. I could only see the back of his head. The rest of him was hidden by the invalid chair he occupied. That explained why he hadn't got up and also why the room was half empty and there were no rugs to impede the chair's progress. Mr Culpeper needed space to manoeuvre.

In a sudden movement the chair spun round with a soft electric purr. He was facing me and I saw the nature of the surgery that had left him disabled. Both lower legs had been amputated and a blanket lay across the remaining stumps. Whether all of this drastic surgery had been carried out recently or over a period of time, or what had necessitated it, I had no idea. But I could well understand why Culpeper had days when he'd no wish to be badgered by people he didn't know and why he chose his grandson as his messenger.

He had not spoken but sat watching me thoughtfully; perhaps wishing to see in my face how the sight of his mutilation affected me. I realised I was expected to make the first move and that a great deal depended on it. I had to get it right. I decided on the more formal and old-fashioned approach.

I walked across and held out my hand. 'Good afternoon, Mr Culpeper. Thank you for agreeing to see me.'

His reply was a question. 'Do you like my view?'

I was a little startled and turned my gaze to the window. It was easy to understand why he sat here. From this vantage point he looked over the long, well-established garden to the canalside mooring. There were trees and shrubs and lawns and a little gazebo. It was beautiful, peaceful and timeless. I did wonder what kind of security was down there to prevent intruders entering property from the rear. Having seen the security gate out front, I was sure something lay hidden among the bushes: photo-sensitive scanners of some kind, floodlights, automatic alarms? There was probably a direct link to the local cop shop and the moment whistles started blowing, bells ringing, lights flashing or whatever would happen if an unauthorised foot was set on the turf, half the local force would be crawling over the place.

I wrenched my gaze away and turned it to my host. He was watching me now with a touch of amusement and also with pleasure. He knew the effect his view had on visitors and liked it. He presented quite an interesting sight himself. He must once have been an imposing figure of a man. Even in the chair he dominated the room. He'd been handsome, too, and still had a fine head of silvering hair and keen eyes pouched in wrinkled skin. Oddly, there was something familiar about him although I couldn't ever have seen him before. It must be a shared likeness with Adam or Becky, I thought.

'It's beautiful,' I said sincerely.

I realised with another start that I still held out my hand. Before I could withdraw it, he took it in a firm grip and held it while he subjected me to a further assessment. Eventually he released it.

'Adam,' he said, 'perhaps you'd tell Alice we'd like a cup of tea?'

I had passed whatever test had been set me. I felt a spurt of relief. But I knew the last thing Adam wanted was to leave me alone with his grandfather. I took great pleasure in seeing him sidle out with a glare at me.

'Pull up a chair,' invited Culpeper. 'I'm sorry to be a poor host.'

'Look,' I said, after I moved over a chair to join him, 'I really am sorry to be a nuisance—'

He waved a hand to interrupt me. 'If you were a nuisance, I wouldn't have agreed to meet you. I'm glad you've come. I am not able to go out so I depend on people coming to see me.'

I decided to get in as much as I could before Adam came back.

'Mr Culpeper, can we get down to business? I understand you engaged the detective agency run by Lottie Forester and her late boyfriend Duane Gardner to find Edna Walters.'

He nodded but said nothing.

I pressed on. 'I've known Edna, on and off, for quite a while.' I explained about the squat and Edna living in the churchyard.

Culpeper began to look distressed and I was alarmed. I didn't want to be responsible for causing him to have some sort of funny turn. He turned his gaze away from me to the window. 'I'm sorry to hear that,' he said quietly. 'No one should be living like that and certainly not Edna.'

A prickle of tension ran down my spine. There was a note in his voice when he spoke Edna's name which indicated some deep emotion. At least his words indicated some far-off old acquaintance with her.

'She's much better off now living in a hostel, as you probably know,' I said. 'The people who run it are quite young and very conscientious. They're nice.'

He moved his thin hands on which the distended veins formed a network of blue-tinged cords beneath the skin. 'So I've learned.'

'Did Duane tell you?' I asked, 'or was it Jessica Davis?'

'Ah, Jessica,' he said. He turned his gaze, sharp again, back to me. 'Have you mentioned Jessica's activities to Adam or to that girl, Lottie Forester?'

'Not to Adam,' I said, 'I didn't think it necessary.'

He smiled, and it was a really charming smile. 'Quite right,' he said. 'It's not necessary. I'd be grateful if you don't mention it to him, or to little Becky.'

I wouldn't but Lottie might.

'But Jessica is, um, enquiring on your behalf?' I persisted gently, just to get the matter absolutely clear.

'In a manner of speaking. Her – enquiries are not quite the same as those I asked Adam to set in train via the agency run by young Lottie. I was far from sure I should employ a private detective. Forgive me, but I've always thought of it as rather a seedy occupation. I've read too many Raymond Chandler books, perhaps!'

'It is a seedy occupation,' I told him. 'But life is pretty seedy sometimes and someone has to get out there and deal with it.'

He nodded. 'Down those mean streets . . .' he quoted. He became brisker. 'At any rate, when Adam told me about Lottie's agency I was happy for him to hire it for me. I've known that girl since she was a baby.' He chuckled suddenly. 'To think of her being a detective! I did fancy she might be my granddaughter-in-law at one point, some years ago. But she and Adam didn't make a go of it and later on she took up with that very strange young fellow, Duane Gardner.'

Henry sat here, a virtual prisoner in this lovely house, but he knew what was going on and who was out there. Who kept him in touch? Adam and Becky? Jessica Davis? A whole network of spies? For a moment I had an uneasy feeling that he was like an elderly spider sitting in the middle of his silken web and waiting.

'Duane was a good detective,' I said. 'He found Edna for you.'

'Yes, and then, as I understand it, you found *him*!' The keen old eyes rested on my face.

Before I had a chance to reply, there was a tap at the door

which opened before Culpeper could call out, and Adam entered carrying a small table. Behind him came Alice bearing the tea tray.

'Here we are,' said Adam rather too heartily, positioning the table by his grandfather and me. He took the tray from Alice and set it down. 'Do you want me to stay, Gramps?'

His grandfather ignored the hopeful plea. 'That will be all right, Adam. Fran and I will just chat for a few more minutes. Thank you for the tea, Alice.'

Adam stalked out.

'Heh!' I wanted to shout after him. 'That's what it's like being dismissed! How do you like it?' I had to content myself with smiling sweetly at Adam as he turned in the doorway to give me a last minatory look. The smile turned the expression on his face to something indicating imminent meltdown.

When we were alone again, Culpeper indicated the tea tray and said, 'Perhaps you'd do the honours, Fran?'

I obeyed. 'Mr Culpeper,' I began again when we had a cup of tea apiece. 'I don't have the right and I don't *want* to enquire into any private matter of yours. But I am concerned for Edna's welfare.'

'That's good of you, my dear. But you need have no fears. I will see that something is done for Edna.'

He wasn't going to volunteer his reasons for his interest in Edna but I couldn't leave it at that.

'Mr Culpeper, it isn't going to be that easy. I realise that you're pretty well informed in general terms. But, forgive me, sitting here and hearing about it isn't the same as being out there . . .' I waved at the window. 'I don't mean to be tactless but I really don't think you'd be so calm about it all if you were able to get a feel of things from being amongst people.'

I feared he might take what I had said as ill-mannered but he didn't turn a hair.

'That's what Jessica is supposed to be doing for me,' he said with a touch of humour.

'Yes, well, maybe she is and maybe not. Has she told you that Edna is currently in hospital?'

The teacup rattled in Culpeper's hand and I hastened to rescue it.

'I'm sorry,' I apologised as I mopped up the tea that had spilled on his jacket. 'That was pretty ham-fisted of me. She's all right. She – she had a fall in the street.'

I thought telling him about the motorcyclist might not be a good idea. Anyway, if he contacted the police or hospital about it, that's what they'd tell him: an old lady had tripped over her own feet. I was the only one who thought someone had tried deliberately to run Edna down.

But I had successfully destroyed the cosy atmosphere.

'I must get in touch with Jessica,' he muttered. He was beginning to sound agitated and fretful, his air of control over the situation evaporating.

It was time I left. I stood up, then leaned over and took his hands in mine. 'Mr Culpeper, don't worry. I'm keeping a close eye on Edna.'

'Thank you,' he murmured, still distracted. 'Thank you very much.'

Adam must have been lurking in the corridor. As soon as my hand touched the door handle it was seized on the other side and the door was pushed open with such force I was propelled back into the room.

He marched past me across to the window. 'Do you need anything, Gramps?'

I could no longer see Culpeper, only the back of his chair again, but his hand appeared to one side, waving a negative. 'No, no, just tell Alice she can come and fetch the tray.' The elderly voice sounded tired.

Adam marched back to me and pushed me ahead of him down the corridor to the stairs. For two pins I think he would have pushed me straight down those as well.

'You've upset him!' he snarled. 'I knew you would.'

'No, I haven't!' I denied, although it wasn't altogether true. 'We got on fine.'

Or we did until I told Culpeper about Edna being in the hospital.

Alice had appeared and Adam relayed the message about the tray. She set off upstairs.

'Well?' demanded Adam as we left the house and Alice couldn't overhear us. 'What did you say to him? What did *he* say?'

But I'd learned a thing from Lottie and Duane. 'Confidential,' I said.

'Bloody hell!' he exploded. 'It's not confidential from *me*! You're working with Lottie and I hired the blasted agency!'

'No,' I told him, 'your grandfather hired it. You were just his mouthpiece. I've made my report to Mr Culpeper and that should fulfil any contractual obligation you have with Lottie's agency.'

He seized my arm in a painful grip and spun me round. 'Don't get clever with me!' he snarled. He didn't look handsome now, just very angry and very unpleasant.

I shook his hand off. 'And don't get stroppy with me, mate,' I returned.

'Street trash!' he almost spat at me.

'Tut-tut,' I said. 'Gramps wouldn't like that.'

'Go to hell,' he said, 'you can make your own way home!'

He got into the BMW and roared away.

* * *

I took my time walking back. I needed time to think. Until I'd met him, there had always been a niggling doubt in my mind as to whether the tale I'd been told, that Adam represented his grandfather in hiring the agency, was true. That Lottie believed it did not make it necessarily correct. She relied on Adam's word. But in the end, it was right. Culpeper had hired the agency even if it had been on Adam's recommendation. I still didn't know quite where Jessica Davis came into all of this. Culpeper's friend, yes, and confidante by the sound of it. But why had he asked her to check separately on Edna? Probably, I guessed, because he had still some lingering unease about using a professional agency, 'a seedy business' as he'd termed it.

I made my way along my home street, my mind turning to cups of tea and the necessity of walking poor Bonnie who had again been left with Erwin. My dog must be thinking that I had abandoned her; she was seeing so little of me lately. The sky was overcast and everything looked grey including the young 'hoodie' standing on the pavement a short way ahead of me. I paid little attention to him; he was just one of these spindly kids who favour dull-coloured tracksuits with hooded top pulled up over the head and obscuring the face. From his general build and the slouch of his posture, I guessed this one to be about thirteen. He was mucking about texting a message to someone on his mobile phone. As I neared him, he stepped off the pavement and began to stroll slowly across the road in front of me, his eyes still on the text message, in his own little world.

Not surprisingly he stumbled, probably helped by the trailing unfastened laces of his trainers. He sprawled full length, but still clutching the phone.

'Hey! Are you all right?' I called and walked out into the road where I made to bend over him. Behind me came the put-put noise of an engine.

He was on his feet and dashed off down the street like greased lightning. I whirled round looking for his mates because this had the look, to me, of a set-up mugging. What I saw and heard, bearing down on me with a now terrifying roar, was a motorbike.

The rider, in leathers and helmet was crouched low over the handlebars, at one with his machine. I was there, stuck in the middle of the road and I had to go one way or the other. I made to go left and saw the rider veer off line to do the same. My God! I thought – he wants to run me down! I threw myself to the right, rolling over and over in the road, scraping my hands and nose on the tarmac, and landed in the gutter. I scrambled up. He had overshot the spot and was turning at the far end of the road to take another run at his target. I threw myself over the nearest low wall and landed amid a collection of wheelie bins which fell over with a clatter and spilled their contents. I was showered by someone's garbage but that was the least of my worries. I heard the bike roar past again and waited, crouched and covered in stinking scraps of food and unknown and probably unmentionable waste.

But he didn't come back. He probably thought the racket I'd made might have attracted attention from inside the house. I rose from my bed of kitchen refuse and nappy sacks which had split releasing their fetid contents and limped home. As I reached the house, the front door opened and Bonnie shot out barking. When she saw me she began to spring up and down and perform a berserk dance round my feet, whining and whimpering in her excitement. She, at least, liked the smell.

Erwin appeared behind her, filling the doorway. 'Hey,' he

observed, looking me up and down, 'the dog heard a noise. What've you been doing?' He leaned forward and sniffed delicately. 'Girl,' he said in awe, 'you stink.'

Chapter Thirteen

'I know,' I said with as much dignity as was possible in the circumstances, which wasn't a lot.

'Hee-hee-hee . . .' giggled Erwin, finding it funny all of a sudden.

I collected my dog and went into my flat. Fortunately Ganesh's mobile was still working. I rang the number Morgan had given me.

'That motorcyclist who tried to run down Edna, you remember that?' I said, and before she could start to argue the point added, 'He just tried to get me.'

'Where are you?' she asked in her practical way, 'and are you hurt?'

'I'm at home and no, just bruised and I have to take a shower and change my clothes. I landed in some dustbins.'

'I'm off duty,' she said, 'but I'll come over straightaway.'

By the time she arrived, I was changed and smelled rather better. The clothes I'd been wearing I chucked in a bin bag to take over to the laundrette. Bonnie was sniffing around it and pawing at it. She still thought it smelled rather interesting and wanted desperately to investigate further.

Janice Morgan had undergone a transformation, or as near to one as mattered. I stared at her in amazement. She wore jeans, high-heeled boots with wickedly pointed toes, and a pink leather biker's jacket. She had pinned her hair up, too, in a knot and wore a bright enamelled pendant round her neck.

'Hey, you look great,' I told her. 'If this is the new Janice Morgan I'm all for it.'

'I'm off duty!' she retorted but she blushed.

'Why don't you dress like that when you go to work?' I asked.

'I have my reasons,' she said in a sinister sort of way.

'Yeah, yeah,' I said. 'You're afraid you'll be treated like a bimbo. That's what comes of working in an old-fashioned sexist environment like a police station.'

'Things are a lot better than they used to be,' she argued. 'Most of that old-time sexist attitude has gone.'

'Most, possibly. All of it, no way. If it had you wouldn't be scared of wearing that jacket to work.'

The red deepened on her flushed cheeks but this time it was anger. 'If I want your opinion, Fran, I'll ask for it.'

'It makes me cross,' I said, refusing to let her brush off the – very constructive – criticism I was kindly sending her way. 'I'll tell you why and then I'll shut up about it. You think you're supporting a woman's right to be plain. I think you are letting yourself down. You're successful. You've made senior grade already and you'll probably go higher. You should do, anyway. Why the heck do you feel you can't dress the way you really want to? Why do you have to keep that wardrobe full of that dreary stuff when you've got gear like you're wearing now? You don't have to prove anything to those dinosaurs down at the cop shop. If they've got a problem, it's theirs not yours.'

'Leave it out, Fran!' she snapped. 'That's enough. If I want to have my ear bent with that sort of thing I can visit my mother.'

That did silence me, I admit.

But I'd released some outpouring from Janice. She fumed on. 'As for my colleagues, whether they're my problem or not, it still *only* concerns me. I didn't come over here to discuss *them* or to discuss me and my clothes, come to that. Put your own house in order and in the meantime stop wasting my valuable and scarce free time. Tell me about this motorcyclist.'

I told her.

'So,' she said thoughtfully. 'Whoever this is, he doesn't act alone. There's the kid you saw.' She leaned back and propped one booted foot on the knee of the other leg. I was by now envying her the pink leather biker's jacket and wondering where she had bought it and how much it had cost. More than I could pay, probably. I didn't dare refer to it again. Anyway, she was right: this wasn't the time for girl talk.

'He could have been paid by the cyclist to decoy me out into the road. Some of the kids round here are a little weird. You won't mention this motorbike business to Ganesh Patel if you should see him, will you?' I added anxiously. 'I'd rather he doesn't know.' *Much* rather he didn't, truth to tell. It would give Ganesh critical ammunition against my activities for weeks to come.

She nodded. 'Sure. I understand he'd be worried.'

'It's his uncle who worries. Ganesh lectures. I can put up with Hari worrying but Gan lecturing gets me down. Would you like a coffee or a glass of wine?'

'If it's the same wine you offered me the last time I was here, I'll settle for the coffee,' she said promptly.

'Yeah,' I mused. 'I should pour the rest of that wine down the sink. It's pretty foul. But it should clean the waste pipe out.'

When I'd brought the coffee, I continued my account of the afternoon's adventures by summarising my visit to Culpeper. 'He knows about my finding Duane dead but I didn't really have much of a chance to discuss that aspect of things. Adam came marching in with the hired help and the tea tray. He didn't like me being there and especially didn't like me talking alone to his grandfather. But I reckon the old boy is pretty devious in his own way. I know Jessica Davis is reporting back to him. He admitted that. Has she been to see you yet?'

Her hands cupped round her coffee mug, Morgan shook her head slowly. 'No, I don't think she's going to come, at least, not unless something else happens to change her mind. After all, she has no reason to call on me. *She* wasn't involved with Gardner directly as far as we know; that was Culpeper, via his grandson. Perhaps I should go and see Culpeper. From what you've said my guess is that before she came to see a police officer like me, Jessica Davis decided to check back with Culpeper and he told her he didn't want anything to do with the police, so she changed her mind. After all, the old man has already got a lot more than he bargained for when he agreed to let Ferrier hire the agency. However, when people don't want the police knowing their business, it always makes me curious.'

She sighed, drained her mug and set it down. 'I am investigating Gardner's death, nothing more, nothing less. That doesn't mean it is the only thing on my desk. I wish a detective's life was like it is in books and on the telly. Off goes the telly-tec with a trusty sergeant and spends his whole time tracking down one villain. If only! I've got half a dozen things on the go, calling on my attention. I know what you want me to do, Fran. You want me to go haring off interviewing each and every person you come across who seems interesting to you. But I just can't do it. I have to justify my time spent. I have to work within the constraints of a budget. I can't afford to look a fool chasing shadows.'

I opened my mouth and closed it again. She was right. I was the amateur and she was the professional. I could pick and choose which hares I chased. She couldn't.

She gave me a sympathetic smile. 'However, it does begin increasingly to look as if Gardner's death has to do with his search for Edna.' She held up her hand to forestall me because a sudden ray of hope had enveloped me and I had sat up. 'Hold on, Fran. That still doesn't mean I can go chasing down every lead you bring me. My biggest problem is this: Gardner *had found* Edna. That's what his employers, Culpeper and Ferrier, *wanted.* They should have been overjoyed and ready to pay the man a bonus! We can count both of them out of the suspicious death scenario. So there I am down a blind alley again. Yes, it's interesting. Is it likely to forward my search for Gardner's killer? No, it isn't.'

'Someone wants to kill Edna,' I countered.

'I still don't agree that anyone does. But, for the sake of argument, let's suppose you're right. Then at least it's not Culpeper or Jessica Davis,' countered Morgan. 'From all you've told me and what they said to you, they are very concerned for her welfare.'

'Edna's no threat to anyone,' I mused. 'She can't possibly be.'

We sat in silence. Then I said, 'You might like to visit Culpeper if only to see the house. It is out of this world. It must be worth a fortune. I don't know if that gives less significance to Culpeper hiring an enquiry agency, or more. I mean, if you're rich, you can indulge yourself in a whim, can't you? It's not like you're breaking open the piggy bank, something you'd only do if it really mattered a lot. Besides, I got the impression Culpeper likes people to report back to him. He's a virtual prisoner in his own home but once upon a time, I bet, he was one of life's movers and shakers and he still likes to keep a finger on the button. Perhaps it gives him a buzz to know he can still get people to jump when he says so.'

Morgan gave a muffled growl.

'He's a nice old boy,' I went on hastily, 'I honestly liked him, but I wouldn't try and fool him. But if someone like that is bored, he might just decide to set Duane the task of finding Edna as a kind of hobby. It *might* just all be an intellectual exercise to him, like a crossword puzzle, something to pass the time. But on the other hand he seemed genuinely upset to learn that Edna had been living rough when I first met her. He didn't fake that. He hadn't known it and he was shocked. He really cared. When I told him she was in hospital he went all to pieces.'

'I'm always interested in what rich people do,' Janice Morgan said simply. 'They sometimes wind up murdered.'

'No one could get to Culpeper. He's surrounded by security – except at the bottom of his back garden. That runs down to the canal but I'm sure there are all kinds of devices hidden in the undergrowth to let you know if there's an intruder. Besides, he doesn't go out and very few people get in to see him – except his family and his spies. It's all a bit like *The Godfather*.'

'Money makes motive,' said Janice.

She sniffed the air. 'Your dog's clawed a hole in that bin bag and is dragging out your dirty clothing.'

'You're very quiet,' said Ganesh.

It was evening and we were on our way to the hospital to see Edna again.

'I've had a busy day, going to see Culpeper. You should see that house, Gan. Poor old chap, he's lost both his lower legs. He's pretty with it mentally, though. He must be really frustrated.'

'Sure,' murmured Ganesh giving me a careful once-over look. 'What happened to your nose?'

I touched my nose and winced because it was tender. 'Nothing.'

'It looks swollen.' His tone grew suspicious.

'Oh? I tripped over Bonnie.'

'Right,' he said in a way which indicated he didn't believe me.

We found Edna sitting beside the bed looking quite pink and chipper in what looked like a brand-new blue towelling dressing gown. Around us other visitors chatted to patients and plied them with grapes and Get Well cards. I handed Edna the bar of chocolate we'd brought from the shop.

'Thank you, my dears!' she said graciously and squirrelled the chocolate away in a pocket of the dressing gown. 'I'm going back to the hostel tomorrow.'

'Are you sure, Edna?' I asked in some dismay. It was what I'd told Morgan I wanted for Edna, to be released from hospital. But I had to admit she was safe in here from homicidal motorcyclists. She looked so much better in herself today that it allayed my fears the hospital would get her down.

'They told me so. She told me so.'

'Who did, Edna?'

Edna's mind had moved on. She leaned forward confidentially and whispered, 'There's such a nice young girl in the bed over there but she's had everything out.'

'Do you mind?' protested Ganesh. 'If the conversation is going to be about women's insides I'm leaving.'

'Edna,' I persisted. 'I'm not interested in any of your fellow patients. Who told you about going back to the hostel?'

'That girl who helps run the place, Nikki, she's called. She was here today. I think it was today.' Edna frowned and pursed her lips, chasing the elusive scrap of memory, trying to fit it into the timetable. She gave up and concentrated on something nearer and more solid. She patted the pocket to check the chocolate was still there and smiled happily.

'Did she bring the dressing gown?'

Edna looked down at the dressing gown as if she hadn't paid much attention to it before and smoothed the surface experimentally. 'I suppose she did. Can't remember. She's all right as those charity people go. I don't hold with charities much. A charity took my cats.' Her air of goodwill faded. She leaned forward. 'I don't forget my cats!'

'No, you don't,' muttered Ganesh beside me.

Edna fished the chocolate from the pocket and studied it. 'I'll keep the wrapping paper,' she said. 'It's pretty.' She stuffed the bar away again.

'Edna,' I began carefully, 'this accident you had in the street . . .'

'I didn't have any accident!' she snapped. 'He ran me down, or he tried to run me down.'

'I believe you, Edna, honestly I do. Can you remember whether you were distracted by anything or anyone just before it happened?'

She turned her gaze on me with a disconcerting alertness. 'Like what, dear?'

'I don't want to put ideas into your head,' I explained. 'I just would appreciate it if you'd think back over the – the incident from the moment you decided to cross the road.'

'There was nothing,' said Edna, sullen now. 'There were people on the pavement on both sides but nothing in the road until that bike came roaring out of nowhere.'

Ganesh, ever loyal even though he hadn't a clue what I was up to, leaned forward. 'Picture it, Edna. An empty road, you . . .'

Edna raised a wrinkled finger and pointed it at him. 'Not just me, no. There was a youngster who crossed just before me. *He* didn't get run down, did he? He went strolling across like he'd got all the time in the world, with his eyes fixed on one of those mobile phone things. If anyone had been run down, it should have been him. He wasn't looking to left or right. He couldn't have seen anything, anyway. He'd got the hood of his jacket pulled right up over his head. It wasn't raining.'

'Thank you, Edna,' I said. 'They call them hoodies, those kids who like that fashion.'

Ganesh gave me a funny look.

'Fashion . . .' mumbled Edna in disgust. 'That's not fashion. I remember when we had fashion. Pencil skirts. You had to have a nice little waist and we wore proper foundation garments. Matching belts and shoes and gloves. My sister had pretty party dresses, lots of stiffened petticoats. I used to watch her getting ready to go and meet her young man. She wore sheer stockings with seams up the back, if she could get 'em. *Are my seams straight, Edna?* They were expensive and if you did lay your hands on a good pair or two you looked after them. None of this throwaway nonsense. If you got a ladder in your stockings you took them to a special shop where they mended them. The girls used to sit in the shop working on it and you could see them from the street, through the windows. The work couldn't have done their eyesight any good.'

Her voice had been growing drowsier and she closed her eyes.

Ganesh was fidgeting. 'Come on, Fran,' he muttered, 'she's roaming down memory lane and getting lost doing it, by the sound of it. She's all of a muddle – you won't get any more sense out of her. Not that we got much before.'

We took our leave, although I don't know whether she realised it or had already fallen asleep.

I checked on the way out with the nurse to make sure Edna

really was going back to the hostel the next morning.

'That's right,' she said. 'We kept her in to run some tests, but everything seems fine. I understand someone from the hostel where she lives will be collecting her in the morning.'

'Did her visitor from the hostel bring that nice dressing gown?'

'I think she must have done,' said the nurse. 'I wasn't on shift at the time.'

'What was all that about whether she was distracted before she started to cross the road?' asked Ganesh, as I'd known he would.

'Just trying to get a clear picture of what happened,' I told him. 'Thanks for your help.'

I was grateful to him. I'd still not told him of my close encounter with the motorcyclist, but he'd chipped in to help me get what I wanted from Edna, even so.

'You'll never get a clear picture of anything from her. Not unless she's rabbiting on about some bygone time when girls mended their stockings, for crying out loud,' he observed.

I said nothing because I was running it all through my head. I'd never known Edna so loquacious and I put it down to whatever pills they were giving her. But had she told me anything of interest, apart from the sighting of the hooded youth? I had a feeling she had but I couldn't pinpoint what it was.

'Good of the hostel to shell out for a dressing gown for the old bat,' said Ganesh a bit later.

That roused me. 'The hostel worker may have brought it in. I'd bet a pound to a penny the hostel didn't buy it. The place is run on a shoestring. They feed everyone there on beans and vegetables. That dressing gown cost money.'

And it was the sort of thing a clothes-conscious woman like Jessica Davis would buy.

'*Clothes*,' I said. 'For more years than any of us knows Edna has worn cast-off bits and pieces she's got from charities and goodness knows where else. So why should she care so much about fashion or the lack of it nowadays?'

'She's old and potty,' said Ganesh. 'She was sane once, I suppose. She remembers something of those days. Old people always remember the past. It's nothing to worry about.'

But I had a feeling it was. 'Damn,' I said. 'I should have asked that nurse how many other visitors Edna had today.'

It was getting late as we made our way homeward but the day was far from over yet. We took the Edgware branch of the Northern Line. I said goodbye to Ganesh at Camden Town and got off the train. It pulled out carrying him on to Chalk Farm, the nearer station for the shop.

I sometimes feel that the whole world meets at Camden Town Tube station. Some people would argue in favour of Oxford Circus being the nation's rendezvous but the people I know favour Camden Town.

That is why I wasn't particularly surprised, when I emerged into Camden High Street, to see Les Hooper lumbering down the pavement towards me with the grace of a hippo escaped from Regent's Park Zoo.

That didn't mean Les wasn't surprised to see me. Dismayed might be the better term. He stopped, looked about him helplessly, and clearly would have turned and run if it would have helped. All he could manage was to stand there flapping his shovel-sized hands and looking miserable.

'Hi, Les,' I said. 'Just the bloke I wanted to see.'

'Oh, 'ullo, darling,' he returned hoarsely. 'What do you want me for? It's not about that poor sod, Duane, is it? 'Cos I don't know nothing.'

'Sure you do, Les,' I said smoothly, linking my arm through his, an action causing him further alarm. 'Come on, let's go and have a drink.'

'Well, I don't know,' he began, trying to disentangle himself from me without actually shaking me off. But, like Bonnie, when I've got a grip I don't let go easily.

'Come on,' I interrupted cheerfully. 'I'm sure you never say no to a pint, Les. My shout.'

'It's not that . . .' he began as I towed him along the pavement. 'It's the rozzers.'

'Police?' I asked sharply. 'Have they been to speak to you?'

'Yes, they bloody have,' said Les unhappily. 'Not just your regular couple of pigs, either, but a smart-mouthed woman inspector.'

'Inspector Morgan?' I asked.

'Yes, that's the one. Here, are you on her payroll or what?'

He stopped and a weight like that isn't easily budged so I had to stop too, but I didn't release his arm. His small reddened eyes were peering down at me suspiciously.

'No, I'm not!' I snapped. 'I'm no kind of grass, Les!'

I must have looked my outrage because he became shamefaced and muttered, 'Didn't think you was.'

We resumed our uneven progress and entered the first pub we came to. Les seemed to rally when his meaty paw encircled a pint glass and he visibly relaxed. Pubs were his milieu. He probably had mates here who'd help him out if things got awkward. I noticed we gathered a couple of curious stares. They probably weren't used to Les coming in here with a woman or, at least, not one like me. I'd bought myself a soft drink because I was on business and needed my wits about me.

Les had seen the stares, too. 'They think it looks funny, you and me,' he muttered.

'Perhaps they'll think I'm your daughter, Les,' I told him kindly.

'If I 'ad a daughter,' retorted Les, 'I hope she wouldn't dress like you. I never did fancy women in boots. I like high heels on a woman, suits her. Shows her legs off.'

Why is it, I felt like asking him, that middle-aged scruffs with a beer gut like Les, liked their women to dress to the nines but made not the slightest effort themselves? Why, in addition, did they think that glamorous fashion-conscious women would be interested in them? I didn't ask partly because I didn't want to alienate Les any further. I wanted information from him. Not that an ego like his was easily dented. But mostly I didn't ask him because he wouldn't have understood the question. Les probably sincerely considered himself a gift to the female of the species.

The pub was filling up and the noise level rising. I didn't want to shout so was forced to snuggle closer to speak in his ear. It probably looked very cosy to the regulars up at the bar.

'Now, Les,' I began. 'I'm not a copper. You can talk to me.'

'You're a copper's mate,' he said, edging away. 'Everyone knows you're pally with that woman inspector, even if you ain't her eyes and ears.' He lifted the glass so that he held it between us like a demarcation line. 'I ain't got anything to talk to you about, girl.'

'I'm not even a copper's mate. You want reminding who I am? I'm the patsy who was left to find the body, remember now?'

'Nothing to do with me!' he said promptly and buried his face in the glass.

I waited until even he couldn't pretend it wasn't now drained. 'I don't like being used like that, Les.'

'No, well, you wouldn't . . .' he agreed unhappily and signalled to the bar.

I knew what the signal meant. Help!

The barman was there in a flash. 'Need another, Les?' He scooped up the glass and gave me a warning look.

'Er, yus, same again,' Les muttered.

'What about your lady friend?' asked the barman, 'or is she just leaving?'

I leaned forward and met the barman's gaze. 'No, she isn't,' I said. 'And Les is big enough to look after himself, right? I'm fine with the drink I've got.'

'Yeah, yeah, she's all right,' muttered the hapless Les, now as red as a beetroot.

'Suit yourself,' said the barman and departed.

'What do you want to do that for?' growled Les. 'Embarrassing me like that?'

'Come off it, Les!' I told him. 'Just answer my questions and I'll be out of here. You can sit here for the rest of the night and with luck you might even meet a woman wearing stiletto heels. But talking of embarrassing situations, let's get back to the one I found myself in when I stumbled over Duane Gardner, as dead as a dodo with a bruise on the back of his head and a socking great needle puncture in his arm.'

A fresh pint appeared before Les and the barman whisked away back to his bar before he had to make eye contact with either of us.

'As Gawd is my witness,' said Les pitifully, 'I never knew anything like that was going down, honest.'

Bingo! So he did know something and I was ready to bet a pound to a penny it had to do with the set of office keys he held – or had held. Susie had surely taken them back into safe keeping or got the locks changed by now and declined to supply him with a new set.

I patted his arm in commiseration and he was so sunk in self-pity he didn't even recoil. 'No, Les, of course you didn't.'

'Old Duane was a mate,' snuffled Les, getting lachrymose. He hadn't had time to drink much with me but I doubted the pint I'd bought him had been the first of the day. 'And we worked together, didn't we? He trusted me.'

More fool Duane, but there, that wasn't his problem now. 'And anyway,' Les was saying, 'I can't be getting into anything like that, can I? I can't have the cops coming round my place and acting like they think I'm up to my neck in something.' Now he leaned towards me and I got a blast of beery breath. 'See, between you and me, darling, I got form.'

'Have you, Les?' I asked, all innocent surprise, as if I'd never suspected.

'Only old stuff!' he hastened to insist. 'I got into a bit of trouble when I was younger. Like kids do, you know. But the cops they never forget, like bleeding elephants they are. They got everything on their records. Use computers these days. It's no use telling them that any trouble you got in when you were a kid was just larking about, being silly. They act like a bloke's a criminal.'

'What sort of trouble?' I had an idea that Les's description of youngsters 'larking about' was a pretty liberal interpretation of events.

'Oh, nuffin' heavy,' Les urged. 'I used to hang round with my mates on match days, we'd go out looking for the other teams' supporters and jump on 'em. A bit of a punch-up, you know. They gave as good as they got. A few times there was a bit of crowd trouble inside the grounds, up in the stands, and I happened to be in the middle of it, just by bad luck. But like I said, it was years ago.'

So here I sat with an ageing ex-football hooligan with a record of convictions for affray and assault. Well, I wasn't interested in ancient history, just the very recent sort.

'So what happened about the keys, Les?' I asked in a kindly tone as used by Sister Mary Joseph when a six-year-old limped in from the playground with bloodied knees. (Whatever the explanation it was inevitably followed by: 'Ah, well, it's your own fault then, so it is. Let it be a lesson to you. Now sit down and stop squalling.')

'Did you lend them to someone?' I coaxed.

'No!' His voice rose in a horrified squawk attracting more curious looks from the regulars. 'No,' he repeated in lower tones but just as vehemently. 'I never lent 'em to no one. But I did, well, mislay 'em for twenty-four hours. I found them again, mind you.'

I invited him to tell me about it. He extracted a promise from me not to tell Susie. I think he was more frightened of Susie than of the police. He wouldn't be getting too much work from Lottie now and he couldn't afford to lose another employer.

'Where was this and when?' I asked.

'It was just a bit of bad luck, not my fault nor nothing. These things happen and I put it right. I got 'em back.' He frowned. 'I hadn't used them for a couple of days but they were in my coat pocket, or I thought they were. You know I recognised old Duane from your description of him. You also know that with Susie not having any work for me, I had to go out looking to see if anyone else had a job for me. Eventually I got out to Teddington. I didn't go to the house. It was getting late. I knew where Duane did his drinking so I went there – and found him. I told him about you asking around about him. He was grateful, like I said. He bought me a whisky.'

Here Les gazed a little resentfully at the beer glass.

'And the keys?'

'Oh, yes. It was hot in there, that place where he was drinking. So I took off my coat and just hung it over the back of my chair.

I reckon what happened was, the keys fell out of my pocket then and they musta landed on the floor. Only I didn't know, did I? I didn't see them lying there because it wasn't very well lit. I wouldn't have heard 'em fall because of all the chatter going on round us. It's a poncey sort of place, all dim lights and fancy food if you want a bite. No sausage and beans, just cass-oo-let.'

'Cassoulet, Les. It's very nice.'

'It's French,' said Les grimly. 'What's wrong with sausage and beans?'

It wasn't the time to discuss international cuisine. 'When did you miss the keys, Les?'

'I didn't,' he said honestly. 'Not right off. I missed them the next day, after old Duane met his end, poor bugger. Susie asked me about them. I put my hand in my pocket and they wasn't there! I didn't let on to Susie. I swore to her they had never been out of my keeping. She was in a fair old state herself and she didn't ask actually to see them, right? It was a near thing, that. I thought that at any minute she would. Usually she's as sharp as a needle but what had happened threw her a bit. The police had been making a nuisance of themselves.'

'Well, when there's a murder . . .' I couldn't help murmuring.

Sarcasm was wasted on him. 'Yeah, you're right. The minute you got a stiff on your hands you can't move for uniforms and plain-clothes. Them SOCO fellers, too, they get in all over the place, looking for fingerprints, scraping up bloodstains. They hoover the dust outa your carpet, you know. They really turned Suze's office over, sealed it off and went through it like a dose of salts. That Michael upstairs, him with the nasty needle, he was doing his nut 'cos he couldn't get up the staircase to his own place.'

'Susie told me,' I said, stopping this flow of information. Les might not like the police but the way they went about their work clearly fascinated him. Probably he had been on hand a few times to observe it.

I was intrigued by his reference to Michael's tattooing activities and wondered if this was based on a less than successful visit to the parlour by Les. But if Les had tattoos, I didn't want to see them.

Les was shaking his head, still wondering at the thoroughness of the Met. Then he got back to the matter in hand. 'Anyhow, I knew I had to find those keys quick before either Susie or the plods asked me to produce 'em. I thought I must have left them at home, so I went straight to my place and hunted everywhere without luck. I was getting panicky, I don't mind telling you. I tried to think where I could have lost them. Then I remembered putting my coat down in the bar where I was drinking with Duane and his mate.'

I sat up so suddenly I nearly tipped the table over. Les made a grab for his glass.

'You didn't say anything about Duane drinking with a mate when you found him!' I said. 'You just said you found him in a place where he drank regularly.'

'Yes, that's right.' He looked at me in a puzzled way. 'He wasn't drinking alone. Nothing odd in that.'

'So tell me about the person he was with, man or woman?'

'Man,' said Les promptly. 'Snappy, stroppy city type. Didn't take a shine to him at all. He looked at me like I was going to ask him for a hand-out.'

Adam Ferrier. So Adam had known almost from the first that I was interested in Edna and that I had spotted Duane outside the Tube station.

I had been silent for longer than usual so Les was getting

curious. 'Do you want to know how I got the keys back or not?'

'Of course I do.' I rallied to the present and pushed aside the interesting line of thought that was developing fast in my brain.

'After I'd looked everywhere else, like I was saying, I began to think I might have lost them out at Teddington in that pub. So I went out there and asked the barman if any keys had been handed in. Funny thing, he told me, not twenty minutes earlier someone had come in and handed over some keys. He didn't know who it was. It was a girl, that's all he could say.'

'A girl!'

Les blinked. 'Yes, that's all I know. The girl said she'd found the keys on the floor there. She'd picked them up thinking they were her boyfriend's but it had turned out they weren't so she'd brought them back.'

But not before they had been used, I thought grimly. Fran, I told myself, you've been made a fool of.

I got to my feet and Les looked relieved.

'You going? Right, then. Here, you promised not to tell Susie!'

'I won't.'

'Nor the cops?' he added belatedly with an anxious grimace.

'Listen to me, Les,' I told him. 'The very best thing you can do is go to Inspector Morgan and tell her all about the keys being out of your possession for the vital twenty-four hours. You can tell her you were unwilling to upset Susie Duke and that's why you didn't own up straightaway. But the longer you keep quiet about it, the worse it will be when the cops do find out. If they pick up someone for Duane's murder the first thing they'll ask the killer is, how did he get in? You might keep quiet. You can't be sure the murderer or his accomplice will.'

'Accomplice?' asked Les, startled.

'The girl who handed the keys in.'

'Oh, yes, her,' said Les, 'I'd forgotten her.'

So had I.

I sometimes feel it takes the quiet of the night and the darkness to get my brain working. I lie there with Bonnie snoring at my feet and the ideas begin to flicker through my imagination with the rapidity of a magic lantern show. Bonnie does have a basket, by the way, but she sneaks out of it and hops up on the bed as soon as she judges I'm asleep and won't know.

That night, after the visit to Edna and the events of the day leading up to it, together with the revealing conversation with Les, my poor brain went into overdrive and fairly buzzed. I wasn't sorry for it because it distracted me from the ache in my shoulder. I must have landed on it when I threw myself to the ground to escape the motorcyclist.

The pieces of the puzzle were beginning to slot together but there were still gaps and also some of my conjectures were leading me down some murky and doubtful paths.

One thing was becoming very clear to me: from the moment poor Duane Gardner and I met at Golders Green and sat talking in that café, he was a doomed man. In fact we both became marked out as threats to someone's plans. It had started even earlier than that, I mused, when I went to Susie's agency and expressed curiosity about the man in the white baseball cap I'd seen watching an elderly ex-bag lady. Duane wasn't supposed to have attracted anyone's attention and no one was expected to ask any questions. That the contrary had happened had alarmed someone deeply.

Even so, why should anyone worry about me, who had just appeared on the very outer edge of Duane's enquiries? Because, I told the darkness, I revealed to Duane not only that I'd known

Edna for some time, but that I still had a personal interest in her. That made me an unknown quantity and caught everyone on the hop.

Duane had either reported the unwelcome development to Adam Ferrier or to someone else. Or Ferrier had found out about it the evening Les had come to the bar, where Adam and Duane were drinking, to tout for business and incidentally to warn Duane about me. Les wasn't to know Duane and I had already met again in Golders Green. But Duane, after Les left them, expressed his belief to Adam that I was also professionally employed to check on Edna. With Les telling them that I was a familiar face at the Duke Detective Agency it must have looked like confirmation.

But was Adam the only person Duane had told? Had Adam picked up the keys which fell from Les's pocket after Les had gone, and realised what they were? Had he slipped them into his own pocket without Duane's knowledge and then suggested to Duane that they might go to the Duke Detective Agency early the next morning and confront me?'

But here my reasoning met a fork in the road. Clearly, someone, at that point, decided to kill two birds with one stone: in Duane's case literally to remove him and in my case, to carry out the foul deed on the premises of the Duke Agency. I would become enmeshed in police enquiries and my watch over Edna disrupted.

But why should it worry Adam – or indeed anyone else – that someone was apparently interested in Edna? Ferrier might be surprised, even puzzled, but *alarmed*? Frightened, even, so much so that he determined there and then to do something drastic about it? More particularly, why on earth would he consider removing from the scene the private detective he had himself hired? Merely because of a perceived incompetence? The answer to that would be to sack him; although it wasn't Duane's fault I'd met Edna outside the Tube station. No, if Duane had been murdered because of his involvement, or so I reasoned, it wasn't just because he had met me. There had to be some other motive inspiring the killer's decision and I couldn't for the life of me imagine what reason Ferrier could have.

So back I came to my second question: who had killed Duane? If Adam had no motive, who did?

Duane was a good detective . . . Lottie's tribute to her late boyfriend echoed in my head. Why did it seem to me that the clue to it all lay in that?

Bonnie was rumbling softly in her sleep. Her imagination works actively at night, too. She dreams a lot. Her paws and nose twitch. She mumbles and mutters in a series of doggy squeaks and mini-growls.

'See 'em off, girl!' I told her. For good measure, I added, '*You'd* better see them off, too, Fran, whoever they are.'

I fell asleep. But my brain must still have been working on autopilot because in the early hours I awoke and sat up with a start, dislodging Bonnie who gave a startled yelp.

'Bonnie,' I said to her. 'It's not always what you see. Sometimes it's what you don't see.'

Bonnie gave a sulky little growl and began to turn round and round, flattening herself a new spot. If I was going to start rambling in the middle of the night, she didn't want to hear it.

But I got very little sleep after that.

Chapter Fourteen

It was time to rattle some old bones. There is no better place to do it than the Family Records Office in Islington.

Mind you, it would be no use my going to any such place to track down my remote ancestors. They were born and buried in Hungary and all I knew of them was from a garbled tale or two recounted by Grandma when she'd been at the apricot liqueur. She had a strong romantic vein in her and might have invented half the tales she told me. According to her our family had once been wealthy landowners. She painted a picture of rolling *puszta* and whitewashed villages, dusty roads and ox-carts and handsome horsemen. She had a few sepia portraits of uniformed figures to prove it – but you can buy old photographs from stalls in antiques markets and I caught her out a couple of times giving different names to the individuals shown. Perhaps she was just getting muddled. Perhaps the bloke with the tight collar and carnation wasn't my grandfather. Perhaps I've always been suspicious by nature. Anyway, true or not, they were good stories. Probably we had all really lived in a boring suburb of Pest, rattling to work nine to five on the trams. There's a sort of heroism in that. About the only thing I do know is that my grandfather was a doctor. Was he the first in the family? Were his parents proud of his achievement? Don't ask me; I'll never find out.

But at the Records office, if you've been born, married or died in England or Wales, you're there. People can find you if they look hard enough and the day I went there the place was stuffed with people looking. There they were, rattling bones like mad. They were seeking out the marriages of people who had been newly-weds when Victoria and Albert were chasing each other around Windsor Great Park. They were requesting certificates so that they could decipher the spiky signatures and gaze on the pathetic laborious 'marks' of the illiterate, which briefly clothed the bones but tantalisingly revealed nothing of the people themselves. Were those marriages happy? Was the arrival of all those babies whose births are recorded here greeted with joy? Were the families recorded as all living at one address on a Victorian census form dwelling in harmony or did the atmosphere seethe with resentment and despair? What old sins and scandals were hinted at? Who had fathered the illegitimate child born to the sixteen-year-old girl whose mother had made a second marriage to a younger man? What on earth did all those obscure causes of death on ancient certificates mean? What misery and pain were indicated by a lingering illness without modern medicines to help? In short, what did the diligent researchers here think they would discover? Why were they all so keen to track down their ancestors?

Probably, like my grandma, they had peopled their imaginations with romantic figures dashing around doing gallant deeds and making fortunes. The reality was more likely to be that if they tracked down anyone, it would be some mild little clerk like Bob Cratchit. But it would be nice to think that even if you are nobody particular, still at some future date someone will spend all day trying to find out when you were born or got married or pegged out.

I told the girl at the counter what I wanted to look up and was directed to shelves and shelves of index volumes. I was there all day, partly because I was sidetracked for a while into looking up my own parents' marriage and my own birth. That sort of research-fever is catching. I had to be stern with myself and stick to looking for what I'd come here to find. I was worn out when I went to meet Ganesh that evening but elated, too, because I was sure I had struck gold.

'I haven't got any birth or marriage certificates or anything,' I said to him as we wandered up the green swell of Primrose Hill to escape the bricks and tarmac. We didn't escape people, the grassy area was filled with them and their dogs, but everyone was relaxing: walking, talking, unwinding. We reached the top and stood there looking across at Regent's Park and at the city skyscape beyond it. 'You have to send away for certificates and it costs money.'

'No proof, then,' said Ganesh dampeningly.

'I had to search the indexes and cross-reference everything, deleting the ones that didn't match up.'

'Indices,' said Ganesh pedantically. 'The plural of index is indices.'

'They've got miles of them there and they call them indexes. They should know.'

'It's sloppy usage.'

'It took me ages,' I went on, ignoring him, 'but in the end I established that in 1957 a Lilian Walters married a Roger Forester at Kingston-on-Thames. I don't suppose she was the only Lilian Walters in the world or old Roger the only Forester male getting hitched at the same time. But that they got hitched to one another makes me sure.'

Ganesh turned slowly to face me, hands in pockets. He wasn't going to let me see it but I knew he was almost as wired by the information as I was.

'You are trying to tell me that Lilian, Lottie Forester's grandmother, and Edna were sisters?'

'You bet they were. You remember Edna talking about her sister to us in hospital? Her sister was a few years older than Edna and very fashion-conscious. She was probably dating Roger at the time. Edna watched Big Sis Lilian making sure her stocking seams were straight before she went off to meet her beau.'

Ganesh frowned. 'Does Lottie know this? Did Duane know it? Is that how Duane got to find Edna?'

'Isn't that the million-pound question?' I retorted. 'I can't believe Lottie knows absolutely nothing. But I do know she's said not a word to me about it, neither has Adam. Why did Adam take his grandfather's search request to Duane and Lottie's agency? Just because Lottie was an old flame or because he also knew that Edna was Lottie's great-aunt? They've been holding out on me, Gan.'

Ganesh was nodding slowly. 'You need to get out of this affair, Fran. Right now.'

I stared at him in astonishment because it was the last thing I'd expected to hear from him. '*Now?*' I squeaked. 'Now when I'm getting somewhere at last?'

'You don't know where you're getting,' he pointed out. 'But you do know now this is family business. I don't understand it any more than you do. But families I do understand. They won't tell you anything, Fran, because you're an outsider, not one of them. They don't want you knowing their business and they will do anything to make sure you keep your nose out of it.'

'Like one of them running me down on a motorbike?' I countered. 'Or trying to run down Edna?'

There was a silence. I knew as the words left my mouth that they were disasterous. But too late.

Ganesh stepped back to survey me better and a faint air of smug triumph crossed his face. 'I knew it!' he said. 'I knew something had happened you hadn't told me about. All that business back at the hospital asking the old lady if she'd seen anyone else around when she had the near miss with the motorcyclist. Come on, out with it!'

I had no choice. I told him about my own near miss.

'I didn't want to worry you, Ganesh,' I said humbly. 'So I didn't tell you and I asked Morgan not to mention it.'

'Rubbish. You didn't want me to know you'd got in way over your head. Not that I didn't suspect it already. How many more good reasons do you want to drop your enquiries? Leave the whole thing to the police, can't you? I don't want to wind up visiting you *and* Edna in hospital!'

He was angry but he was really worried to think I'd been in danger. An apology was in order for keeping him in the dark. I delivered one handsomely.

'And now will you promise me to stop meddling in this?' he demanded passionately.

'I can't, Ganesh. If they were after me before, they are still after me now. They missed me once. They may try again. They will try to get Edna again. Why should they want to kill her? And why is Culpeper so interested? Is *he* in danger? I'd hate to think that vulnerable old man has a dangerous enemy. I don't mind telling you I'm really pleased he's shut up in that house and can't get out. No one can get in either – the place is like Fort Knox.'

Ganesh said slowly, 'If this is down to people close to the principals in the case, being shut away is no guarantee of safety *if* anyone means him harm. On the other hand, as so few people have access to him, the list of suspects would be pretty short and the police would be checking them all out before you could say "inside job".'

'Let's hope you're right,' I said, not convinced.

'Culpeper may even be a part of the conspiracy, for all you know', Ganesh went on.

I sighed. 'That's the worst thing. They may all be in this together. Culpeper may not have his legs but he has his brain and likes to control things. Well, I don't scare off easy. They may think it's family business. I think it's mine.'

'I know you do,' he said. 'So are you going to tell Morgan?'

'No,' I said and seeing his mouth opening in protest, I went on quickly, '*You* are.'

'Me?' he was horrified. 'Leave me out of it.'

'Please, Gan! I haven't got time to go and see her. I've something else I've got to do first, just to make sure I'm not doing like my grandma and making it all up.'

'You might be creating all this out of a handful of very thin clues. Goodness only knows how your imagination works but it seems to go crazy at the drop of a hat,' said Ganesh dolefully. He frowned. 'What's your grandmother got to do with it?'

'If *I* go to Morgan she'll tell me to stay home and do nothing and let her take over. I won't be able to refuse her because it will be an official request. So the only way I can do it is by *you* going to her and gaining me a little more time. Please, Ganesh.'

'I can't just take time off in the middle of the morning and leave the shop,' he argued.

'Why not? Business is slow. Hari owes you some time off, anyway.'

'Hari doesn't believe in anyone having time off. But you are right; he does owe it to me.'

There was a silence. A pair of large dogs appeared and frolicked round us. Ganesh looked alarmed but luckily the owner called them back and they lolloped off. Ganesh relaxed.

'What's this very important thing you've got to do?' he asked. 'If I go to see Morgan, where will you be going?'

'To Teddington. To Fulwell, actually, to Lottie's place.'

'You're going to confront her? Look, Fran, this really isn't a good idea. If she's kept information from you deliberately she's going to be anything but pleased to find out you know it.'

I shook my head. 'No, I'm going to take a very discreet look around. Don't worry, Ganesh, I will be very, very careful.'

'That'll be a first,' said Ganesh. 'I can't stop you. But I will go and see Morgan and tell her where you've gone. That's not because I want to oblige you by winning you more time to get into serious trouble . . . but because you'll go to Teddington anyway and I'd rather Morgan knew it.'

'Give me the time,' I begged. 'Don't tell her before I've had a chance to look the place over. And don't worry, I will keep out of everyone's way.'

Chapter Fifteen

I got up early. To be honest I'd hardly slept. I lay awake thinking out my strategy and hopped out of bed raring to go. It was too soon to knock on Erwin's door and wake him to ask if he'd take Bonnie. I knew he'd been playing at a gig for most of the previous night and hadn't come home until about three in the morning. I'd heard the slam of the van door and the farewells of his band buddies. So there was nothing to it but take her over to the newsagent's and ask if I could leave her in the storeroom at the back.

We set off round there at a brisk trot but when we got to the supermarket which was the cause of all Hari's woes Bonnie and I came to an abrupt halt. Blue and white tape across the entrance announced this was a crime scene. A notice on the door apologised to customers for temporary closure. Inside I could see a couple of figures at the far end of the place by Dairy Products but they weren't stacking shelves. One was writing in a notebook and the other, in a managerial white shirt and tie, was waving his arms around.

I barrelled into Hari's shop agog with curiosity.

Hari, busy serving a small queue of customers, beamed at me above their heads.

'Ah, Francesca, my dear! Ganesh is in the stockroom! Yes, yes, twenty Silk Cut . . .'

Bonnie and I shot through to the stockroom where I demanded, 'What's happened at the supermarket?'

Ganesh looked round at me. His face was haggard as if he hadn't slept either. He certainly wasn't sharing Hari's good humour. 'Oh, that,' he said. 'They had a break-in. The robbers got in round the back somehow and moved out all the wines and spirits. They had a go at breaking through the grille protecting the cigarettes but the alarms were going by then and they had to scarper. Hari and I heard the din about three in the morning and we didn't get any sleep after that. Cops have been there since early on. They must be nearly finished now.'

'So, how long do they reckon they'll be closed?'

'Oh, I shouldn't think more than one day. Then all the customers will go back there and we'll be doing no business again. But for today Hari is dead chuffed to see all the punters come back even if only temporarily. He's hoping it won't be temporary. He argues that when they realise they have been missing the personal service they get here, they won't go back to the supermarket. Hari's idea of personal service being what it is, I wouldn't bet on that. Anyway, he's shaking his head and lamenting the high incidence of crime, but he's beaming from ear to ear at the same time.'

'It's an ill wind,' I observed. 'Bad luck for the supermarket, though, and not a nice thing to know people are hanging about the area breaking into places.'

'We don't stock booze,' said Ganesh laconically. 'And there aren't enough cigarettes in there –' he indicated the shop – 'to make it worth their while bothering us. We get light-fingered kids but that's about it. The supermarket is part of a chain. The chap who runs it is only a manager. It's not like it's his business and they've got insurance against that sort of thing. It will affect his receipts, of course. Main thing is, no one is hurt, isn't it?'

'I must say, you're pretty laid back about it.'

'It's got nothing to do with me. I'm not Hari. Sorry if I can't get delirious over a minor break-in on another premises.'

Oh, dear, sour mood. Hari chirpy: Ganesh glum. It seemed to be always the way. They were like those toy figures predicting the weather. One comes out of the little wooden house when it rains and as soon as it clears up, the other comes out but the first one shoots back inside.

'OK if I leave Bonnie while I go out to Teddington?' I asked.

'You're going through with it, then?' Ganesh folded his arms and leaned back against a shelf stacked with bottled water.

'Yes, and you're going to see Morgan and tell her what I found out, aren't you? You said you would, only don't rush off and do it before I've had a chance to get out to Teddington and do what I want to do.'

Ganesh eyed me rather as though I was some sort of display offering discounted chocolate bars and he wasn't quite sure where in the shop I'd be positioned to best advantage.

'I'll take an early lunch break. Hari will kick up a fuss because we're busy for once, but I'll go. What will you do if you run into this dodgy female or that bloke, Ferrier?'

'If I do find myself face to face with Lottie, then I'll catch her off guard. I'll put it to her point blank and see what sort of explanation she comes up with. She's held out on me. I am supposed to be working with her on this. As for Ferrier, he won't be around. He works in the city. He'll be sweating away on his next bonus.'

'Make sure *you're* not caught off guard,' he warned.

Hari called to him at that point and I was spared further delay.

I settled Bonnie in the storeroom and promised her that when all this was over, I wouldn't keep dumping her nearly every day while I went off and did interesting things without her. She stared at me with reproachful brown eyes, sighed and settled down on her cardboard bed, her shiny black nose resting on her forepaws. She knows how to make me feel guilty.

I retreated through the shop at indecent speed, waving an airy hand at Hari who was busy selling ciggies to a labourer in a yellow jacket. The jacket was smeared with black streaks and reeked of something chemical. I hoped when the guy lit up one of his fags he didn't combust. Hari was looking at the customer as if he feared he might incinerate the shop.

I spent the train journey out to Teddington thinking what I'd be doing if I were Lottie. I wouldn't stay in the house the whole day, of that I was fairly sure. I doubted she was doing any detecting at the moment. She was never the one who went out and hoofed it round the streets digging out the dirt. She sat back in the office and kept the books straight. She wouldn't know where to start doing the practical stuff and she'd have to look for another business partner for that. She still had Les to call on, of course, but I had the feeling she'd be calling on Les somewhat less. But she was on her own, there wouldn't be any book-keeping or telephoning to speak of – and she must miss having someone there to talk to. Time would be heavy on her hands and I was sure she'd go out, either up to town to trawl the big stores or maybe to meet a pal for lunch somewhere. I had been careful when getting off the train at the Fulwell stop to watch out for her. My luck had held and she wasn't hanging about on the platform. I had, just in case, taken the precaution of donning Susie's black wig again. It wouldn't have fooled Lottie close up, any more than it had fooled Duane for more than a few minutes, but the chances were she wouldn't look that closely – if she did happen to be there.

Trusting to the wig, I walked briskly down the street past the house without slowing or showing any interest in it. There was some sort of brightly coloured advertising circular sticking out of the letter box. I couldn't see anyone going from house to house distributing the leaflets so I reckoned it had been there a while and Lottie wasn't there to remove it. The one thing which might interfere with my carefully calculated scenario was if she was out back in the kitchen busy painting the walls duck-egg blue in preparation for the ceremonial hanging of Duane's portrait. But I was inclined to bet she would keep that for the evenings.

Nevertheless, I had to be sure. I would watch the house for a little while and see if there was any sign of life at a window or any callers.

It's not a simple thing to keep watch even on a supposedly empty house in a residential street, especially one in a fairly prosperous area. Neighbourhood Watch fanatics are peering from behind their blinds and au pair girls are ringing their employers or the police to insist in fractured English that someone is planning to kidnap them and force them into the sex trade.

I couldn't therefore position myself right opposite Lottie's place but there was a small café down the road on a corner. I went in and found I was the only customer as they had just opened up. They looked a bit surprised. I asked if they did breakfasts. They didn't do fry-ups, they told me. They could manage croissants and coffee if I didn't mind just waiting for a bit until the croissants arrived. I was delighted to wait a bit and settled myself at a window where I could see down the street and just about keep Lottie's front door in view if no one parked in front of it.

I could see that the woman behind the café counter was a little bit suspicious of me so I went out of my way to chat to her cheerfully and tell her I was out looking for a flat in the area and the best way to do that was to explore it first, wasn't it?

She agreed. 'It's a nice area to live in, dear, but the rents are high.' She set down my coffee which smelled fresh and delicious. 'You could advertise in the local press,' she said. 'Or there is a newsagent in the next street might put up a card for you.'

'I might get some funny replies,' I said direly, as one who had learned from bitter experience.

'That's true,' she admitted. She retired to dust off her rock buns.

I sipped my coffee and then let out a yelp.

'All right?' asked the café woman anxiously. 'It is a bit hot.'

I assured her I was fine. It wasn't hot coffee that had caused my involuntary exclamation. It was the sight of Lottie, outside in the street. Well, so much for all my elaborate deductions about her catching the train into town. Just as well I hadn't walked straight on to the property. She *had* been in the house. I hadn't been prepared for her sudden appearance. I was barely settled in and the croissants hadn't turned up yet. I leaned back away from the window and prayed she wasn't coming into the café too. But no, she was all kitted out in a tracksuit with her hair tied up in that bandanna affair. She broke into a steady jog as she went past the café, then carried on down the street in the general direction of the golf course. I would be surprised if they allowed her to pursue her exercise routine on their hallowed turf but wherever she had gone, I guessed she'd be gone for a while.

I got up and went to pay for my coffee. 'Nice coffee. I'll come back for the croissants later,' I said.

'Good luck!' called the woman as I left.

I remembered I was house-hunting and thanked her.

I could not be sure the woman at the café might not come to the window and watch which way I went, so I took myself off briskly in the opposite direction to Lottie's place, made a tour of the block and came back to approach the house from the other direction.

I tried to look as normal as possible as if I had every right to enter the premises. I ignored the front door and walked down the side of the house towards the detached garage at the end of the drive. I saw as I approached it that it was padlocked.

Surely I wasn't to be foiled by something as basic as a padlock? I prowled round the garage's exterior walls. There was a small dusty window in one side overlooking the neglected garden. Beneath it in an untidy pile was a job lot of gardener's hardware: a rusty lawn roller, stacks of empty plant pots, plastic sacks which had contained compost and now seemed to contain rubbish and propped against it all an ancient wooden sawhorse. You know the sort of thing: it's constructed from a pair of X-shaped ends with a bar between them. I dragged it out, trying not to pepper my hands with splinters, and gave it an experimental shake. It seemed solid enough to support my weight. I'm not that big. I hauled aside a couple of the rubbish sacks to make more room beneath the window. It was only a matter of time before someone looked out of a neighbour's window and spotted me so I had to act fast. If challenged I'd try and get away with telling anyone interested that I was being paid to clear out the garden. I scrambled cautiously up onto the sawhorse. It groaned in protest and one of the X joints gave an ominous little crack.

The ground beneath it was soft and the horse shifted without warning so that I wobbled dangerously and grabbed at the windowsill. I didn't want to spend any more time up here than I had to. My precarious perch might give way at any minute. I pressed my face against the cobweb-festooned glass panes. At first I couldn't make out anything in the gloom inside the garage. And then my eyes adjusted to the poor light, I caught a gleam of polished metal and there it was: a lovingly maintained powerful motorcycle.

It was what I had hoped to see, the last little thing which would tell me I was absolutely on the right track now.

'Well, well, Fran,' said a voice behind me. 'Scouting round prior to doing a bit of burglary? Allow me to help you down.'

It was Adam Ferrier.

Chapter Sixteen

I felt a fool and I felt angry. What was worse, I was momentarily stumped. I had very little time to concoct a plausible explanation. But it wouldn't wash, whatever I said. He knew exactly what I had been looking for – and exactly what I'd seen.

As I jumped down the sawhorse toppled away beneath me and I lurched forward to land inelegantly in his arms. He took hold of my elbow in a very professional policeman's hold, pushing the shoulder joint upward so that it was almost impossible to twist away. I wondered where he'd learned it or maybe experienced it.

'We'll go into the kitchen,' he said, 'and wait there for Lottie to come back.'

He pushed me towards the back door and, still keeping a tight grip on my elbow, fished a bunch of house keys from his pocket.

'Oh,' I gasped, 'so you've got the keys to Lottie's house, too? You're a great one for collecting keys, aren't you?'

'Shut up!' he said in a cold little voice and pushed me through the opened door.

It was at that moment I felt the first small spurt of fear pushing aside all the other emotions I'd experienced when he'd discovered me teetering on that sawhorse. Now I realised I wasn't just in his power alone but at the mercy of them both. They had worked together in a neat little conspiracy. They wouldn't allow me to let the world know about it. If Adam had sounded angry I would have worried less; but that cold little voice reminded me I was dealing with a killer.

My ever-active imagination raced ahead. How would they do it? As they dealt with Duane, with a hypodermic? I saw my body being found in some deserted spot. How would I be identified? Would they leave Ganesh's mobile phone on me? Would my photo appear on television crime prevention programmes? Would the woman at the corner café remember me as the girl who never came back for the croissants?

'Take a seat,' invited Adam with a sarcastic grimace. 'Take off your wig and make yourself at home, why don't you?'

I sat down at the kitchen table. The room smelled of fresh paint. Lottie had made a start but hadn't got very far. What looked like an experimental few brush strokes decorated the surround of the door frame. Perhaps she'd abandoned the work because she hadn't liked the colour, after all. I can't say duck-egg blue is my favourite shade.

Adam seated himself near me, where he could cover any attempt I might make at escape either through the back door or into the hall towards the front door.

'Why aren't you doing something financial in the city?' I asked resentfully. 'What are you doing here this morning?'

I pulled off the wig, not because he had suggested it but because it made my scalp sweaty and scratchy. Glad to be free of it, I tossed it on the table as nonchalantly as possible and it lay there looking like some sort of road kill.

He raised his eyebrows. 'What am *I* doing here? Oughtn't I to be asking you that?'

I tried to brazen it through. Fat chance of success, I knew, but

I had to try. It's the actor in me. 'I came to see Lottie. She's not here. I took a look round the garden. It was just curiosity.'

'Curiosity killed the cat,' said Ferrier unpleasantly.

Well, it didn't matter if he believed my explanation or not. Once he knew I'd seen the motorbike, *how* I'd come to see it was immaterial. He wasn't a fool, though. He knew I hadn't taken a sudden interest in gardening.

His mind was running on, too.

'What tipped you off?' he asked with a frown.

I pointed at the wall behind him but he didn't turn his head. 'She took the family photographs down,' I said. 'She should have left them there. I noticed them when I first came into this kitchen and talked about her grandmother. She realised afterwards that I might remember enough about that wedding photo of her grandmother to spot a likeness to Edna, the next time I saw Edna. They were sisters, weren't they, Lilian and Edna, I mean?'

'Had you,' he asked, without answering my question, 'spotted a likeness?'

'No, not then. She needn't have worried. I probably wouldn't even have looked at them again. But when she took them down it got me wondering. I didn't buy into the story of hanging a memorial photograph of old Duane up there. That's his motorbike, isn't it, out there in the garage all nicely locked away from prying eyes? His pride and joy, I bet.'

This time he nodded. 'Yes, the poor sap fancied himself as a ton-up boy in black leathers. He used to take it out at weekends and burn rubber down to Brighton or Bournemouth or some such seaside spot. Sometimes Lottie went with him pillion but she wasn't keen on travelling like that.'

'But she did ride it herself from time to time?' I raised my eyebrows. 'As you've been riding it since Duane hung up his leathers for the last time, thanks to you.'

He still said nothing.

'I'm guessing you were riding it when Edna was nearly knocked down and Lottie was riding the day I was the target. Only it didn't quite work either time, did it? Killing Duane was the easy part. Getting rid of Edna and me has proved a bit harder, hasn't it?'

Adam smiled then and I rather wished he hadn't. 'Practice makes perfect,' he said. 'I'll get it right next time – which will be fairly soon.'

My only hope, as I could see it at the moment, was that he wanted to wait for Lottie to come back and she might have a different idea. His unwillingness to act without her told me that she made the decisions. One of them had been that they should kill her boyfriend and business partner. My blood seemed to stop circulating for a moment. I think I must have looked my horror because Adam smiled again. He probably thought I was contemplating my own death. But I was thinking of Duane and of Lottie's treachery. It's happened before that love's died and, when it hasn't been easy for one party to disentangle him or herself, then murder has suggested itself as a solution. The lurid details make a double feature in the tabloid press. Usually it's a shotgun blast in a lonely farmhouse turned luxury home. This time it had been a syringe in the arm in Susie Duke's office.

'I suppose,' I said, 'Lottie and Duane never really had that much in common, other than a desire to set up this agency.'

'You met him,' Adam said with a dismissive shrug.

'Whereas you were an old flame who had come back into her life. You are doing well and living in Docklands and your elderly infirm grandfather is worth a few millions. Suddenly, Duane was inconvenient. Even more inconveniently, he was a *good* detective. I mean he wasn't just efficient; he was honourable, too.'

'He was a prat,' said Adam.

There are people who see having a conscience as a weakness and Adam was clearly one of them.

'You had a bit of luck,' I mused, 'being there when Les came to tell Duane about me. Even luckier, Les managed to lose the Duke Agency's keys at the same time. How did you know they were the keys to Susie's office?'

'Les,' said Adam thoughtfully, 'the bruiser with the personal hygiene problem? Yes, I saw the keys on the floor and was going to call after him, but then I saw the wally had tied a little tag on them reading "Duke". No address or anything but they had to be the office keys. I suddenly saw that Fate was playing into my hands. It all seemed rather *meant*, you know. I just slipped them into my pocket. Duane was up at the bar and didn't see.'

'You and Lottie plotted together,' I said dully. 'Lottie phoned Susie Duke to arrange a set-up meeting to get her out of the office. You, meantime, persuaded Duane that a visit to the Duke Agency to confront me there or to quiz the owner might be a good idea. So he went trustingly with you to what, you knew, would be an empty office. Wasn't he a bit surprised when you produced the keys?'

'I didn't,' he said crossly. 'Give me a bit of credit, will you?'

'No, of course, you didn't. Lottie had got there first and had been hanging about waiting for Susie to leave. She nipped up the stairs and opened up the door so that when you and Duane arrived, you could just walk in, as if the place was occupied and Susie sitting in there waiting for business. Am I right?'

He only gave that grimace which I could no longer call a smile. 'You seem good at working things out. Perhaps you and Duane should have set up in business.'

There was a pause and I got in a dig of my own. 'You know,' I said, 'you'll never be able to trust her. Whatever Lottie's motives, to betray Duane like that . . . That's abnormal. They had been together for years. Not just boyfriend and girlfriend but business partners. They shared this house. They shared their lives. She just abandoned him, cut herself loose, and agreed to let him die. She doesn't function like other people, Adam. You'll always have to watch your back.'

'Function like other people?' he retorted mockingly. 'That's a bit rich coming from you. What would you know about normality?'

There was a distant rattle from the front door.

'Ah,' said Adam pleasantly, 'here's Lottie now.'

Footsteps echoed out in the hall as the front door slammed. The kitchen door opened and Lottie appeared red-faced, shiny with sweat, and panting from her run. She froze in the doorway with her eyes popping as they took in me and her jaw dropped.

'What the hell is *she* doing here?'

As the words left her lips she suddenly swivelled to look back over her shoulder.

Lottie hadn't returned from her run alone.

The person who had been standing in the hallway behind her moved forward. Lottie backed away into the kitchen as if mesmerised to allow the newcomer full view.

'*Jessica!*' Adam leapt to his feet and his chair toppled over backwards with a crash to the floor. 'What the devil . . .'

'I met Lottie at the door,' Jessica Davis said, coming further into the room. 'I was just about to ring her doorbell when she jogged up and so we came in together. Just as well, I fancy.' She nodded at me. 'Hullo, Fran.'

'You know Fran?' Adam's voice rose to a squeak of incredulity.

'Look,' Lottie had rallied and now burst into a gabble of

speech. 'I don't know what's going on here. I met this woman at the door. She says she's a friend of your grandfather's and she wanted to talk to me, so I asked her in. I have no idea what she wants. I don't know what Fran is doing here and what the hell you've been saying to her?'

The full force of her accusing glare fell on Adam.

'She—' Adam broke off and his self-possession gave way to confusion and anger. 'She was snooping round the back by the garage. I thought she was up to no good so I invited her to come in and wait for you so she could explain herself. That's all. Whatever she chooses to tell you I've said, she's lying. Not that I've said anything.'

Jessica moved in to take smooth command of the situation. She was as elegantly turned out as the previous time we'd met. This time she wore caramel slacks and quilted jacket and another pair of what were probably her trademark big earrings. Not a hair strayed out of place and she showed not a faintest sign of being discomposed mentally in any way. I wasn't surprised Lottie and Adam were both momentarily at a loss. As a wild card, Jessica was a trump.

'I came to talk to Lottie because there is something I believe she should know – and indeed you should know too, Adam. I've discussed this with your grandfather and he agrees, you should both have been told long ago.' Her voice was as calm and modulated as her appearance and demeanour suggested it should be.

'What?' Adam and Lottie chimed together. They both looked and sounded completely at sixes and sevens. They didn't know what was coming.

'Shall I sit down?'

I had to hand it to Jessica for coolness under fire. I also handed it to her for stagecraft. She knew when to make the audience wait for a punchline. She pulled out a chair and seated herself elegantly; after a second or two, Adam retrieved his fallen chair and followed suit. Lottie, left alone on her feet, unwillingly took the fourth chair. They stared at Jessica in the kind of immobilised fascination rabbits are always supposed to show when faced with a stoat. A trickle of sweat ran from Lottie's hairline down her brow and along her nose. I don't think she was even aware of it.

As for me, my heart was pounding like a drum. With Adam and Lottie's eyes and attention completely fixed on the newcomer, I should take my chance to bolt out of there but I didn't intend to miss whatever revelation Jessica was about to make. Whatever it was, as a result of it, all those loose pieces of the jigsaw would fall into place. Nor could I abandon Jessica. The other two could deal with one of us at a time, but not both of us together.

'You know me as the daughter of old friends of your grandfather's,' Jessica addressed Adam. 'As such I'm also a friend of your grandfather's.'

'I don't know about friend,' Adam said stiffly. 'I know you visit him and sit up there in his room chatting with him. It's always seemed downright weird to me, what with the age difference and everything. He hasn't even got his legs, for crying out loud! It's downright indecent.'

I opened my mouth and closed it again, not wanting to draw attention back to myself. But indecent? As if Adam Ferrier knew anything about decent behaviour!

She wasn't fazed. 'I suppose it would to you, Adam. But, you see, I'm a little more than Henry's friend. I'm Henry's natural daughter – and my mother is Edna Walters.'

Chapter Seventeen

I was as thunderstruck as the others.

None of us seemed disposed to break the almost palpable silence that seemed to hang in the air. I stole a look at Lottie. Her beautiful face was frozen, as regular and expressionless as marble. She put me in mind of one of those large white angels that tower over Victorian graves.

Adam's features, in contrast, were twitching in an alarming manner. I hoped he wasn't going to have some kind of heart attack.

He was the first to speak. 'Rubbish . . .' he croaked.

'Perhaps I should tell you the whole story?' Jessica replied sympathetically.

'Bloody hell!' he burst out, her tone unlocking whatever paralysis had momentarily seized him. 'You better had and it had better be convincing!'

'You can check it all with Henry.'

Lottie spoke up then in a tight little voice. 'This has nothing to do with me.'

'Oh, but it has, dear,' said Jessica, turning to her. 'Because if I am Adam's aunt, then I am also your cousin at one remove, am I not? We're all family here.'

Lottie licked dry lips. 'She's not!' she snapped, jabbing a finger towards me. 'Get her out of here!'

'No!' Adam leapt up and grabbed my shoulder although I had made no move to leave. 'She can't go—' He broke off, his mouth working soundlessly.

'You *have* been blabbing to her!' Lottie shouted at him.

'No, I haven't! She's been rabbiting on but I've said nothing, not a bloody word! If she thinks that meant I was agreeing with her, she's as barmy as she looks.' He was fighting for self-control as he spoke and it was returning to him. One could almost hear the mechanism clicking round in his brain. 'There is nothing she can tell the— tell anyone. I found her snooping round, trespassing. She doesn't know – she can't prove anything!'

'*Shut up!*' yelled Lottie furiously, swinging the finger she had pointed to me, towards Jessica. 'Not in front of *her*!'

I was sure then, even if I'd had few doubts before, who the brain of this outfit was. Treacherous, clever, without any natural feeling or decency but ever resourceful, Lottie Forester, if anyone, would get the conspirators out of the unexpected jam they were in. But not if I had anything to do with it. What's more, Jessica's arrival and her shattering news had thrown all the ingredients into the cauldron anew. I decided to give the brew a stir.

'Sometimes the first ideas are the best ones,' I observed. They all turned their heads to stare at me. 'I guessed from the first this might be about a will,' I went on. 'And it is, isn't it? Or even two wills? Because your grandfather must have made his will, too, Adam, and probably you and your sister hope to be the main beneficiaries.'

Lottie was shaking her head. 'I still don't believe you,' she said in an obstinate little voice to Jessica. 'I won't believe you whatever yarn you spin us here. How can you be – how can you be the daughter of that crazy old bag lady?'

Adam had become as pale as a ghost and in a manner of speaking I think everyone knew we were in the presence of the spirits of the past. We had rattled the bones and they had risen from their rest to confront us all.

'I should explain,' said Jessica. 'I know this is a shock for you and I do understand that. But when I've told you all about it, you'll understand.'

'I'm with Lottie, I won't believe it, whatever you claim.' Adam's features were pinched and angry, 'Frankly, I don't *care* what you say. I don't care what my grandfather says. He's an old man in poor health and you've influenced him. I'll go to court over that if necessary. You may have got him to believe you're his natural daughter, but I never will.'

Jessica gave him a patient smile. A nerve jumped in his throat and Lottie's alabaster-pale face darkened to puce in suppressed rage.

I spoke up then. 'I've been finding out a few things, too, about families.' I looked Lottie full in the face. 'Your grandmother Lilian and Edna were sisters. What's more, you knew it.'

She said nothing. Her face kept that marble whiteness and immobility.

'Did you tell Duane?' I asked her. 'Is that the clue that set him on the trail of Edna and allowed him to find her?'

That angered her. A dull red tinge crept into her white cheeks. 'No! I didn't tell him a thing! How the hell do you know?'

'Records Office,' I said simply.

'Nosy-parker, aren't you?' Adam sneered.

'No, I'm a detective.'

He shrugged and turned to Jessica. 'We can get back to the

Walters sisters later, if at all. I want to know how you mean to persuade me you are Edna's and my grandfather's daughter. I knew my grandmother. She and Henry had a very good marriage. There was never any talk of his sleeping around. Anyway, I've known him all my life and he was always a very proper and upright sort. He made his money peddling church vestments, for crying out loud! He sold them all over the world. Name your brand of religion and he'd supply you with everything from cassocks and surplices to birettas and skullcaps – a bishop's mitre if you wanted one, designed to order! You're going to tell me he had a secret life? I don't believe it.' He thrust out his chin pugnaciously.

'Then let me explain,' Jessica said, unfazed by this onslaught. 'My mother and Henry met in the late nineteen fifties. Edna was only sixteen and so pretty. You can't picture it now, of course, but I've seen photographs.'

'Where?' rasped Adam.

'Henry has several. He kept them hidden away for years, all through his marriage. He couldn't bring himself to part with them.'

Adam looked thunderstruck but Jessica looked sad. We were about to hear a tragic tale of star-crossed lovers, not that it would make any impression on either Lottie or Adam.

'Henry was seventeen years older than Edna when they met but he fell for her hook, line and sinker. He was married, of course, married quite happily in lots of ways, as you rightly say, Adam. But passion takes over, doesn't it? It knocks all the rules out of the way and won't answer to any reason. He and Edna fell madly in love. He told me she made him feel as young as she was and that it was the first real love for him just as it was for her. Yet he didn't have a bad marriage. It was what the French call a *coup de foudre*.

I don't think Henry understands to this day just how it all came about. He asked his wife for a divorce but she refused. It must have given her a terrible shock.

'She fought back. She said she'd contest any divorce action bitterly and there would be a hell of a scandal. Anyway, she was the injured party and in those days if she chose not to ask for a divorce, there was little Henry could do about it. His wife took the view that Henry was temporarily infatuated and he would get over it. Her solution was that they take a holiday abroad somewhere, repair the crack in the marriage, and return home just the way they'd been before the hiccup in relations.

'As for Arnold Walters, Edna's father, well, his reaction was even worse! He was a martinet of the old school.'

Jessica shrugged and said almost apologetically, 'Arnold's wife had died when the girls were young and perhaps he thought he had to be extra strict because the girls had no mother to watch over them. Perhaps, if their mother had been alive, it might all have gone so differently, but we'll never know, will we?

'Predictably the old man hit the roof and wouldn't even discuss any possibility of Henry getting a divorce and marrying Edna. In those days the age of majority was twenty-one. Even if Henry *had* got his divorce, they'd have needed Arnold's permission to marry. If they had applied to a court they would have been unlikely to receive a sympathetic hearing, given the age difference and everything else. It's more likely that my mother would have ended up as a ward of court.

'Henry's business partner stepped in then and put the case pretty crudely. Word was getting round and it wasn't doing the firm any good. They were in the church supplies business, just as you said. Scandal would mean cancelled orders on a big scale. Henry had to put his house in order sharpish, which meant reconciliation with his wife and dumping Edna. Otherwise, he would be obliged to sell out to his partner. Henry couldn't afford to do that. He'd have been forced to accept a miserly amount for his share of the company and, even if he got his divorce, he would have alimony to pay and there would still be his children to educate – plus the cost of starting up anew with Edna.

'As for Edna's elder sister, Lilian, she was in a panic because she had just got engaged, very respectably, to just the sort of chap her father approved of, strait-laced, old-fashioned principles, family to match. If they got to hear of Henry and Edna's affair, her fiancé's family would be horrified. They were all so dreadfully respectable in those days. We tend to forget. They didn't care who got crushed in the process so long as an outward appearance of all being absolutely normal was maintained. It was a kind of hypocrisy but it sprang from fear of being ostracised by society.'

Lottie glanced up at the wall as if still expecting to see her grandmother's wedding photograph there and then, when her gaze fell on the blank patch, frowned as if she had forgotten she'd removed it.

'Then Arnold played his trump card. He told Henry that with no possibility of marriage, Edna's reputation would be ruined. It was Henry's duty to put an end to the affair. With everyone ganged up against him and being told he was set to ruin Edna's life, Henry gave in. He patched things up with his wife and business partner. They even went off on that holiday his wife had suggested. They went to Switzerland. By the time they returned, Edna had been discovered to be pregnant. But by then it was too late and no one was going to give an inch.

'Lilian's wedding day had been named. Lilian, her fiancé, Henry's wife and business partner and Arnold Walters all almost went into orbit. The whole affair had to be hushed up. Abortion was illegal then and Edna refused point blank to go along with any of the ploys for getting round the law. So she was sent to a Mother and Baby Home for her confinement. It sounds a cosy name for it, doesn't it? But they were far from cosy places. All the girls were there because their families had rejected them or wanted to hide the "shame" of an illegitimate birth; and because the fathers of the babies couldn't or wouldn't marry them. Few of the girls would be allowed to keep their babies. Everyone assumed they would be put up for adoption, as I was.'

I also looked up at the empty patch on the wall, remembering the photograph and the bride's tense expression and brittle attitude. The whole wedding had come within a whisker of being delayed and probably even eventually cancelled, all because her little sister was in a Mother and Baby Home and the father of the child caught in a web of his own making, as novelists used to write.

Jessica shook her head. 'You'd think it couldn't get worse but it did. Edna suffered a complete nervous breakdown after the birth. She had been parted first from the man she loved and then from her baby. She probably had what we now call "baby blues", postnatal depression. How could that poor little sixteen-year-old, sitting in that cold and unwelcoming Home surrounded by censorious faces and the misery of the other girls, cope with such a dreadful situation? So from the Mother and Baby Home she was moved to the first of a string of psychiatric wards.' A bitter expression crossed Jessica's face. 'That's how they dealt with depression then. They locked you up.'

'And her family rejected her completely,' I said, unable to keep silent any longer.

Jessica nodded. 'Oh yes, a daughter or sister off her trolley was as bad as one with an illegitimate baby. Old Arnold Walters never mentioned Edna's name again and wouldn't allow anyone else to mention it in his presence, either. The years went by and the old fellow died. In his will he left everything to Lilian and because by then Edna had been forgotten, left to rot in a psychiatric ward, no one contested it. Lilian chose to say nothing.

'As for me, things turned out rather better than they might have done. It was still possible back then to arrange adoptions privately. A childless couple, who knew Henry and what had happened, asked it they might adopt me. I was never to know, of course, that was the agreement. Henry and his wife moved to a different area. Henry was at least satisfied that the couple who adopted me were decent people. It was the best of a bad job.

'Times change and so do ideas. By the time I was eighteen my adoptive parents – of whom I can't speak too highly – had rethought the decision that I should know nothing of my origins. They now decided I ought to be told. Arnold Walters was dead. They were all more afraid of him than of anyone else.'

Unexpectedly Lottie murmured, as if to herself rather than to any of us, 'His daughters were scared stiff of him. Lilian told me so.'

Adam shifted uneasily in his chair and gave her a hard stare. 'Shut up!' it ordered but I don't know if Lottie saw it. Adam then turned his attention to Jessica.

'You,' he spat with sudden venom, 'decided to trace them! Were you just meddling? Or did you think there might be money in it? My grandfather is worth quite a bit.' His face and neck had turned an ugly brick red.

I thought the accusation might shake Jessica's calm but she just shook her head and carried on as if he hadn't spoken. 'I did nothing for years. I felt that while my adoptive parents were alive, I couldn't. Later it got put off until after my divorce. Then I thought, I've got no one now, no husband, no children. But I have got natural parents somewhere, so why not seek them out? I still hesitated but I eventually set out on the trail.

'My mother appeared to have vanished off the face of the planet. She had finally been released from the last psychiatric ward in the early nineteen eighties. No one knew where she had gone.

'My father *was* traceable. I was wary of approaching him at first because his wife was still alive as was his legitimate daughter, the mother of Adam and Becky. Poor Henry, he lost both women in quick succession, his wife to cancer and your mother, Adam, as a result of a skiing accident. For a while it seemed unfair to intrude on his bereavement. Eventually I plucked up courage five or six years ago. He was delighted to see me. But we decided not to tell you or Rebecca, Adam, at least not for the time being. In retrospect, that was a mistaken decision. But I suppose, like our families all those years ago, we thought it was for the best. You might say we never learn. It's always better to tell the truth, however awkward.'

Lottie had been listening intently to all of this and her mind was racing ahead. 'This house is mine,' she said sharply. 'Lilian made it over to me just before she died. She wanted to avoid inheritance taxes. The necessary seven years passed between her doing it and her death, so the tax people have nothing to say about it.'

Jessica nodded. 'But also,' she said quietly, 'because Lilian was about to make a new will and she didn't want you to feel that you had been overlooked. In the new will she made generous provision for her sister and she feared you might contest it. It suggests that by then she had reason to believe my mother was still alive out there somewhere. Perhaps she attempted to find her only to lose the trail. But whatever she found, it was enough.'

'We can't know,' I interrupted, 'but I think she *did* find Edna, that is, she found out that Edna was living as a bag lady on the London streets. I think that old respectability kicked in again. She couldn't tell any of you that, Lottie, you or your dad, her son, of the shocking state of affairs. But she did try and fix things up, just like they fixed them up all those years ago. But Edna had bitter experience of people making decisions on her behalf and running her life. She said something about it to me once. If Lilian came forward, Edna would've told her to take a running jump. Lilian backed off and later she died, only Edna didn't know her sister was dead now. How could she? She just knew that Lilian had found her once and might do so again.

'So, when Edna discovered someone *was* following her – Duane – she thought it was Lilian again, trying to get in touch. But it wasn't Lilian. After all these years it was her ex-lover, the man who had, even if he hadn't meant to, ruined her life.'

We all sat silent for a while until I added, 'I always believed Edna had some idea who might be following her. She was wrong about the instigator, as it happened. The man she'd spotted and feared was her sister's granddaughter's boyfriend but he'd been set on the track by the grandson of her old flame.'

Adam muttered, 'Rubbish . . .' but he didn't sound convincing.

Lottie's eyes were flickering round our group, studying first one of us and then another.

She spoke now. 'It was just a job,' she said. 'I had no personal interest in it. Adam said his grandfather wanted the old woman traced, so we said we'd do it. We were professional private investigators. We did – do – anything legal. Duane said it was a good piece of business, paying well. It didn't even depend on results. We'd be paid a daily rate plus expenses. What did I care about the old bat or who she was? I never knew her.'

'Oh, I think you cared very much, Lottie,' Jessica told her. 'And I know why.'

Chapter Eighteen

'Henry and I . . .'

Jessica paused to give a wry little smile and added, 'I've never called him "Father" and to do so now would be pointless and confusing. Henry and I, then, agree with you, Fran. Towards the end of her life Lilian suffered pangs of conscience where her sister was concerned. She set out to find her and she did. If she had discovered Edna living happily somewhere, her mind would have been easy. But Edna was living as a homeless person. Lilian knew she ought to try and make some amends for the years of neglect, also for the way Edna had been deprived of any inheritance from Colonel Walters's will, years before, an inheritance to which she was entitled. Had she contested that will at the time, a court would almost certainly have awarded her some part of it. Or Lilian might have been obliged to make some settlement to avoid protracted and public dispute. The scandal thing again, you see.

'Lilian had failed her little sister then. If she made her own will not mentioning her sister, then Edna would be cut out for the second time, and Lilian would have failed her again. She made over the house to you, Lottie, because that was something she could settle in a straightforward way and there were tax advantages. A decent legacy still went to your father, Lottie, didn't it? I have been to the probate office, by the way, and got a copy of the will. The residue of her considerable estate was left to her sister Edna Walters. Lilian didn't feel she was being unfair to her own descendants. You'd been taken care of. Besides, you weren't in need. You were young, Lottie, and your father not short of money. But Lilian knew Edna was in desperate need and she carried the extra pressure of guilt. The nearer you get to death, the more the sins of years ago return to haunt you.'

She hesitated and we all waited. 'Lilian felt she had cheated her sister,' Jessica said softly. 'After she herself was widowed she had a long time, sitting alone in this house, to think about it.'

Unexpectedly Lottie burst out, 'It was that damn solicitor! I told him, when Lilian's will was read, that there was no one else, only my dad and me. Dad's Auntie Edna must have died years ago. But he said that in the absence of a death certificate we must make all effort to trace my grandmother's sister. We could apply to have her declared dead if all attempts failed, but that could be years from now. I thought it stupid and told him so. But he put a notice in *The Times* and some other papers. You know the sort of thing, you've seen them. "Anyone knowing the whereabouts or having information . . ." That sort of thing. Mad old Edna didn't see it, of course.'

'But Henry Culpeper did,' Jessica said softly.

'He bloody would,' said Lottie bitterly. 'If he hadn't, none of this . . .'

Jessica looked at me. 'It gave Henry a terrible shock to read it. He'd never forgotten my mother. He'd always hoped that eventually she'd found happiness with someone else somewhere. The thought that Edna might still be alive began to obsess him. He needed to know not just where she was but if she was happy or if she needed help. The idea came into his head that he could hire detectives himself. But at the same time, he wanted to keep it in the family.'

Jessica shrugged. 'Henry is a man of his generation, after all. The instinct to bury scandal is still there. It's not so strong but it's like the remains of a once-virulent disease lingering in the body. We don't throw off the way we were brought up. Then he remembered that you, Adam, knew a young couple who ran a detective agency locally. What's more, one of them was Charlotte Forester, Lilian's granddaughter. You couldn't keep it more in the family than that. The Forester family also had a powerful interest in finding Edna, so no effort would be spared.'

'He wrote to my father and to the solicitor,' mumbled Lottie. 'He told them what he meant to do and my dad said that was all right then; Duane and I would look into it without letting the whole world know about it. My dad's got a way of burying bad news, too. He didn't know the whole world in the shape of her . . .' A ferocious glare came my way.

'It was a bad choice, anyway,' I said. 'Henry didn't stop to think how much the prospect of Edna turning up might horrify Lottie or his own grandchildren. Lottie envisaged money from her grandmother's estate being handed over to someone she'd never heard of. Adam and Becky feared he might write some provision for Edna into his own will. They didn't know the details of the relationship between Henry and Edna, of course. They just thought she must be an old flame.'

'We feared more than that! Old flames have got married before now,' rasped Adam. 'Look at the websites and magazine features that reunite old pals. Middle-aged and elderly people, who haven't given one another a thought for years, get in touch and suddenly decide they can't live without each other. Gramps sits in that great house all on his own except for Alice. He tolerates her because he needs her, but she bosses him around and he doesn't really like it. Becky and I know he's lonely. We visit him but it's not enough. It was bad enough when Jessica appeared a few years back with some tale of being the daughter of old friends. We thought it fishy then and should have done something about it. But well, her visits kept Gramps happy so we decided not to interfere. But there's a limit to how many people we could accept turning up on the doorstep! Who knows what he might do? He might grab a chance to remarry and give Alice the boot.'

He shrugged. 'Anyway, even if all Jessica tells us is true and Edna and Henry had a child together, it still gives that crazy old bag lady no right to batten onto him for money and it certainly doesn't entitle her long term to any part of my grandfather's estate.'

'Nor to Lilian's!' snapped Lottie.

Adam was still in full flow. 'It doesn't give you any, either, Jessica! I don't care what a lawyer might say about the law regarding illegitimate children. Gramps didn't even know you existed until comparatively recently. I, for one, shall be insisting on a DNA test.'

'You're a fool,' said Jessica to him in that kindly tone which I now realised she knew was far more devastating in dealing with opposition than any shouted words. 'As it happens, I have made it clear to Henry I don't wish to be named in his will. I don't need the money. When my husband and I divorced years ago he made me a very generous settlement. I still earn money of my own from teaching dance and mime. My reason for contacting Henry was only ever to meet my natural father. That we get on so well together is a bonus. I couldn't ask for anything more.'

'That's very noble of you!' Adam sneered.

'What about me?' Lottie burst out. 'I didn't think Duane

would find Edna! No one knew anything about her! She might even have been dead, after all. Living rough all those years, her health ought to have cracked up years ago like her brain. But Duane was so damn efficient and dedicated. He reckoned she'd be in the London area because that was where she'd last been released from hospital all those years ago and where she'd grown up before that. He checked out retirement homes, the Salvation Army, charities, council records, the lot! And would you believe it? He found her!'

'And he wouldn't damn well keep quiet about it!' Adam almost howled. 'We pointed out to him he might after all have found the wrong woman. Until Gramps identified her, we couldn't be sure. The next move would be to persuade the mad old crone to meet my grandfather. It gave us time—'

He broke off.

'To engineer some kind of fatal accident for Edna?' I asked.

He stared at me coldly. 'It gave us time to think what we should do next. Gramps didn't deal with Duane directly so if I said nothing, it should have been all right for a while. All we had to do was keep Duane's success from Gramps and from that family solicitor dealing with Lilian's will. We tried every argument we knew to persuade Duane to go along with what we'd all decided. He ought to have been able to see it was in his interest, too! Lottie's father would have been generous with Lilian's money. Duane and Lottie would have had plenty to invest in the business and keep them going until they got into profit. Lottie's father wouldn't have refused her. But no . . .'

'But no, he wouldn't agree to keep it all quiet,' I said, 'because Duane Gardner was a *good* detective, in both senses of the word.'

'You were mistaken, anyway, Adam,' Jessica added, 'in thinking Duane didn't ever meet Henry directly.'

Her words acted on the heated atmosphere like a bucket of cold water thrown over fighting dogs. Lottie gaped.

Adam blinked. 'What? Why, the sneaky little— Duane never said a word to us!'

'Perhaps Duane had summed you up pretty well,' I told him. 'He never trusted you, Adam.' I turned to Lottie. 'His mistake was to trust his girlfriend.'

She turned brick red. 'I shouldn't have trusted him! He went behind my back to consult Henry Culpeper in person.'

Jessica shook her head. 'Henry likes to see for himself where his money is going. Duane went to see him two or three times, at Henry's own request, and on the last occasion he told us that he had traced Edna to that hostel. Henry asked me to go along there and see what it was like and, if possible, to see Edna. I went but missed my mother, who had gone out. I did meet Fran.'

'I don't know why you had to interfere,' Lottie said bitterly to me. 'The old woman is nothing to you.'

'Think of me as a friend to watch over Edna's interests,' I said.

Adam snorted. 'To think Gramps went behind my back like that! I never suspected it.' He shook his head as though some insect buzzed around it.

Jessica spread out her hands. 'It wasn't that he didn't trust you, Adam, but Henry was hedging his bets, as I suppose you'd call it.'

And perhaps, I thought but didn't say aloud, Henry had had time to consider that Adam and his sister might not be over-delighted when Edna walked back into Henry's life. He wanted someone else to know what was going on and he chose Jessica because she, too, had an interest.

Adam was doing some rapid thinking. 'I didn't kill Duane. I went with him to that detective agency's office but only to search it, once we'd got Mrs Duke out of the way. We didn't find anything and I left. I thought Duane left, too, but he must have gone back. I don't know what happened after that.'

'So who did kill him?' I countered.

'I don't know, do I?' he yelled at me. 'Ask her!' He pointed at Lottie.

'You shit!' She leapt out of her chair and began to pummel Ferrier around the head and shoulders with her clenched fists. 'You lying, two-faced, spineless creep! You're worse than Duane!' She whirled round and before we could stop her grabbed a kitchen knife from the display on the dresser behind her.

Jessica and I threw ourselves at her. The table crashed over. Adam's chair fell back with him in it and landed on the floor for a second time with a deafening clatter. Lottie, screaming like a banshee, flung herself on top of him. Trying to hang onto her and her knife-wielding arm and pull both away was like trying to hold back a runaway horse.

Eventually I managed to twist her wrist and the knife clattered to the floor. Jessica wrapped both arms round Lottie's upper body, clamping her elbows to her sides. Lottie squealed and kicked backwards but dancers are strong. Jessica hauled her away sufficiently to allow Adam to scramble to his feet and scuttle to the far side of the kitchen out of Lottie's avenging reach. Blood was streaming from the side of his head, not from a knife wound as far as I could see but from colliding with the floor or furniture in his fall.

'She's crazy!' he gasped, pointing at her wildly. 'For pity's sake, don't let go of her.'

'I should never have relied on you!' snarled Lottie at him. She no longer looked beautiful. Her features were distorted and hate-filled. 'You all let me down, you, Becky, Duane, everyone! You couldn't take care of the old woman and you hadn't a clue what to do about *her*!' Her head jerked sideways to indicate me. 'I *should* have killed Duane myself. At least then I'd have known it was done and I wouldn't have to worry that anyone else knew about it. But I relied on *you*!'

'Fran!' Jessica gasped. 'Have you a mobile? Can you call the police? Then help me hold Lottie till they come?'

'It's already sorted . . .' I replied, dodging another wild kick from Lottie.

'Oh, hell!' cried Adam and turning, bolted out the kitchen door while Lottie screamed imprecations after him.

'You're spot on,' I told her. 'You can't rely on him.' I looked at Jessica. 'It looks like we've lost him.'

'Oh, he won't get far,' observed Jessica. 'But are you sure about the police?'

Lottie had gone limp in her arms, not from surrender, but temporary exhaustion. She'd have another go at wresting herself free at any moment.

'Sit her on that chair,' I suggested. 'You can keep your grip on her upper body and I'll hold her legs.'

Lottie found some quite astonishing language to tell us what she thought of that and resisted us vigorously. Jessica got a clout in the eye which would turn into a real shiner and I got clobbered on both shins. I'd be hobbling for days afterwards.

'I hope you're right about Adam!' I panted to Jessica when we had Lottie immobilised between us at last.

'Oh, yes,' she gasped. 'He's not fool enough to hang around his flat in Docklands and he can't go to his grandfather. But wherever he goes, Adam can't operate without money. He'll have to use his credit card or access his bank account in some way.'

'There's his sister,' I said. 'He might go to her for help.'

Lottie gave a sinister little chuckle. It made my spine prickle.

'Becky,' asked Jessica in a surprised voice. '*She* never has any money! She's permanently broke and begging handouts from everyone she knows. She's never done a day's work in her life and is living in expectations of Henry's will, if anyone is. She must have been more frightened than Adam when she heard about my mother.'

Lottie said unexpectedly and in quite a reasonable tone, 'Talk about a skeleton in the cupboard.' She twisted her head to look up at Jessica. 'I hope Henry marries mad old Edna and leaves her and you the lot in his will. It would serve Adam right.'

She sagged slightly and appeared to have relaxed. 'I'll deny it all,' she said. 'You won't prove a damn thing. Adam and Becky have more reason to want Edna to stay missing than I did. Duane was my boyfriend. We were together for a long time. Why should I agree to any plot to kill him? It's nonsense. No jury would buy it.'

Her eyes met mine and she smiled. 'I'm going to put his portrait up on that wall,' she said. 'Just like I told you.'

Chapter Nineteen

That was when the doorbell rang. We looked at one another.

'Oh,' I said, 'that will probably be the police.' I had fished Ganesh's mobile from my pocket but I put it back. 'I told you it was sorted. I'll just go and let them in.'

Lottie's whole body gave a convulsion. 'What do you mean, police?'

'I forget to tell you,' I explained. 'You haven't met my friend, Ganesh. But while I've been here having this interesting conversation with you and Adam, Ganesh went to see the cops to tell them about Lilian and Edna being sisters. You know, Inspector Morgan herself said to me not long ago, "Money makes motive." '

I walked down the hall past the neglected plant and opened the door. Morgan stood there with a plain-clothes man I didn't know. Possibly he was a sergeant from the local station. He looked at me as if there was no difference between the plant and me.

'There you are, Fran,' Morgan greeted me in a way that boded ill for me at some later date. 'Mr Patel said you would be. You've been playing hotshot amateur detective again, I hear. All right, what's going on? First Les Hooper came to see me this morning with some garbled tale about keys. He was hardly out of the door before your mate Ganesh turned up with some yarn about your ferreting around in the Records Office. Typically, I might add, instead of bringing your information to me, you scurried out here to do things your own way as usual. Patel insisted I should get out here immediately so here I am and oh, boy, this had better be worth the trip or you are in serious trouble! Where's Lottie Forester?'

'Lottie's in the kitchen. Jessica's keeping an eye on her but it might be a good thing if we hurried back there. She's awfully angry, Lottie I mean, and she can be violent. She tried to knife Adam Ferrier. He's got away.'

'Bloke in the car that burned rubber going past us?' observed the sergeant as we all three hastened down the hall. 'I tried to get his number to pass it on to traffic. Speeding in a built-up area and driving without due care, if ever I saw it.'

They drove off a little later with Lottie in the car. She went quietly enough and it worried me.

'I want to see both of you,' said Morgan to Jessica and me before she left. 'In my office tomorrow, please, nine o'clock. Mrs Davis?'

'I'll be there,' Jessica promised. 'I should have come to you before. I realise that now. I can come today if you want.'

Morgan shook her head. 'I want to interview Lottie Forester first and get her statement. She's asked for her solicitor to be present so we have to wait until he gets there. In the meantime, we need to pick up Ferrier. I'm going to be busy for the rest of today. But tomorrow, nine o'clock, right? Fran? Don't let me down.'

'When have I ever?' I demanded indignantly. 'Inspector, there's one thing you must do.'

'Oh?' Morgan raised an eyebrow. 'Going to tell me my job again, Fran?'

'I'm not telling you your job and there isn't time for us to argue about it!' I retorted, suddenly angry and not caring that she knew it. 'I've flushed out Lottie and Adam for you and you ought at least to be polite and thank me for my efforts. Not that anyone ever does thank me! And please don't tell me all that stuff about budgets and accountability and the rest of it. I know that you work under constraints. I know you don't want to be chasing shadows, as you put it the last time we spoke. But I also guess you won't want to have your bosses asking you why you took no action to protect an elderly, vulnerable and very wealthy member of the community like Henry Culpeper.'

Jessica looked understandably startled at hearing me harangue an officer of the Met like this. But Morgan didn't turn a hair.

'Culpeper is at risk?' She twitched an eyebrow.

'What do you think? Adam Ferrier is zooming round like a disturbed hornet out there looking for someone to sting! Please, Inspector, put a police officer in Henry Culpeper's house until you pick up Adam. The old gentleman has to have protection. Adam is a loose cannon. I haven't time to explain now but part of this is all about wills. Adam must be a main beneficiary of his grandfather's – but he won't remain so for long once Culpeper learns what he's been doing. It's in Adam's vital interest that his grandfather doesn't get the chance to call his lawyers and tell them he wants to change his will.'

Morgan nodded. 'Point taken. I'll see to it, straightaway.'

We watched them drive off. Lottie gave us one long look through the car window as it drew away – it gave a whole new dimension to the saying 'If looks could kill . . .'

'Jessica,' I said. 'Morgan's the best and most reliable copper I've ever come across. She'll send an officer over to the house. But that doesn't mean you and I can sit on our hands. We have to go and see Culpeper, right now. We have to tell him all of this. He has to order Alice, or whatever she's called, not to admit Adam Ferrier to the house under any circumstances. If necessary, you and I will stay there, all night if need be, to back up Alice.'

'Adam wouldn't harm his grandfather!' Jessica looked and sounded deeply shocked. 'I listened to what you told that police inspector and I appreciate your concern for Henry. But I honestly think you're going too far. I know Adam is a rotten apple but there are limits.'

'What limits? After this, do you think Henry Culpeper won't change his will? Once he learns what Adam has been up to, the first thing Henry will do is send for his solicitor. Until Adam is in custody, Henry's not safe.

'Don't you see, Jessica? A murderer can't inherit from the will of his victim, right? But having killed *Duane* wouldn't prevent Adam inheriting under Henry's will – unless, of course, Henry changes the will when he hears the news! He's almost certain to do that. If Adam can get into that house and take some action or other to stop Henry being told the truth and contacting his lawyers, he will. Provided he slips into that house, does the deed and slips out again without anyone seeing him, who can prove he did it or was ever there?'

Jessica was still unconvinced although shaken. 'But by your own argument, Fran, the risk Adam would take is enormous. He would automatically be suspected of killing his grandfather. If it were proved he'd lose the right to inherit, anyway.'

'Suspicion and proof are two different things, ask Morgan!' I countered. 'Adam doesn't have to break into the house; he's got keys and a remote to work the security gate. The house is already full of his fingerprints and traces of his DNA from his many previous visits so none of that could be used later as evidence to prove his presence. Provided he isn't seen in the house tonight, what's to prove he's been there, no matter what anyone suspects? Jessica, Henry would normally be alone in that house all night with only Alice and she probably sleeps like a log. That's why the cops have to put in an officer as protection until Adam is picked up and we have to be there, too. Adam has nothing to lose. Henry will change his will if he's told the truth. So Henry must not be allowed to know the truth. Adam runs a big risk going to the house. But it's a dead cert he'll be disinherited if he doesn't take some desperate action. One way he certainly loses. The other way, as he'll see it, there's a chance to protect his long-term interests.'

Jessica looked miserable. 'Explaining this to Henry . . . he is a sick man, you know. He'll take it badly.'

'All the more reason for you to be the one to tell him. We'll spend the night keeping watch downstairs. Alice knows you? She trusts you? She'll let you in?'

Jessica took a decision. 'Yes, Alice knows me. She also knows *who* I am.'

'What?' I yelped. 'She knows you're Henry's daughter?'

Jessica pulled a rueful grimace. 'I didn't tell her. The sort of job she's had looking after Henry she's done before in other families. I imagine she's seen it all. She recognised a resemblance between Henry and me. There was something in my attitude when I was with him, she told me. She guessed I was his daughter.'

Alice looked relieved when she saw us. We needn't have doubted she would let us in. She practically pulled Jessica through the front door and I trotted in behind her.

'Oh, Mrs Davis, I am glad you're here! The police have phoned and said they are sending over two officers to stay in the house.

They seem to think someone may try and get in and harm Mr Culpeper. What *is* going on?'

Jessica patted her arm. 'It's all right, Alice. I'm going to stay, police presence or not, and so is Fran. You remember Fran?'

'Yes, I do.' The gaze Alice turned on me was far less welcoming. 'Mr Culpeper hasn't been the same since you came to see him. He had a really bad night last night, hardly slept. This morning I sent for his doctor. He came about an hour ago and said Mr Culpeper was stressed. I should say he is! He keeps talking about someone called Edna. He keeps saying he must see Edna. Who is Edna? Was she his wife?'

'Is anyone with my father now?' Jessica demanded.

'He's asleep, Mrs Davis. The doctor has given him something to settle him and what with being awake nearly all night, he just went off to sleep like a baby. It's the best thing.'

'Then we can't talk to him – or the police, they can't either?' Jessica demanded.

'Believe me, Mrs Davis, he's out for the count. No one will be able to talk to Mr Culpeper before tomorrow morning, that's my guess.'

I caught Jessica's eye. 'Perfect for Adam . . .' I muttered. 'The old boy is lying up there unconscious.'

She looked frightened.

'Are there any other staff in the house?' I asked Alice.

She shook her head. 'I sent Mrs da Souza, the cook, home. She comes in daily and clearly she wouldn't be needed today. If Mr Culpeper had wanted a snack, I could have prepared it for him but the doctor's pills have just put him out. The only other staff member is the cleaner. She comes in twice weekly and today isn't one of her days.'

I thought that Alice had a pretty enviable job. A lot of

responsibility, of course, but she didn't cook or clean and she lived here in luxury. She had a strong interest in preserving her employer safe and sound. Nor was Mrs da Souza overburdened. There wouldn't be many dinner parties here to cook for, just old Henry and Alice with the occasional family lunch when the grandchildren visited. I bet the twice-weekly cleaner didn't suffer repetitive strain injury in her dusting arm, either.

'Is there a gardener?' I asked, remembering the immaculate view from Henry's window.

'Landscaping firm does it,' said Jessica. 'They come every six weeks and just keep it ticking over.'

Another set of people doing nicely out of Culpeper. If you're rich, you can buy all you need, but it struck me these people were a little like parasites.

The two officers turned up about half an hour later. Morgan didn't let grass grow under her feet. They were a man and a woman, and neither of them was pleased to see Jessica and me. They suggested we go home and leave this to them.

Jessica insisted she wouldn't leave her father and she wanted me there for moral support. She exhibited an unexpectedly steely attitude and eventually, after telephoning for instructions, they gave in. They told us to stay downstairs and should there be any trouble 'which we are not anticipating. This is purely a precautionary exercise,' we must keep out of the way.

Jessica went upstairs with the woman police officer and cautiously looked in on her father. He was still asleep.

It was a funny sort of afternoon. Alice fixed us something to eat at one point, ham sandwiches and sponge cake, but I didn't eat much myself. Neither did Jessica. The two cops tucked in placidly. It was just another job to them. I found some books and started to read but my mind wasn't on it. I wondered if it would be in order to phone Ganesh but realised it wouldn't. No one was supposed to know we were here.

From time to time either Jessica or Alice checked on Henry but he slept on. The pills must have been strong enough to knock out a horse.

The unreality lasted until about ten that night when Alice, after producing a second lot of ham sandwiches, went up to bed. Two different officers replaced the original ones, both men this time. They sat in the kitchen reading tabloid newspapers, eating the fresh lot of sandwiches and drinking endless cups of tea. Occasionally one of them would take a walk round the house checking windows and then go back to his mate. Eventually, even they switched off the lights and found themselves armchairs in a sitting room to snooze in.

Jessica and I remained wide awake. The place was creepily quiet. You wouldn't have believed you were in the middle of London, or not far off the busy heart. We had retreated to what Jessica told me had been Henry's den before the operations on his legs had left him marooned upstairs. There was a big old leather chesterfield sofa in it and I clambered up on that. Jessica took a reclining chair. Neither of us spoke much. I knew she was awake, although I couldn't see her, and she knew I was sleepless.

Once she whispered, 'No one can get in, Fran.'

'The burglar alarm is off,' I pointed out. 'Otherwise we or those two coppers would set it off, moving around downstairs.'

'But the security grilles are over all the downstairs windows and the main gate is shut.'

'Adam has a remote control to operate the gate.'

'Well, yes. But we'd hear it. The gate squeaks and it's so quiet now. I think we'd know if he operated it. And even though the burglar alarm is off, the security lights outside are working. If anyone is out there, they'll switch on automatically.'

'What about the river edge of the property?'

'There's an electronic trip. If anyone passes through the beam all hell breaks loose.'

It was what I'd expected. But something still worried me. I wished I knew what it was.

The air was warm and stuffy. The leather of the chesterfield had a soporific odour all of its own. Eventually I dozed off.

I don't know what wakened me. It was no more than a creak of wood. Overnight as temperatures change and cool, wood settles and emits its own range of muted sounds. But this was a sharper sound. I opened my eyes.

'Jessica?' I whispered.

A faint snore answered me.

I slid off the chesterfield and crept to the door, letting myself out into the hall. I couldn't hear either of the cops but possibly the sound I had heard came from one of them doing the rounds, checking. The creak came again. It was overhead and if I was right in my orienteering, it came from the corridor leading to Henry's bedroom, adjacent to the day room in which I'd visited him.

'Our protection squad, Fran, just doing their job,' I told myself, 'patrolling the house.'

Outside the house no security lights had come on but I still went to the window and peered out between the diamond lattices of the security grille. The garden was bathed in silvery moonlight, as bright as day except that all colour had been bleached out. If any prowler had been out there I'd have seen him. Even so it would do no harm to check indoors.

I moved slowly up the staircase, keeping to one side to minimise any creaks caused by my own progress.

On the upper corridor the same bright moonlight shone in through a window at the far end. By it I could see that the door of Henry's bedroom was ajar.

I told myself it had been left like that so that either of the officers could check on the room's occupant without disturbing him, but I still didn't like it.

I tiptoed softly towards it and on reaching it, put out my hand and gave it a little push.

Henry's curtains were drawn back. The silver moonlight bathed the room, the bed and its occupant – and something else standing by Henry's bed and bending over him.

For a second I froze in horror. I couldn't tell what it was my terrified gaze fixed on, only that it appeared the kind of monster you are sure you will see in your bedroom when you are a kid, if you are rash enough to pull your head from beneath the bedclothes. It wasn't tall but it was bulky, strangely misshapen, a Quasimodo of a figure, partly human but animal-like in its curious bulk. It hovered there filled with silent menace.

The paralysis which seized me lasted only that second. I let out a purely involuntary yell and at the same time threw out my hand and switched on the light.

It showed me Becky Ferrier. Her hands gripped the large pillow which had given her outline the strange bulky shape. She was standing by the bedside of her grandfather, crouching forward ready to place the pillow over the face of the sleeping man.

She stared at me open-mouthed, the blue doll's eyes wide in shock. Her horror at seeing me was as great as mine had been a few instants earlier on beholding her. Then she flung the pillow at me and as I automatically put up my arms to ward it off, she barged across the room and full into me, striking me in the midriff.

The muscles of my diaphragm went into a sickening spasm, the air whooshed out of my lungs and I folded up on the floor, gasping. Somehow I managed to throw out a hand and grab at her ankle. A rib-crunching kick was the response and she had freed herself.

Old Culpeper was stirring, struggling against his medication to wake up. But my yell had been heard below. Stout police footwear pounded on the stairs and along the corridor behind me. I rolled over onto my hands and knees, although what I thought I could do in that position I had no idea. I crawled into the corridor, drawing painful breaths, determined to be a part of whatever happened next.

Becky had started to run down the corridor towards the head of the stairs but stopped, seeing the phalanx of opposition, both protection officers and Jessica hard on their heels, bearing down on her. She turned back towards me. But this time I wasn't letting her escape. I wrapped my arms round her legs and hung on.

There was a confused mêlée in which I managed to avoid, by the narrowest of margins, being trampled by police footwear. Then a male voice shouted in my ear, 'All right, all right, we got her! You can let go now!'

I released my grip and managed to stagger to my feet. Becky was held fast between the two police officers and squealing on a high long note, like a small mammal in the grip of a hunting owl. It was unearthly and I could only stare at her in horror.

Jessica showed more presence of mind and ran past us into her father's bedroom. I blocked out the sound of Becky's wail and followed Jessica. She had crossed to the bed and was leaning over it. The old man was struggling against his drugged state, moaning and rolling his head back and forth as if aware of the disturbance but unable to locate it.

'It's all right, Henry. Everything is all right.' Jessica soothed him, placing her hand on his forehead. 'It's me, Jessica, I'm here.'

That seemed to get through to him and he stopped rolling his head in that distressing way.

Behind us, out in the corridor, Becky had stopped the eerie screeching to attempt a justification of her presence. 'I only wanted to see Gramps. I wanted to make him more comfortable . . .'

Her plaintive voice tailed off as the protection officers frog-marched her away. I heard the trio clattering downstairs and then Alice's voice, sleepy and frightened, asking what had happened. Jessica looked up and my gaze locked with her wild stare.

'Is he all right?' I asked.

She nodded but still looked white-faced and bewildered. There was no trace of her former self-possession. 'She . . . little Becky . . . Not Adam . . . She was going to use that pillow, wasn't she?' Jessica pointed at the pillow lying on the floor between us. 'How did she get in?'

'She was in the house all the time,' I said bitterly. 'Bet my last penny on it. Adam must have phoned her on his mobile and let her know what happened at Lottie's house. They've always worked together. Adam told her it was too risky for him to come and do the deed himself and she had to do it. She came over here – she must have a remote for the gates too – slipped in either before we got here or the cops arrived. She must know every inch of this house. She's tiny and could easily hide in something like a cupboard. Or she could have concealed herself somewhere in the grounds first and got indoors later while we were all here with the alarm off and before Alice locked up for the night.'

An image of the little gazebo came into my head. Had that been her hiding place?

Jessica shivered. 'Little Becky . . .' she repeated.

* * *

It had not been so difficult for Becky Ferrier, so Morgan explained the following morning when Jessica and I went to see her. Morgan had calmed down and was prepared to overlook my rummaging at the Records Office and my dash out to Teddington. Overlook it for the time being, anyway. I dare say the next time I upset her she'll bring it up. Les Hooper was right in saying that coppers have memories like elephants.

'Adam had phoned her immediately and she hurried to her grandfather's house, letting herself in through the front security gate with her own remote control and hiding, as you guessed, Fran, in the gazebo. She was in place before our people got there. They checked the house but she waited until later and when the protection teams were changing shift, slipped in through, of all things, a narrow disused coal chute into a cellar, a legacy of the house's Victorian past. As children she and her brother had often come and gone secretly by that route and Becky is still tiny enough to squeeze through it. The burglar alarm was off in the house. The outside defences had never been triggered.'

'We were worried about Adam Ferrier,' added Morgan ruefully. 'We forgot his sister.'

One always did forget little lisping Becky with the baby-doll eyes and apparent complete absence of working brain cells. Just goes to show.

'They had always worked together, just as I told Jessica,' I said to Ganesh later. 'Becky was the hoodie kid I saw in the street and Edna had seen earlier, the one who set us both up for the onslaught by the motorcyclist. With her slight build, to disguise herself as a young boy was simple. She pretended to fiddle with a mobile phone and lured me out into the road by sprawling headlong. Good Samaritan that I am, I ran out to help as they knew I would. In Edna's case the hoodie attracted her attention in some other way.

'It must have been his sister to whom Adam gave the keys Les had dropped in the pub. It was Becky who phoned Susie and invited her to go out to Richmond to see about a job. It was Becky, not Lottie, who got to Susie's office first and opened the door to make it look as if Susie was inside and then left. Later it was Becky who returned the lost keys to the barman with the tale of having picked them up in error. I should have realised that immediately because the barman didn't speak to me as though he had recognised the girl. But if Duane drank regularly there, then it's a fairly sure bet that Lottie had been in there with him from time to time. The barman would have known her.

'Lottie knew about it all. I'm sure of it. They wouldn't have dared risk any of it if Lottie hadn't been on side. She'd have pulled the rug out from under them. She's swearing blind she didn't know a thing, of course. Who was it wrote that the female of the species is more deadly than the male?'

'Rudyard Kipling,' said Ganesh. He'd recently added a book of quotations to his reference library. At least it wasn't a collection of football trivia.

Chapter Twenty

In one way, Jessica Davis had been more correct in her predictions made in Lottie's kitchen than I had been in mine. As we later discovered, not daring to go to his grandfather's house himself, Adam had phoned his accomplice, his sister, to set up her murderous attack. For himself, he'd set off driving hell for leather in that company car of his, heading towards the south coast. But, as Jessica had foreseen, he hadn't got very far, although it wasn't lack of cash which did for him. He seems to have intended to cross to the Continent. But he piled himself up in a motorway smash on the way. He had to be cut out of the wreckage by the emergency services. He's still in hospital at the time of my writing this and it will be a very long time before he stands trial. Becky is pleading duress. Her brother dominated her and she was scared of him etc. She'll have a job persuading a court. I saw her standing there with that pillow ready to smother a defenceless old man. However, I suspect Becky can be very persuasive.

Lottie, just as she said she would, is sitting tight and denying all knowledge of any of it. And do you know? She might even get away with it, at that. Duane will have his portrait up on the kitchen wall, after all.

* * *

A few days later I accompanied Jessica, at her own request, to the hostel where Edna lived. What might turn out to be the most difficult moment of all had come.

'I have to tell my mother who I am. You're her friend. She trusts you, Fran. I don't want her to be frightened.' Jessica, uncharacteristically nervous, fiddled with one large enamelled earring.

But Edna wasn't at the hostel. She had already gone out. I'll swear she knew that we, or someone, were on the way. Like the cats whose company she'd kept for so many years she was attuned to danger. Her whiskers had twitched and she was off.

Simon was bewildered and grouchily apologetic.

'Nikki and I just don't understand any of this. Inspector Morgan and some sergeant called Parry have been here and it's upset all our residents. Sandra is huddled in her room upstairs and won't come out. It took us months to get her as far as the front steps. Now we'll have to start all over again.' A pettish note entered his voice and he looked at me as if it was all my fault.

'Edna!' I said firmly, letting him know Sandra was his problem.

Simon shrugged. 'Oh, she'll be walking round the streets somewhere. You didn't tell us you were coming, you know. We could have tried to keep her here. But it's always very difficult. She'll be back tonight with any luck.'

I was worried about that. Morgan's visit must have frightened her. No wonder she had taken off. Would she return? I knew we had to find Edna at once.

Thought of delay clearly frustrated Jessica, who'd psyched herself up to this meeting though I had warned her you couldn't ever count on Edna.

Nevertheless, I touched her arm. 'I think I know where she might have gone. Come on, I'll take you there.'

Sure enough, Edna was there, sitting on the same stone bench amid the headstones in Golders Green cemetery. The sun was shining and she had turned her face up to it. Her skin looked smooth, unlined and almost young. There was even a cat with her, a little black one with green eyes. Goodness knew where it had come from. Perhaps it had been mousing in the long grass. But it had joined Edna and they sat together like a couple of old friends.

Jessica and I stood a little way off and watched.

'It won't be easy,' I warned her softly. 'She's happy this way. She doesn't trust anyone who tries to help her. Some pretty horrible things happened to her in the past when people organised her life for her. I know some people might pity her now and say she doesn't have much of anything. But when you look at her like she is now over there, you could say she has everything. She's happy. There is nothing more she does want.'

'I understand,' Jessica returned. 'But she can't go on like it, Fran. No one will force her to do anything she doesn't want to do. Neither Henry nor I want that. But somehow we will find a way. I'll look after my mother.' She hesitated. 'Thank you,' she said. 'Thank you for everything you've done. Henry is grateful, too. He'd like you to go and see him so that he can tell you so himself.'

She set off towards the seated figure. I remained where I was, watching for a few minutes in case I thought it necessary to intercede. The cat blinked its eyes at the approaching woman and then got up and trotted away. Jessica bent over the seated form and, after a moment, Edna turned her head and looked up at her.

'Hullo, dear,' she said amiably.

'Hullo, Edna,' replied Jessica hesitantly. 'Do you know who I am?'

Edna made an odd little sideways movement with her head. 'I think so. You have Henry's eyes.'

I saw the relief flood Jessica's face. 'My name is Jessica,' she said and took a seat beside Edna on the bench. After a momentary hesitation she reached out and took Edna's hand in hers.

I thought the older woman might resist the gesture but she didn't. She seemed content to allow Jessica to have possession of her hand.

'Jessica,' repeated Edna. 'That's a nice name. I like that.'

I crept away.

I did go and see Culpeper. I took Ganesh with me for moral support but to be honest there was an element of wanting him to see that extraordinary house. I didn't just go to hear Culpeper's thanks; I owed him a sort of apology. Actually I felt pretty embarrassed and sad.

'Becky and Adam are your grandchildren,' I said. 'Perhaps you would really have preferred I'd found out none of this. It must distress you more than any of us could possibly understand. I really am so sorry.'

'It's not your fault, my dear.' Culpeper smiled at me and then raised his thin shoulders in a shrug. 'If it's anyone's, it's mine, all of it. I fell in love with a sixteen-year-old innocent, when I was married and couldn't be free, and was too selfish to walk away immediately and not let things get out of hand. I ruined Edna's life. I destroyed my wife's trust in me. I set up the situation which Adam tried to resolve in his own wrong-headed way. Becky was under the influence of her brother. She's always been of a malleable character. Wrong-headedness seems a trait in our family.'

He tapped his fingers on the arm of his chair and gazed from his window down the length of his beautiful garden. 'You might even say I cost that unfortunate young man his life.'

'No!' I interrupted. 'You're not responsible for anything that happened to Duane Gardner.'

He turned back to me. 'Well, even so, I don't intend to fail Edna again. Thank you for coming to see me.' He held out his thin, blue-veined hand. 'It has been very nice to meet you, Mr Patel.'

'He still wants to believe in his granddaughter,' said Ganesh as we made our way downstairs. He shook his head. 'It's incredible after what she tried to do.'

'You haven't met her,' I said. 'I have. I hope she gets a woman judge and a nearly all-woman jury. I wouldn't trust a set of men not to buy the "influenced" theory.'

'Now, now . . .' said Ganesh.

'Still,' I added, 'in a funny sort of way Culpeper probably *needs* to believe at least one of his grandchildren wouldn't cheerfully bump him off. Whatever happens, it wouldn't surprise me a bit if Becky eventually worked her way back into his good books, if there's time and he doesn't drop off the twig too early. I don't know about Adam. I don't think he'll be forgiven quite so easily.'

Alice met us at the bottom of the stairs and shook our hands. 'It was a good job you came along that night, after all,' she said to me graciously.

'Glad we could save him,' I replied, biting back the observation that a fat lot of help she'd been, turning up when it was all over.

'Poor old bloke,' observed Ganesh with a sigh as we walked out through the opened security gate. 'Shut up with all those memories making him feel like shit and thinking he's responsible for everyone's bad deeds.'

'He's got Jessica,' I said, 'and with luck he'll get Edna back again. He's got a chance to put some things right. It's not often anyone gets that, a second chance.'

* * *

Ganesh and I, with Bonnie at our heels, climbed Primrose Hill again later that day to take in the sunset.

'*Indices?*' I asked Ganesh. 'Who the heck ever says *indices*?'

'The plural of index is indices.' Ganesh is like me, obstinate. He never wants to give way.

'Who cares? No one ever *says* it. They say indexes.'

'Then they're wrong. The plural of index is indices, it's Latin.'

'No, it isn't. I looked it up in a dictionary. OK, yes, it *is* from the Latin and there *is* a plural indices, but it isn't used for books. That's indexes. The plural indices is only used when the word "index" is being used in one of its other senses.'

'The Latin language was around long before that dictionary was printed. If Julius Caesar said indices, then it's still indices.'

'Nobody goes round talking in Latin any more.'

'What's the plural of addendum?' demanded Ganesh, changing tack.

'Addenda,' I admitted.

'And what's the plural of erratum?'

'Give over, Ganesh. I know it's errata. Have you been reading one of those reference books again? What are you trying for? Brain of Britain?'

'So the plural of index is indices.' Ganesh wasn't sidetracked. 'You don't say "erratums" or "addendums". Why say "indexes"?'

'Because that's what people *do*. It's called usage.'

That's the nice thing about old friendship. You can wrangle for hours about nothing and it doesn't matter a jot.

'*Jot* is from the Greek,' said Ganesh.